Praise for
The Measby Murder Enquiry

"A pleasant read, evoking Saint Mary Mead and Miss Marple with its atmosphere of surface calm and hidden demons. It's a solid book, cleverly plotted and tightly structured, with all the makings of a perennial favorite."
—*Curled Up with a Good Book*

The Hangman's Row Enquiry

"A delightful spin-off." —*Genre Go Round Reviews*

"Full of wit, venom and bonding between new friends."
—*The Romance Readers Connection*

"Purser's Ivy Beasley is a truly unique character, a kind of cross between Jessica Fletcher, Miss Marple and Mrs. Slocum from *Are You Being Served?*—just a delightful, eccentric old darling that readers are sure to embrace. Pair this with Purser's charming storytelling technique, and you have a fast-paced tale that will keep readers guessing to the very end."
—*Fresh Fiction*

Praise for the
Lois Meade Mysteries

"First-class work in the English-village genre: cleverly plotted, with thoroughly believable characters, rising tension and a smashing climax." —*Kirkus Reviews* (starred review)

"Well paced, cleverly plotted and chock-full of cozy glimpses of life in a small English village." —*Booklist*

"Purser's expertise at portraying village life and Lois's role as a working-class Miss Marple combine to make this novel— and the entire series—a treat." —*Richmond Times-Dispatch*

The
Wild Wood
Enquiry

ANN PURSER

BERKLEY PRIME CRIME, NEW YORK

THE BERKLEY PUBLISHING GROUP
Published by the Penguin Group
Penguin Group (USA) Inc.
375 Hudson Street, New York, New York 10014, USA

Penguin Group (Canada), 90 Eglinton Avenue East, Suite 700, Toronto, Ontario M4P 2Y3, Canada
(a division of Pearson Penguin Canada Inc.) • Penguin Books Ltd., 80 Strand, London WC2R 0RL,
England • Penguin Group Ireland, 25 St. Stephen's Green, Dublin 2, Ireland (a division of Penguin
Books Ltd.) • Penguin Group (Australia), 250 Camberwell Road, Camberwell, Victoria 3124, Australia
(a division of Pearson Australia Group Pty. Ltd.) • Penguin Books India Pvt. Ltd., 11 Community
Centre, Panchsheel Park, New Delhi—110 017, India • Penguin Group (NZ), 67 Apollo Drive,
Rosedale, Auckland 0632, New Zealand (a division of Pearson New Zealand Ltd.) • Penguin Books
(South Africa) (Pty.) Ltd., 24 Sturdee Avenue, Rosebank, Johannesburg 2196, South Africa

Penguin Books Ltd., Registered Offices: 80 Strand, London WC2R 0RL, England

THE WILD WOOD ENQUIRY

A Berkley Prime Crime Book / published by arrangement with the author

PUBLISHING HISTORY
Berkley Prime Crime mass-market edition / May 2012

Copyright © 2012 by Ann Purser.
Cover illustration by Griesbach/Martucci.
Cover design by George Long.
Interior text design by Laura K. Corless.

ISBN: 978-0-425-24804-1

BERKLEY® PRIME CRIME
Berkley Prime Crime Books are published by The Berkley Publishing Group,
a division of Penguin Group (USA) Inc.,
375 Hudson Street, New York, New York 10014.
BERKLEY® PRIME CRIME and the PRIME CRIME logo are trademarks of
Penguin Group (USA) Inc.

PRINTED IN THE UNITED STATES OF AMERICA

10 9 8 7 6 5 4 3 2

ALWAYS LEARNING   **PEARSON**

For Philippa and her little boys.

One

"FOR GOODNESS' SAKE, scram!"

Ivy Beasley pulled the duvet over her head and vowed that she would not rise from her bed until the cleaners had finished the corridors of her residential home. They had been outside her door for hours, filling the morning with loud vibrations, which she could feel all the way down to her toes. "They do it on purpose," she muttered. "We've got the cleanest carpets in Barrington!"

Katya, the Polish care assistant, would be knocking at her door any time now with morning tea and plain digestive biscuits. Only then would she sit up, take deep draughts of hot tea, and dial her fiancé on an extension number to wish him a fond good morning.

Ivy Beasley was in her seventies or early eighties—she varied the number according to who was listening—and her fiancé, Roy Goodman, was roughly the same age. Both lived in Springfields Luxury Retirement Home, in the

Suffolk village of Barrington, where they had met, fallen in love, and become engaged. Grumblings from the home's manager, Mrs. Spurling, about having enough trouble without romance rearing its ugly head, were countered by her assistant, Miss Pinkney. She considered Ivy's love affair with Roy the most lovely thing she had experienced in half a lifetime of caring for old people.

The engagement was not the only Beasley thorn in Mrs. Spurling's flesh. Ivy had arrived at the home from Round Ringford, a village in the Midlands, full of complaints and requests for special privileges, and then to everyone's astonishment, she had set up a private enquiry agency with a mysterious and, thought some, decidedly suspect character, Augustus Halfhide.

The third and fourth members of Enquire Within were Roy and Ivy's cousin, Deirdre Bloxham, much younger, rich and flighty, who lived in a large house not far from Springfields. It had been Deirdre who persuaded Ivy to move, and at first she was quite sure she had made a grave mistake. Ivy was a pain and a pest. But then, as she grew to appreciate the old lady's courage and persistence, she realised that her own life since she was widowed some years ago, which had been filled with good works and hairdressers' appointments, was now much improved.

"GOOD MORNING, MY love! How are you? Well, I trust?" Roy had been awake for some time, thinking about how his life had changed since Ivy arrived at Springfields. He had been coasting to a dismal end, and now he greeted each day with enthusiasm.

"Fighting fit, thanks," said Ivy. "Ready for breakfast?" She had already had two cups of Katya's tea and cleared the plate of biscuits but was looking forward to a smoked kipper with lots of white bread and butter, real butter. Mrs. Spurling had advised wholemeal bread and Bertolli healthy spread, but Ivy had replied tartly that at her great age it wouldn't matter much, would it?

"So, down to business," said Roy when breakfast was finished and they were enjoying a final coffee. "It's time we took on another case, don't you agree? Our Gus is looking gloomy, and Deirdre says she is spending far too much time gardening, instead of leaving it to the man who comes in regularly and, without asking, uproots all her hard work."

"You mean we should advertise? I thought we had agreed that publicity would draw too much attention to ourselves. Experience working on cases has shown us that keeping our heads down is good practice. As my old mother used to say, 'If you keep your head down you won't get shot.'"

Roy laughed. "No, I've had a request from James at the village shop," he said. "He's lost his old tortoiseshell cat. I think it's a she. He was apologetic about asking but says she means a lot to him, and he can't bear to think of her caught in a trap in the woods or shut in somebody's outhouse to starve to death."

"Surely nobody would do that." Ivy's own cat, Tiddles, had been a birthday present from Roy and was a much-pampered animal.

"James seemed to think it possible, and he's had no replies to the notice he put up in the shop. What d'you think, Ivy? Dare we ask the others to take on a missing cat?"

"Not sure. After murder and embezzlement, they might think it a bit tame. If you ask me, we should do it together, just you and me."

"Mm. Not a good precedent, surely. We are a team, after all. It has worked very well in the past. Deirdre and Gus might not approve of a splinter group taking on a case without consultation, do you think?"

Ivy did not answer, and at that moment, Deirdre Bloxham, mistress of Tawny Wings and funding member of Enquire Within, stalked across the dining room to where they sat. She sat down heavily and thumped one hand on the table, causing cutlery and crockery to shiver and jump.

"Deirdre! What on earth's the matter with you?" Ivy rescued a fork from her lap and glared at her cousin.

"I've had enough!" Deirdre answered. "He's moved them, without so much as a by-your-leave!"

"Moved what, my dear?" said Roy soothingly.

"Six forsythia bushes, just little ones. I planted them on Sunday afternoon! There's a gap in the hedge at the front of the house, and I thought it would look so cheerful, all golden yellow, in the spring. And he's taken 'em out *and,* what is more, started a bonfire and chucked them on top!" She looked first at Ivy and then Roy, and burst into tears.

"Now, now, Deirdre. Pull yourself together, girl, do. You've got things all out of proportion. Roy, ask Katya to bring some fresh coffee. And just stop it, Deirdre, you're making an exhibition of yourself."

With a cup of strong black coffee, and more admonishment from Ivy, Deirdre became calmer and more like her normal, even-tempered self. "Sorry about that," she said. "I guess I haven't got anything more important to think about."

"Then you came to just the right place," said Roy. "Ivy and I were discussing a possible new case for Enquire Within."

"That's right," said Ivy. "Now, Deirdre, here's what we're going to do."

Two

"BEST COME UP to my room, and we can discuss matters," said Ivy. "We should get Gus along, too, so perhaps you could give him a ring, Deirdre? And for heaven's sake, wipe your nose. Spoils your merry widow image."

In spite of herself, Deirdre laughed, and they proceeded out of the dining room where they were met by an irritated Mrs. Spurling.

"I have offered Mr. Halfhide coffee and said he would be welcome to join you in the lounge with other residents," she said. "But he claims he is doing research into foreign workers in this country and needs to talk to Katya and Anya in the kitchen. I shall be glad if you would have a word with him, Mr. Goodman. I really can't have these irregularities."

Deirdre winked at Roy and said they had all heard about Mr. Halfhide's research methods. "Much better if we all decamp to Tawny Wings," she added. "Stay to lunch, all of you."

This sent Mrs. Spurling into another paroxysm of irritation, as she said all missed meals had to be booked the previous day. How could she be expected to run an efficient home if certain residents who should be nameless were constantly disobeying the rules?

Roy smiled winningly at her and promised they would try to remember in future. He went off to the kitchen to find Gus, and Ivy looked speculatively at Mrs. Spurling.

"If you had lost a cat," she said, "where would you look first?"

"I wouldn't look," said Mrs. Spurling acidly. Last year, when Ivy had had a birthday celebration, the sorely tried manager had, against her better judgement, allowed Roy to buy a kitten for his beloved. He had said Ivy had always owned a cat in Round Ringford and missed the companionship here in Springfield. In a moment of weakness, Mrs. Spurling had agreed, and now it turned up all over the home, tripping up the elderly residents and prowling about in the kitchen looking for scraps.

"Just checking," said Ivy. "I need to be prepared."

When Roy and Gus appeared, looking sheepish, Ivy suggested they start straightaway for Tawny Wings.

"A new assignment?" Gus said eagerly.

Ivy looked at Roy. "You could say that. But let's listen to what Roy has to offer."

After a short interval, when Roy's motorised trundle, as he called it, was brought round to the front door, the three were on their way through the village, en route for Tawny Wings, the eccentrically V-shaped house where Deirdre and her late husband had lived ever since he had made a fortune with a string of car salerooms in nearby Oakbridge and around the county.

"Let's have lunch first," Deirdre said, "and then we can

go up to the office and have a proper meeting. Is there a lot to discuss?"

Ivy said nothing. Gus had been given a quick rundown by Roy whilst waiting for the trundle and now said, "Could well be a complicated operation," but added that the details would keep until they had all eaten the delightful salad that Deirdre had prepared.

"Rabbit food," Ivy announced, and although Deirdre heard and bridled, she soon regained her good humour at the thought of the four of them working together again.

Three

WITH VERY BAD grace, Deirdre had finally agreed to help in the search for Posy Moon—"Ridiculous name!" she had said huffily—and the atmosphere at Tawny Wings was distinctly cool as the others set off to return to Springfields.

"It's not as if we have anything else to do at the moment," Roy said defensively.

"Best thing to do in this weather," said Ivy, taking off her cardigan and putting it safely on Roy's lap, "is to stay in the shade and get on with our knitting."

"I don't knit," Roy said.

Ivy looked at him, neatly dressed in lightweight jacket and panama straw hat, gallantly driving his trundle over the bumps and hollows of the path back to Springfields. She reflected that she, and most others there, forgot that Roy had been an active and successful farmer locally and did not appreciate how hard it must be for him now, when every day farm vehicles roared past, the young drivers waving gaily. She patted his shoulder and said that he was quite right. It was the least they could do for James at the shop.

"We'll probably find the cat quickly," she said comfortingly, "or else it'll come back on its own. Cats do, you know. Then we can settle down until autumn, when the cool weather comes. That'll be the best time to do some more enquiring. Something's bound to come up."

Gus was following behind them, walking slowly and thinking hard. He did not agree with Ivy and thought much the best thing for all of them would be to tackle a really juicy enquiry as soon as possible. He was sure it was only too easy to vegetate in homes like Springfields. In no time Ivy and Roy would join the ranks of oldies sitting in comfy armchairs, the telly blaring for the deaf, and most of them fast asleep.

Time to get in touch with his contacts, he decided, and quickened his pace, pulled along by his small grey dog, Whippy. "I don't altogether agree, Ivy," he said. "I had a call this morning from an old colleague, and it looks like something for us could well be in the pipeline." A white lie in a good cause, he reassured himself, and jogged back home with renewed enthusiasm.

As he approached the Hangman's Row terrace, where he rented the end cottage from the squire, he saw his spinster neighbour, Miriam Blake, knocking at his front door. He stopped. Ever since he moved in, she had persisted in a campaign to snare him into marriage, pointing out that they could knock through and have a much bigger house as a result. She had wooed him with hot suppers, bottles of primrose wine, bunches of sweet new carrots and, in season, tiny scarlet tomatoes from her greenhouse. He had held out without much trouble. Miriam was not bad-looking, but she couldn't hold a candle to Deirdre Bloxham. Without any pangs of guilt, he strung Miriam along, enjoying her hospitality and making excuses for keeping her at bay when she became too overwhelming.

Now he walked on, knowing that in any case she would turn and see him, and decided that if she was offering supper, he would accept. Deirdre's salad had been all right in its way, but Miriam was a meat and two-veg cook. The thought of it made his mouth water.

"Ah, there you are!" she gushed. "Just when I had given up hope. Now, Gus, how would a roast chicken and all the trimmings appeal for your supper?"

IVY SAILED PAST Mrs. Spurling who was glowering at her from the reception desk, not forgiving her for being out to lunch with half an hour's notice. Roy parked his trundle and followed. He and Ivy planned to retire to their rooms for a snooze. This had become a pleasant habit since they became engaged. "If we spend all day every day glued to each other," Ivy had said, "we shall soon be fed up. It ain't natural, you know. But in this place . . ."

She hadn't finished her sentence, because Roy knew exactly what she meant and had applauded her common sense.

Upstairs in her room, Ivy did not lie down on the bed as usual, but sat by the window watching the harvest traffic filling the air with dust and noise, and thought about Posy Moon. Two alternatives, she reckoned, could account for her disappearance. Either she was off hunting rabbits and had become trapped or stuck in a burrow or she'd been stolen.

Then another thought struck her. She *could* be shut in

somewhere. A little used garage, perhaps, or somebody's potting shed. James would have looked all round his own property, but cats wander. Farmyards were good hunting grounds, and there were at least two within striking distance for a cat. Then there was the stable yard up at the Hall. Rats and mice galore. That would be a good place to start, Ivy decided, and retired to her bed to make a plan.

GUS RETURNED TO his cottage, replete with chicken and trimmings, followed by gooseberry pie and custard. He was in a good mood. Perhaps now would be the time to start his memoirs. Nothing much else to do, except look for a mislaid cat, but he could safely leave that to Ivy. She was the expert on cats. His eye was caught by the message light winking at him. He picked up the receiver and his heart sank. It was his ex-wife, and whenever she telephoned, it meant digging into his pocket for money he did not have.

"Hello, Gus. It's Katherine here." There was urgency in her voice, and he listened more closely. "Gus, something terrible has happened, and I need your help. It's serious, Gus, and I think I might be in danger. Ring me back, please, as soon as you get back. Please."

He frowned. He had never heard Kath sound so scared. "Oh God, what now?" he groaned, and dialled her number.

"There is no one here to take your call at the moment," the mechanical voice said, and he put down the phone. Her mobile, then, would certainly be on. She never switched it off. He pressed the right button, and again a message service clicked in.

How unlike Kath! he said to himself. And her voice, sounding so frightened . . .

Gus left a message on her mobile and began to worry.

Four

NEXT DAY, A brilliant summer morning with clear blue sky and a light, cool breeze had enticed Ivy out into Spring-fields garden before breakfast. As she stood looking over the fence and across open fields, she felt a pang of home-sickness for Round Ringford. Her garden at Victoria Villa had similarly looked over fields, and sometimes young horses had been there, waiting at her fence for fallen apples or an occasional Polo mint.

"Penny for 'em, my love," said Roy's voice behind her. He knew from the way she was standing that her thoughts were far away. That's love, he said to himself. I know her better than she knows herself.

"You made me jump!" she said. "Isn't it lovely, Roy? Mind you, if you ask me, it'll be fine before seven, rain before eleven."

"Then it's lucky we decided to visit the Hall first thing,"

he said. He took her arm. "Come on, Ivy girl, let's go and see what our jailer has dished up for prisoners' breakfast."

Ivy felt it was only fair to defend Katya and Anya in the kitchen, and said she had caught a whiff of frying bacon, which, she said, could be the best smell in the world.

Roy laughed, and said he was pleased his beloved was in such a good mood, and hoped nothing would dampen their outing this morning.

As they set forth, with Ivy walking at a slow pace beside the trundle, they met Gus outside the shop. "Morning!" said Roy cheerfully. He was surprised at Gus's reaction. He looked at Roy as if he had never met him before and said absently, "Oh yes, good morning, um . . ."

"What's up with him?" said Ivy as they continued on their way.

"Too much primrose wine?" suggested Roy. "Probably wined and dined by Miriam Blake last evening. That homemade stuff is lethal, you know."

They arrived at the main gates to the Hall and found them shut. "Ah," said Roy. "First hurdle. What do we do now, Ivy?"

But Ivy was already fishing in her capacious handbag for her mobile phone, an advance in technology that she had at first regarded with deep suspicion but soon relied on for what she called "private chats" almost every day.

"Mr. Roussel? Miss Beasley here. I wonder if you could help us. Mr. Goodman and me are looking for a lost cat, and your stable yard is a favourite hunting ground. Do you remember my Tiddles being found there? You don't. Well, never mind. Now it is the shop cat, and we are commissioned to find it. I am sure you would allow us to look around the stables? Ah, well, that's the thing. Your gates are shut. Five minutes? That would be most satisfactory. Thank you."

Theo Roussel, hereditary squire of Barrington Hall, stood at his study window, looking down the long drive to where the gates had opened. He saw an intriguing sight. A very smart Roy Goodman, one of the farming family Theo remembered, now driving along in his motorised shopper, accompanied by an old lady in a good grey suit and black straw hat. He smiled and went downstairs to meet them.

"Morning!" he said, and Roy raised his hat. "Nice to see you again," Theo continued. The old lady was, of course, Miss Ivy Beasley. The pair of them had been part of an odd investigating team who had efficiently sorted out the very nasty drama featuring the death of old Mrs. Blake and his former housekeeper.

"We shall not keep you long," said Ivy firmly. "Come along, Roy, we'll go straight round to the stables."

"Not sure you'll find anything," said Theo. "No murder victims this time!"

Roy smiled, but Ivy said severely that she hoped not, and if anyone asked her, she would say the death of a cat was just as tragic as that of an evil-minded housekeeper.

She began to open stable doors, and Roy signalled to Theo to stand back and leave her to it. They began to talk about old times, when Theo was a boy and Roy still farming at School Farm.

"Ah!" interrupted Ivy. "Just as I thought." She had opened the old tack room, seldom used nowadays, and out stalked a very pale version of Posy Moon, the shop cat. Ivy picked her up and stroked her, talking in the special voice she kept for Tiddles.

"Well done, Miss Beasley!" said Theo, and Roy added his congratulations.

"Enquire Within triumphs again," he said. "But how

strange she looks. All her lovely tortoiseshell colouring has gone."

"Not for good," said Ivy. "She's been in the dark. You'll see, once out in the sunshine she'll soon be her old self. So, thank you, Mr. Roussel," she added. "We won't keep you any longer. I shall carry her safely back to the shop and suggest to James that he takes more care of her in future."

Five

GUS HAD LISTENED to the news from Ivy and Roy with a pronounced lack of enthusiasm. "Jolly good," he had said. "James must have been thrilled. Free boxes of chocolates all round?" He dreaded that awful feeling of having nothing of importance to do and nothing to think about but Katherine.

His solution, one he had made many times before, was to start writing his memoirs. Now he sat staring at his ancient portable typewriter, and having typed "Chapter One," he was stuck. Then, with determination, he began again: "One snowy evening . . ."

The telephone rang. He rushed to answer it, hoping it would be his ex-wife to set his mind at rest. It *was* Kath, but he had hardly said hello, when in a peculiar sort of disguised whisper she said, "Gus, don't say anything, and don't ring back. Am on my way. Should be with you by six."

Gus got to his feet, pushing his chair back so violently

that it fell, narrowly missing Whippy, who had curled up behind him as he worked.

"What?" Gus yelled so loudly that the little dog scuttled out into the kitchen and through the old cat-flap, which just about accommodated her, into the garden at the back of the house.

Miriam Blake heard Gus's voice, witnessed the quick exit of little Whippy, and at once pushed open the gate between the two houses, knocked loudly at the back door and walked in.

"Gus? Are you there? What happened? Are you hurt?"

"No," groaned Gus, now returned to his typewriter with his head in his hands. "Don't worry, Miriam. Just writer's block, you know. All we writers get it at some time. Could you shut the door as you go out? And perhaps you could check that Whippy is all right. Now I must get on. Bye, dear."

Somewhat mollified by being called "dear," Miriam returned to her house. She had said nothing more but was not fooled. Gus's yell had been one of great alarm, much more than not being able to think of a few words. She decided to go back around teatime to make sure he was quite fit.

ABOUT SIX, KATH had said. Gus did not move for several minutes. He went over and over what she had whispered in that stupid voice. Was it all some foolish game? Something to amuse her idle friends. Well, maybe it was, and perhaps this would be the best explanation. The last person in the world he wished to see stepping over his threshold was his ex-wife, Katherine. She never communicated unless she wanted something from him or was cheering herself up by abusing him with blistering words. If she really intended to tackle him face to face, then it would be a matter of such grave importance that he should start running for the woods straightaway.

But first he must finish his first sentence. "One snowy evening, a dark-haired, slim woman stepped on to a train at Liverpool Street Station, and . . ." He swore, ripped the paper from the typewriter and screwed it up. He threw it across the room, and it landed in Whippy's basket.

"Good dog," he said as she began to chew it to pieces. "We'll watch a bit of telly," he told her. "Take our minds off ex-wives," he added, and sitting down in his scruffy armchair he found the remote control and switched it on. In minutes, he had shut his eyes and drifted into a troubled sleep.

AT TEN PAST six, Gus woke to a sharp rapping at his window. His befuddled brain told him he was sleeping at Wuthering Heights and it was the ghost of Catherine Earnshaw at the window, begging to be let in. Then his sleep cleared away, and he realised it was his very own ex-wife, Katherine Halfhide, peering in and gesticulating to be admitted.

He felt sick. He had not seen her for God knows how long and had almost forgotten what she looked like. Slender, tall and dark-haired, that much he remembered. He braced himself and went to open the door.

"You took your time, Gus!" she said, and then glanced along the terrace. "What on earth are you doing in this hole? And don't tell me you can't afford to live anywhere else. Aren't you going to ask me in?"

She came into his sitting room and looked around with

an expression of distaste. "My goodness, how are the mighty fallen!" she said. "Have you got water laid on? If it doesn't come out of a bucket in the garden, I'd love a cup of coffee."

"What do you want, Kath?" he said, without moving.

"Oh, come on, Gus. I'm not here to fight for my alimony, you'll be relieved to hear. I just need a place to stay for a few days. Please." Her voice had changed, no longer the old challenging Katherine but more vulnerable and pleading.

"Stay? Are you tired of your old friends? Which one now have you misled?" he asked stiffly. He remembered now how well she could dissemble.

"Doesn't matter who. I do need to rest awhile, just for a bit. Friends have told me there's a hunt ball up at the Hall, so I might go to that if I feel like it."

At this moment, there was a knock at the back door, and in came Miriam, saying as she came into the room that she was just checking that Gus was all right. She faltered as she saw the elegant Katherine staring at her. "Oh, sorry," she said. "I didn't realise you had visitors."

"I'm not a visitor," said Katherine in icy tones. "I'm his ex-wife. Who are you?"

Miriam looked helplessly at Gus, who took pity on her and said, "Let me introduce you, Kath, to my very helpful neighbour, Miriam Blake. Miriam, this is Katherine, my ex-wife. She is calling in on her way back to London."

Katherine looked at him in surprise. "But you said I could stay for a few days. I need some country air, you see, Miss Blake," she said apologetically.

Gus shook his head at the barefaced lie. "Try Switzerland," he said.

Then Miriam coughed in an embarrassed way and said

she quite understood that Gus must not be disturbed in his writing work, but next door she had a very nice spare bedroom and would be delighted to have Mrs. er . . . as a lodger for a week or so, if that would help. Gus could vouch for her cooking skills.

"Not possible—" Gus frowned deeply, but Kath said at the same time that she was most grateful and smiled winningly at Miriam.

That smile! Gus had fallen for it the first time they met, and now here she was, intruding on his hard-won peace of mind, guaranteed to turn his world upside down once more.

"If you would like to fetch your things, Mrs. er . . ."

"Do call me Kath. Everyone does, except Gus when he's cross with me. Then it's Katherine."

Oh God, please help me, Gus groaned inwardly. She'll be bosom pals with Miriam in no time, and then what shall I do? Vanish, he told himself. You've done it before and it would be easy. Then he thought of Deirdre, and Ivy and Roy, and Enquire Within. How could he leave them in the lurch? No, this would have to be got through, and he must make the best of it. Country life would soon pall with the urban Katherine, and she would be gone again.

The two women went off chatting happily, and Gus watched them go. He knew Kath was putting on a false and rather cruel act of friendship, and he had a pang of guilt. Miriam had never shown him anything but kindness and hospitality. He hated to see her so gullible in the face of the famous Kath charm. Ah, well, if she hadn't gone in a week, he would get rid of her himself. Somehow.

UP AT TAWNY Wings, Deirdre was thinking about Gus. Their relationship had rather cooled off lately, with no investigating to bring them together. She still spent pleasant evenings, and sometimes whole nights, in the company of Theodore Roussel up at the big house. She had been close to him as a young woman, though the difference in their social standing had prevented anything serious from developing.

Now, in these days of equality for all, she had renewed a light and affectionate friendship. The fact that she was a rich widow had more than a little bearing on Theo's attentive attitude. He was an impoverished aristocrat, and Deirdre, still pretty and fun, and wealthy to boot, was an attractive proposition. He would cheerfully have married her now, but she made it clear she was not interested.

She looked at her bedside clock, saw that it was ten o'clock, and decided to phone Gus, just for a chat. He answered after some time, with an abrupt "Yes?"

"Hello, Gus. It's me, Deirdre, calling to see how you are. How are you?"

"Terrible. Was that all?"

"Gus! What's wrong? Are you ill? Shall I come down?"

"No, for God's sake don't! I'll explain it all tomorrow."

"Gus, I'm worried about you. Can't you tell me now?"

"Okay, here it is. My ex-wife, Katherine, has turned up, asking to stay for a few days. I refused, but dearest Miriam from next door has offered to put her up. Need I say more? No. Right then, if you see a strange, hangdog-looking man creeping into Springfields tomorrow, it'll be me. Good night, Deirdre."

Six

FOR A FEW minutes, Gus felt cheerful. The sun was streaming through his bedroom window and last night's weather forecast had promised another hot, dry day. "Never mind about the farmers praying for rain," he said to Whippy, curled up at the bottom of his bed. "You and I will take our ease in my untended garden, served with refreshment every so often by our friendly neighbour, Miriam—"

He sat up suddenly, remembering all the horrors of yesterday evening, and shot out of bed yelling, "Miriam and Kath!" There would be no solitary lazing in the sun with Whippy for him. He had lain awake for a long time last night, trying out all the scenarios that might have driven Kath out to Barrington and Hangman's Row, to him, her ex-husband. An exclusive hideaway hotel on a remote island would be more in her line. In the end he had given up. He had no idea who her friends or, come to that, enemies, were these days.

When he had married her, he foolishly thought she had been the undoubted best of the year's debutante set, birdbrained and fit only for the pleasures of the season. But he soon learned that he had misjudged her. She was far from birdbrained and had several moneymaking little businesses on the side. Agencies for exclusive tableware, costly fabrics, that kind of thing. He discovered that one or two of them were not entirely snow white but not seriously dodgy enough to cause her to flee her beloved London.

"Now then, Whippy," he said, as he pulled on his clothes, "we have to make a plan. You and I are going to ignore the Honourable Katherine next door, and carry on with our routine as usual. If necessary, we shall proceed incognito." He looked down at her enquiring little face and shrugged. "Well, perhaps not," he said, and they went down to breakfast.

DEIRDRE ARRIVED AT Springfields at ten o'clock to find Ivy and Roy sitting in the lounge playing cribbage. They looked up and nodded. "Sit you down, for a minute, Deirdre," Ivy said. "I've nearly won. We've got ten matches on this game."

"One of these days," said Deirdre, "you'll play for real money and break the bank."

"Don't be ridiculous," Ivy answered. "And what's all this about an emergency meeting of Enquire Within this morning? We got a message from Gus. Something about his ex-wife. Is it our new assignment?"

"Not sure, but I think I should prepare the way before we meet." Deirdre then gave them a blow-by-blow account of her conversation with Gus last evening, and suggested they have coffee and discuss the likely outcome of the meeting.

"We're not agony aunts," said Ivy, scooping up her

matches. "It can't be anything to do with a marriage recon-ciliation or some such rubbish."

"Not likely," said Deirdre. "Gus's ex-wife is a tricky customer from the sound of it. He's more likely to want us to get rid of her, I should think. In the nicest possible way, of course."

"Trust that Miriam Blake to stick her oar in where it's not wanted," said Ivy, and Roy shook his head. "She's not a bad sort, Ivy," he said. "Been a very good neighbour to Gus up to now."

"And now she's gone too far, most likely. Ah well, we shall see."

GUS SET OFF for the meeting just before eleven o'clock, and by this time had seen nothing of either Katherine or Miriam. As he went by his neighbour's house, the curtains in the front bedroom window were still drawn across. He frowned. He knew that Miriam would be in the shop by now. Very likely she had left Kath in bed, expecting her to be up and around by lunchtime.

As he approached the shop, he slowed. He was already late, but perhaps he would pop in and buy some of the chocolates that Ivy loved, just to oil the wheels. The shop was empty, apart from Miriam behind the counter, and she greeted him with a tentative smile. "Morning, Gus," she said. "Lovely morning."

"Is it? Can't say that I've noticed," he said glumly.

"Ah, that's because you wish you'd given hospitality to your wife, I expect," she said. "We had such a lovely talk last evening. She really opened her heart to me, you know."

"She hasn't got one," Gus said. "But she's very good at pretending."

"Now, now," said Miriam, as if to a recalcitrant child. "I found her an extremely pleasant companion. I think she was exhausted. Still fast asleep when I left. The rest will do her a power of good."

"Mm. I'll have these chocolates, please," Gus said.

"For Katherine? Oh, how nice!"

"No, not for Katherine. They are for Miss Ivy Beasley at Springfields, which is where I am heading. Thanks, Miriam. Good morning."

Miriam watched him until he vanished behind the trees outside Springfields. It was just as if she was in the centre of one of those lovely stories in her women's magazine, where husband and wife have had an acrimonious separation, and then, little by little, helped through by an understanding friend, they come together, and live happily ever after. "And I am the understanding friend," she said aloud, feeling a warm glow of anticipation.

But then, as she said later to her friend Rose Budd, who lived at the end of the terrace, she came to her senses. The last thing she wanted was Gus reunited with his wife! Hadn't she spent months softening him up, ready for the time when he decided he couldn't do without her? No, she must be pleasant to Katherine but get her out of the way as soon as possible. Rose Budd had advised caution. "Never come between husband and wife," she had said.

BY THE TIME he reached Springfields, Gus was fully functioning and quite certain of the plan he would suggest to Enquire Within for their next assignment. He was unsure how they would take it but hoped his powers of persuasion had not completely deserted him.

"Better late than never," Ivy said, greeting him without a smile. "The coffee must be cold, Deirdre."

"Oh no, not in my new machine," Deirdre said. "Hi, Gus. You look as if you need a strong black injection. Here, this'll help you to tell us all. We're consumed with curiosity!"

"Not much more to tell," Gus said, sitting down and placing his cup on the table in front of him. Deirdre noticed how his hand shook, rattling the cup in its saucer.

"My ex-wife, Kath, has turned up with only a couple of hours' notice, asking for asylum from an unnamed threat. I know her only too well to accept her brief explanation and flatly refused, but unfortunately Miriam Blake turned up and, no doubt thinking she was doing us a favour, offered her sanctuary for a few days."

"And is that all right, then, old chap?" said Roy sympathetically. He was fond of Gus, in spite of his irritating habit of making a mystery out of everything, and he too had noticed the shaky hand and tired-looking eyes.

Gus shook his head. "No, Roy, I'm afraid it is far from all right. Kath would never arrive to ask a favour of me unless she had nowhere else to go. There is certainly something serious afoot, as they say, but she's not likely to tell me yet."

"Would she tell that silly Miriam Blake woman, do you think?" Ivy had never had a high opinion of poor Miriam and thought it extremely unlikely that someone in big trouble would confide in her.

Gus shrugged. "Who can tell? I never knew if Kath was telling the truth when I was married to her and certainly don't know now." He looked round at the eager faces and said that he appreciated their concern, but they should get on with Enquire Within business.

"But isn't this what we're concerned with?" Deirdre said.

"Ah, now that's where it gets difficult and why I called us together," said Gus. "There may well be something for us to take on, but until there are further developments, I can't really say. It might be useful to itemise what we know. Kath is a divorcée, mixing in society circles in London and carrying on a number of small businesses. Some of these may be shady. She is attractive and clever, and she is in trouble. Possibly big trouble. She has landed herself on an unsophisticated, unsuspecting woman, who has a history of unwise romantic associations and poor judgement. Miriam Blake is very vulnerable, and I feel partly responsible for her, since Katherine was my wife. And in spite of everything, I wouldn't want harm to come to Kath."

"That was a long speech, Augustus," Ivy said, and continued, "I don't know about you others, but if you ask me, I say we should support Gus as a member of our team and prepare ourselves for a crime that hasn't happened yet."

Roy looked at her admiringly. "Well said, my love. Though quite how we do that, I am not sure. Can you help us out, Gus?"

Deirdre interrupted, and looking directly at Gus, she said, "And is that really all you know? All you can tell us?" She asked without much hope of a constructive answer, knowing from past experience that Gus always knew much more than he intended telling them.

Gus ignored her question, and suggested that he outline a plan of action. "This may seem a risky first step," he said, "but I would like to enlist Miriam's help. I shall persuade her to relay anything that Kath might say relating to her flight from London, and at the same time assure her of our support if needed. I might even suggest one or two seemingly innocent questions Miriam might ask."

Silence. Then Roy cleared his throat. "Oh dear me," he said. "I am not at all sure that Miriam Blake would be the right person. . . ." He tailed off and looked at Ivy. She nodded and said that if anyone asked her, she wouldn't trust Miss Blake to add two and two and make four, let alone take on a complicated task like Gus was suggesting.

"Oh, I don't know, Ivy," Deirdre said. "She's not stupid. Well, not very, anyway. I think it's worth a try. But I would like to say this," she added firmly. "It may well be that Katherine ex-Halfhide has had a row with a boyfriend and needs to get out of his way for a bit. Something really unimportant like that. I don't want to be a wet blanket, but I suggest we wait for a few days, and see what happens."

Seven

DEIRDRE HAD FELT sorry for Gus, and even though she suspected that his ex-wife might have some right on her side, she took pity on him and asked him to stay and have lunch with her. He accepted with gratitude, but said he must dash back and give Whippy her midday meat and biscuit. Deirdre said surely the dog could wait a couple of hours, but Gus insisted. "Back soon," he said.

The lunch was duly prepared, and Deirdre sat down with the morning paper, glancing at her watch now and then, and finally getting up to turn down the heat under a pan of soup, swearing that it was the last time she invited Gus Halfhide to lunch.

"Sorry I'm late," he said, puffing back into the house. "Whippy had escaped somehow, and I had to search everywhere. She has no road sense, so I couldn't leave her to find her way home."

"So did you find her?" Deirdre's tone was sharp.

"Yep, I met her on her way home from the woods, carrying a baby rabbit. Dead, of course."

"Gus! Please, spare me the details! Anyway, the soup's burnt now, so I'll open another carton and you can calm down in the garden. It's lovely out there. I'll bring lunch out."

Gus wandered out, and stared down into the dark depths of the goldfish pond, dug out by hand by Deirde's late husband, Bert. His head was still full of this morning's meeting, and then his treacherous memory took him back to the fashionable church of St Paul's, Knightsbridge, where Katherine had stood, slender and lovely in her long white dress, her father in his colourful uniform by her side. Both were waiting nervously for Augustus Halfhide, brilliant scholar and fledgling spy. A glowing future before the pair of them, everyone said, and until it all went wrong, he had believed them.

"Gus! Lunch is ready!"

He looked up, disorientated for a second or two, and then waved. "Coming!" he shouted, like any suburban husband summoned by his loving wife in a frilly pinny. What was it Katherine had said so cruelly? *How are the mighty fallen. . . .*

"WELL, THAT MEETING was a waste of time," Ivy said as she and Roy sat in Springfields' lounge. "Something and nothing, if you ask me."

"I thought it might well be interesting," said Roy mildly. "If Gus's wife is really in trouble, we might be able to help her out with the added bonus of inside knowledge. After all, although they have been separated for years, he must still know something about her present life. Were there any children, Ivy?"

Ivy shook her head. "As far as we know, none. But then, when you think how little we actually *do* know about Augustus, he could well have a tribe of six assorted offspring. As for being interesting, I think it's much more likely to be dangerous. Besides, I don't really approve of Enquire Within team members asking for help with personal problems. Doesn't seem right, if you ask me."

Roy smiled at her fondly. "I am sure you are right, dearest, but at the moment, and until we know more, I tend to think it is probably even more important that we help our close friends."

"*Close* friends?" replied Ivy. "Would you call Gus a close friend? He may be a close friend of Deirdre's—"

"Very close," interjected Roy, with a grin.

Ivy ignored the interruption. "But I wouldn't say we knew enough about him. Still, you may be right. After this investigation, if Miriam Blake worms dark secrets out of that Katherine woman, we may know a whole lot more. Perhaps more than he would like."

MIRIAM BLAKE HANDED over duty in the shop at half past two and set off for home in a very different mood from the elation she felt on leaving her visitor sweetly sleeping this morning. She had not had many customers, leaving her plenty of time to think. How could she have been so silly? She had plans for Gus, and of course she did not want Gus and Katherine to be reunited! No, she would do her very best to prevent it.

She walked swiftly down Hangman's Lane and up to her front garden gate. There she stopped, frowning. Good heavens, the lazy woman had not even drawn back the curtains. Determined on a different regime designed to get rid of Katherine as soon as possible, she opened her door and went through to the kitchen. She felt the kettle. It was stone cold, so she was probably still in bed.

"Well, Mrs. Ex-Halfhide," she muttered to herself, "if you think I'm waiting on you hand and foot, you have another think coming." She walked through to the foot of the stairs and listened. No sounds coming from the spare room. "Yoo-hoo!" she called. "Time to get up?"

There was no reply, and Miriam sighed. This was going to be more difficult than she had thought. She climbed the stairs, stamping her feet to warn Katherine of her approach and knocked firmly. No answer. With rising anger, Miriam pushed open the door and looked inside. There was nobody there, not in the unused bed or in the small bathroom next door.

Miriam looked carefully around upstairs, including in the cupboards, which made her smile. Don't be ridiculous, she told herself, Katherine's up and dressed, made her bed, packed her bag and dumped it with Gus and gone out for a walk or something. . . .

She returned to the kitchen and walked out into the garden. No sign of her. Ah well, she thought, the woman is a townie and probably went out in search of what she insists on calling "air like champagne." She could have gone anywhere round the village or up through the woods. No food for her, then, Miriam decided, unless she's back here in the next half hour.

After a solitary snack, eaten with little appetite, Miriam felt she had been taken for a ride by Katherine Halfhide. She had been so friendly last night, telling her all about Gus's early life when they were married. Some of it she should probably have kept to herself! But now, this morning, there had been no note of explanation, no indication of where she had gone or when she might return. She had behaved as if Miriam were running a boardinghouse for travelling salesmen. Well, two could play at that game. There would be no cooked tea if she came back hungry. Miriam was off to the Women's Institute meeting this evening, calling for her friend Rose Budd on the way, and would have a quick sandwich before leaving.

Perhaps she would just nip along to Rose's cottage at the end of the row and check on what they had to take with them. A demonstrator was booked for this evening, showing members how to make delicious dishes from ingredients collected from the countryside. Nettle soup, thought Miriam with a shudder, and mushroom omelette made with poisonous toadstools and pigeon's eggs! Still, they had to show willingness. Numbers were dropping from the membership, and Miriam couldn't bear the thought of Barrington without a WI.

Rose Budd was in her back garden but heard Miriam calling. Her hands were covered in sand from the children's sand boat, a new trendy toy supposed to be cleaner than the usual sand pit. "Some hopes!" Rose had said to her husband, David. Her two boys were capable of messing up the *Queen Elizabeth* cruise liner, let alone a boat-shaped wooden box with a climbing mast, filled with sand and plastic buckets.

She heard Miriam and sighed. Miriam Blake was years older but a good friend. Rose knew she wasn't overfond of children but always willing to babysit or stand by if Rose had to rush out on her own. She called out to her to come around the back and watch out for buckets and heaps of sand strewn around the garden.

"What are you taking tonight?" Miriam asked, picking her way over to the sand boat.

"Oh goodness, haven't thought," said Rose, pushing her fair hair out of her eyes with sandy hands. "Ouch! Oh blast, have you got a tissue, Miriam," she said, blinking and shaking her head.

Miriam produced a neatly folded handkerchief with *MB* embroidered in one corner and handed it over. "Poor you," she said. "I suppose you don't fancy a walk to pick some whatevers, just to show we care."

Rose nodded. "Anything to get me away from sand," she said. "Can you wait a few minutes while I clean up, and then we'll go up to the woods. Should be something there, if it's only a half-eaten sandwich left by picnickers."

"I need to lock up," Miriam said. "See you in five minutes?"

"Yes, okay. We must be back in time for me to pick up the boys from holiday club."

Miriam returned to her house, gave a cursory look-around for any signs of a returning Katherine but quickly gave up. She wrote a note to Gus, telling him she assumed he knew where his ex-wife had gone, but in any case, she could no longer put her up as a guest. She collected a basket from her garden shed, locked up and made her way back to meet Rose.

THE WOODS WERE pleasantly cool and shady, with dappled sunlight spreading over grassy patches between the trees. Miriam and Rose walked along chatting, with eyes to the ground for likely looking plants, and both agreed that even if they found nothing useful, it had been a good idea to have a walk. "There's always something to do in the house," Miriam said, brushing aside undergrowth in search of young nettle leaves.

"You could spend your whole life cleaning," agreed Rose. She had picked up a fallen branch and broken it into pieces to have a strong stick for whacking her way through bracken and thorny twigs. "Some people say the curled tips of new bracken are edible," she said, and then suddenly stopped with a gasp.

"What's up?" said Miriam.

"Oh my God, look here," Rose said in a hoarse voice. "What's that, under the bracken? Look, just there!"

Miriam walked forward gingerly, and peered down. "Ah, I see," she said calmly. "Looks like a hand, doesn't it. Perhaps we'd better—"

She got no further but turned back to where Rose swayed, deathly white. Miriam reached her, arms outstretched, and caught her just as she fell.

Eight

MIRIAM HAD LOOKED back at the whitish glimpse of the hand but decided the most urgent thing was to help poor Rose back to her own house. She had settled her down in a chair by the window and now busied herself arranging for a friend to pick up and keep the boys until Rose could collect them. This done, she bustled about like the community nurse on a visit.

"I'll put the kettle on and make you a nice cup of hot sweet tea. That's for shock. And then I'll phone the police."

"Shouldn't you do that first?" Rose whispered. She could not get out of her mind the sight of that hand, sticking out so pleadingly from the bracken. Miriam wouldn't touch anything but said they must leave it for the police. She was so calm! Of all people, Rose would not have thought Miriam a heroine in an emergency. She was usually all of a dither at the slightest thing. But now she was making tea as if a dead body in the wood was an everyday occurrence.

"Now, you drink this," Miriam said. "And I'll dial 999. I suppose I should ask for police rather than the ambulance. It's not as if that woman's in a hurry."

"How do you know it was a woman?"

"I don't, but it's usually women who get murdered. Hello? Police, please. Well, yes, I suppose you'd say it was urgent. Murder is usually urgent, isn't it? All right, all right! Keep your hair on. I'm not joking. It's in the woods up Hangman's Lane in Barrington." Miriam gave her name and address and said she would be at home for the rest of the day.

"That's that, then," she said tidily, filling up Rose's cup. "Drink that up, not too quick. There's plenty of time before you collect the boys."

"I don't want them frightened by the police," Rose said anxiously. "You'd be the best one to show them the, um . . ."

"Don't worry, I'll certainly do that. And anyway, I don't suppose they'll be in Farnden all that soon. They obviously thought I was having 'em on. Practical joke, you know."

In Rose's imagination, the hand was already being attacked by foxes and carried off to their earth. Ugh! She wished David was not miles away helping with a neighbour's harvest.

"You'd better go now," she said. "I'm feeling okay, thanks to you. I mustn't alarm the boys, though I expect there'll be police cars and all that quite soon. Thanks for helping me out, Miriam. I'll be fine now. Bye. Oh, and if you want, you can come up and have supper with us later. Don't sit there brooding on your own. Bye."

* * *

DETECTIVE INSPECTOR FROBISHER was weary from a long interview with a woman who was clearly guilty of repeated shoplifting but had clever excuses and explanations for each crime. He only half listened to the latest reports coming in but caught the name Barrington and knew immediately that it was somehow significant. Then he remembered. "Enquire Within," he said aloud.

"Sorry?" said his fresh-faced young assistant.

"Enquire Within," Frobisher repeated. "An enquiry agency consisting of two ancient pensioners, one jolly divorcée, and a mystery man not long arrived in the village of Barrington. That's the name I recognised. Barrington, a lovely Suffolk village on our patch, and up until the last case solved by Enquire Within, with no help from the police of course, it was a quiet, law-abiding place, never requiring any attention from us."

"Ah, yes, now I've got it, sir. Barrington. That was the call that came in an hour or so ago. Hoax call, we reckon. Some woman reporting a dead body found in the woods. I blame the telly, sir. Gives people ideas they'd never think up themselves."

"Speaking from long experience, are you, Paddy?" Frobisher said blandly. "So who's gone to investigate?"

Paddy was embarrassed. "We sort of hoped you'd look in on your way home. Not far from your village, is it, sir? I'll give you the woman's address." He checked his watch. It was past his off-duty time, and he had planned to meet his girlfriend after work.

"Right. Get us a car, then, and we'll be on our way."

"Um, sir."

"What is it?"

"Nothing, sir. Ready when you are."

MIRIAM WAS IN her kitchen, sitting at the small, scrubbed table, cleaning odd pieces of silver her mother had collected over a lifetime of service at Barrington Hall. She heard the rat-tat-tat at the front door and knew at once it would be the police.

"Good afternoon, madam," Inspector Frobisher said. The woman looked familiar, and he was sure she had figured largely in that Enquire Within case. "I understand you reported finding what purported to be a dead body in the woods at the end of this lane?"

"It didn't purport anything," Miriam said. "It was past purporting. And it wasn't a body, it was a hand, as I reported. I could see where it ended. And it was dead." She had decided not to mention Rose at this point. After all, there was no need to involve her in these early stages. Miriam would not have admitted it, but she was enjoying herself, feeling important in the eyes of the police. It was heady stuff. No doubt Rose would have to be questioned, but that could be later.

"Very well," said Frobisher, taking a deep breath. "Would you be kind enough to accompany us to the exact spot where you found this, um, hand?"

"I'll just lock up," said Miriam. "You can't be too careful these days, Inspector."

Frobisher wished he could say that if her story was true, then that was a statement of the obvious. But he nodded politely and said he would wait by the gate.

In no time, Miriam reappeared and led the way to the

woods. "It was just along here," she said, a hundred yards into the trees. "I remember where it was exactly, because I was looking for the tightly curled ends of bracken and had just found some."

In God's name, thought Frobisher, what is the woman talking about? He began to sympathise with the others back at the station. A right nutter, this one!

"You can eat them, you know. But when they're older, they can poison you! Funny, that. Maybe the woman had—"

"Sorry to interrupt," said Frobisher sharply. He had had enough of this and for two pins would go straight home and release poor young Paddy. "Are we anywhere near the spot?"

Miriam looked about her. She saw the place where Rose's shoes had trampled down the undergrowth and then stopped short. "That's it," she said, triumphantly pointing. "There's the bracken I was telling you about. See the curls?"

"That's all I can see, Miss Blake," said Frobisher. "No hand. Perhaps you could show us?"

Miriam peered down into the bracken, frowned and parted the fronds with her boots. "It *was* here, right here!" she said. "It's gone!" She began to stamp down the surrounding brambles.

Frobisher took her arm. "Please don't do that, Miss Blake. We may need to inspect this whole site. But for now, as you so perceptively observe, the hand has apparently gone."

They returned to the cottage in silence. As the policemen prepared to depart in their car, Frobisher leaned out of the window and said, "Miss Blake, over here, please." Miriam walked towards him and stood abjectly by the car.

"I'm very sorry, Inspector," she said. "I know you think

I'm having you on, just for a joke. But I promise you there *was* a hand sticking out of the bracken. It was a horrible whitish colour, sort of dead looking. . . ."

Miriam tailed off, as the car began to move away.

"Let us know if you have anything else to report," Frobisher called back to her, and then they were gone. It was not until Miriam was back in her house that she remembered Rose. Of course! She could back her up. She'd seen the hand and had fainted at the sight. She was going to look a right fool, not telling the police about Rose straight-away. Well, the hand had gone, so a phone call could wait until tomorrow.

Nine

MIRIAM ARRIVED AT the Budds' cottage in time for an early supper before she and Rose set off for the WI meeting. She had spent the last few hours turning over in her mind what she would say. Rose would certainly have told David about the hand in the woods and would want to know what happened when the police arrived. They would have been expecting an ambulance and police cars and sections of the lane cordoned off from the general public. The whole business, in other words. But there had been nothing, just a police car driving away and not returning.

"Hello, Miriam! Come in—we're dying to know how you got on with the police!"

So, thought Miriam, in at the deep end. She had finally decided to tell the exact truth; then there would be no complications when the police would be bound to return.

"Let the poor woman sit down, Rose!" said David Budd. "And you two boys, sit still and behave yourselves at the table. Pepper and salt, Miriam?"

She began slowly, explaining how she had intended to spare Rose from police questioning until they had seen the site. Rose had been so upset, she told David, and she was hoping to avoid both of them having to go back to the grisly scene. So she had escorted the two policemen up to the woods, and—here she paused dramatically—the hand had gone. There was no sign of it. "I could see then that they didn't believe me. They had me down as one of those nutty spinsters with nothing to do but make up fantastic stories. They couldn't wait to go off home."

"Didn't they suggest talking to Rose? She could have supported your story," David said.

Miriam flushed. "I still hadn't told them about Rose. I was going to, and then the fact that the hand had disappeared made me look a proper liar and knocked me sideways, so I forgot. I remembered after they'd gone that all they would have had to do was ask Rose. I'll ring them tomorrow, if that's okay with you."

David looked at Rose, and she frowned. "Well, I suppose that'll be all right," he said. "If the hand really had gone, the police will keep until tomorrow. It is possible, I suppose," he continued, looking from one to the other, "that a person might have been alive and hiding under the bracken for some unknown reason. I suppose there weren't any film cameras about? Sounds like the plot of a horror film to me."

"What's a horror film?" piped up one of the boys.

"Never you mind. Just eat your supper, and then we'll go out and shut up the chickens."

* * *

WI MEMBERS HAD gathered in the village hall, most of them carrying bunches of nettles and a few tentatively handing in mushroom-shaped toadstools. The expert on foraging for food in the wild, a hairy man with deep blue eyes and a winning smile, tactfully pointed out suspect features of these and put them to one side.

"Later, in a month or so," he said, "the hedgerows will be full of colourful berries and leaves, but I am glad to see someone has found wild garlic, and—" He stopped and picked up from the table a ready plucked and drawn pheasant. "Now, did this fall or was it pushed?" The ladies laughed, and one of them said she was driving along, and the pheasant ran across the road and under the wheels of the car in front of her.

"It's okay to pick it up if you didn't run over it yourself," she said, winking at the expert, who nodded and suggested they move on to a heap of fresh dandelion leaves. "Delicious with a little lemon juice and olive oil," he said.

Miriam could not concentrate, until Ivy Beasley announced firmly that if anyone asked her, it was asking for trouble, picking up dead things from the road and nasty poisonous plants from the woods. Miriam, along with the rest, listened with bated breath to hear what Miss Beasley would say next.

"In fact," said Ivy, "if you stick to things in packets and tins, you can't go wrong. That's what I always say." She folded her hands in her lap and looked pointedly out of the window.

Miriam smiled. She was reminded of Miss Beasley and her friends in Enquire Within. After she had telephoned the police tomorrow morning, she would go to see Ivy at

Springfields and ask for help. She did not accept David's suggestion that it might have been anybody, alive and well, hiding under the bracken. Although she had seen only the hand, there was something unquestionably dead about it.

After the business of the meeting, when the expert had dismembered the pheasant, braised it and served it up with a dandelion salad and nettle sauce, and each member, except Miss Beasley, had had a taste and pronounced it delicious, Miriam and Rose walked back to Hangman's Row together.

"So will you let me know what the police say tomorrow?" Rose said. "I do need to go into town to do some shopping, but I can put it off if necessary."

Miriam had thought long and hard about tomorrow and now said she wondered if Rose herself should make the call to the police. "They'll realise you're a young mum with two boys to look after and a farm-manager husband and be more likely to take you seriously. Do you mind, Rose?"

"Um, no, I suppose not. Can you come round, and we'll do it together. I'll do the talking and you can stand by."

"That's great," Miriam said, as they reached the cottages. "I'll see you tomorrow—about ten? You'll be back from taking the boys to holiday club then. And then I have to go out myself, unless the police have other ideas!"

She returned to her house and turned on the television, now feeling much more relaxed. It would be much easier with Rose making the call, willing to describe what they had seen. She looked at her watch and saw that it was nine o'clock. Too late to telephone Miss Beasley? She feared Ivy's sharp tongue and decided to do it first thing in the morning. The idea of private enquiries going on, whatever the police decided to do, appealed to Miriam, and since her lovely Gus next door was part of the Enquire Within team, she looked forward to working with them.

As she locked up the house, she remembered Katherine Halfhide. She went upstairs to check the spare room and found no sign that she had returned. Miriam guessed she had gone back to London, without saying good-bye or offering to pay for her bed and board. Well, good riddance! It was unlikely, but if she came back and was unable to get in, she had been told where the spare key was hidden. Miriam continued to lock all the doors and finally went upstairs to bed. With a violent murderer about, she was taking no chances.

Ten

IVY AND ROY had finished breakfast and were sitting in the lounge reading the newspapers. A royal engagement had just been announced, and all the papers were full of photographs and details of the couple's private lives, down to the brand of toothpaste they used.

"If you ask me," Ivy said, "they should be stopped."

"Who?" said Roy, peering at Ivy over the top of his *Times*. "And what should they be stopped from doing?"

"These newspapers, of course. How would we have liked it when we announced our engagement, if journalists had come pushing in here, wanting details of our private lives? And look at these family trees! What does it matter if dozens of her ancestors have been street sweepers? Jolly good thing, I say. Put a bit of new blood into that family. It's like dogs. If you interbreed them, they end up weak in the head."

Roy started to shake, and then he put down his paper

and roared with laughter. He leaned forward and took Ivy's hand. "I don't think the big wide world is in the least interested in us, my beloved," he said. "But as to dogs, you are quite right."

At this point, Mrs. Spurling approached. "Telephone call for you, Miss Beasley," she said. "Will you take it in your room, or would you like to come into the office?"

"I'll take it in my room, thanks. I am safe from eavesdroppers up there." She got to her feet and made her measured way up to her room. "Hello? Who's that? Speak up, do!"

"Good morning, Miss Beasley," said Miriam. "I wonder if I could come to see you on a possible job for Enquire Within. It is quite urgent, so if you could see me this afternoon it would be really helpful."

Ivy had known Miriam for some while and was familiar with her overactive imagination and love of drama. "Better come straightaway, if it's that urgent," she said. "And I hope you won't be wasting my time, Miss Blake," she added. She contacted reception and told them to show Miss Blake up to her room when she arrived and also would they please ask Mr. Goodman if he could come up at once.

"You'd think we had nothing more important to do than run around after her!" Mrs. Spurling said to her assistant. "Go and tell poor Mr. Goodman he's wanted upstairs, please, Miss Pinkney."

Miss Pinkney obeyed, wondering why Mrs. Spurling had not yet realised that Roy Goodman would happily do Ivy's bidding, whenever and whatever it proved to be.

MIRIAM SET OFF from her cottage, calling in to tell Rose not to ring the police until she was back from Springfields.

"Shouldn't be late," she said. "Miss Beasley isn't a great one for idle conversation."

She passed the shop and then stopped and turned back. Juicy Jellies might be a good idea to sweeten up the old thing. James was in the shop, stacking supplies and listening to news of the engagement on the radio. He turned it off and greeted Miriam. "Not your morning here, is it?" he said, smiling. Miriam was a good shop assistant, and he relied on her completely.

"No, I'm a customer today. Juicy Jellies for Miss Beasley," she said. "Most of the old ladies like these."

"That's why Miss Beasley loathes them. I recommend these Devon clotted cream toffees."

"Hope her teeth are good, then," she said.

As she turned to go, James said, "No trouble down Hangman's Lane, I hope. I heard there were police cars down there yesterday."

"*One* police car," said Miriam. "I can't tell you more at present. Tomorrow, if you don't mind, I'll know more then. I'm sworn to secrecy at the moment."

James, too, was familiar with Miriam's love of a drama, and he laughed. "Fine with me," he said. "Just as long as everybody's still alive and kicking. So I'll see you as usual tomorrow. Give my regards to Miss Beasley. I don't suppose the secret had anything to do with Enquire Within?"

Miriam shrugged and left quickly, before James could break down her defences.

When she arrived at Springfields and was shown up to Ivy's room, she was surprised to see Mr. Goodman there, too. Miss Beasley explained that he was part of the team, and it was always useful to have a second pair of ears to pick up anything she failed to hear.

"Not that I am hard of hearing, goodness me, no. But

you are a real mutterer, Miss Blake, so we would appreciate it if you could speak clearly and not into your boots."

Not a good start, thought Miriam, but asked if Miss Beasley was aware that Gus's ex-wife had been staying with her. Ivy replied that of course she knew, and what had that to do with anything.

"Nothing, I hope," said Miriam, and explained as clearly and loudly as she could, looking Ivy straight in the eyes, that she and Rose Budd had been collecting plants and things in the woods and had seen a hand under the bracken. At this, Ivy chuckled. "The hand of the Baskervilles, I suppose," she said, and Roy smiled at her witty riposte.

Miriam frowned. "It is not a joke, Miss Beasley," she said. "I naturally told the police and took them to the place where we'd found it. But, to my horror, it had disappeared. Needless to say, the police were not impressed and went away, as good as saying I had imagined it."

"Not surprising," commented Ivy, but Roy was not so sure.

"Didn't Mrs. Budd substantiate your story?" he said.

So Miriam had to explain why she had not told the police about Rose and what they planned to do next. "But I have a feeling it won't make much difference," she said. "They'll think it's a practical joke. I reckon Rose will get the same dusty answer as me."

"So what would you like us to do?" Roy said. He had a soft spot for Miriam Blake, suspecting that, for all her faults, her heart was in the right place. What is more, he believed her.

"I would like you to find out who that hand belonged to and who killed him or her. I'm sure it was a human hand," Miriam answered.

"And are you sure it wasn't one of those plastic things

from a joke shop?" Ivy said, still sceptical. "It wasn't a sev-ered hand, was it?"

Roy smothered a smile, and asked seriously if they had tried to uncover an arm attached.

"Look here!" said Miriam crossly. "I have come here with a genuine job for you to do. I'm prepared to pay good money for an investigation, so if you don't want to take it on, just say so, and I'll get back to what me and Rose have to do."

"Of course we'll take it on," said Roy hastily. "It is just part of our professional approach to make sure we shall not be taking your money with no chance of success. Now, if you are agreeable, we'll get our full team together, and per-haps you will by then be able to tell us what further steps are being taken by the police."

Mollified, Miriam said she would be in touch, and left Springfields with a lighter step. Everyone said Miss Beas-ley's bark was worse than her bite, and Miriam knew that the team had had some real success in the past. She had no confidence in the police taking it further, even with Rose's call, and Ivy's question about a joke hand had convinced her that this was probably what the cops had thought.

By the time she reached the Budds' house, she had begun to have doubts herself. There *was* a gang of youths in the village who found it hilarious to frighten old people living alone. But she was not old! And anyway, the ringleader had been warned by the police, and there had been no recent incidents. Besides which, why would the kids half bury a joke hand in a place where it was most unlikely to be found?

ROSE DIALLED 999 and waited for the answer. "Police, please," she said, and nodded to Miriam. "She sounded really nice," she whispered.

After that, Miriam said nothing while Rose told her story. She had obviously taken trouble to give a clear and truthful account, probably rehearsing it with David, and Miriam's heart sank. It sounded exactly like a rehearsed speech, and when questions were asked, Rose stuttered and hesitated and said she was sorry, but she had fainted and could remember no more.

She did not want to upset Rose again and so said she thought that had been fine and no doubt the police would want to take the matter further. What had they said before she finished the call?

"Nothing much," Rose said. "They thanked me for calling and said they would look into it. That was it."

"I thought as much," said Miriam, and told Rose about her meeting with Ivy and Roy. "If we don't hear anything more from the police," she said, "at least we'll be doing something on our own account. Don't think you have to be part of this, Rose, if you'd rather not," she added. "I'm quite capable of handling it myself. And I've always got Gus next door."

Eleven

DEIRDRE SWORE. WHEN the telephone rang, she had been struggling with her head stuck in the slinky evening dress she planned to wear at this evening's grand occasion at the Hall. She was to act as Theo Roussel's hostess, and the great and good of the area had bought expensive tickets, comforted by the thought that profits were to go to the local branch of the RSPCA. As many of the guests were members of the Barrington Hunt, and since hunting with dogs was officially banned, this was a blatant attempt to sweeten the opposition.

Her dress now had a smear of lipstick on the front, and she grabbed the phone and said crossly, "Hello? Oh, Ivy, it's you. What do you want? Yes, I am going to the ball. And no, not at all like Cinderella. No, I do not have to be home by midnight!" The old thing was losing her marbles, Deirdre thought. But Ivy's next words reminded her that whatever else was aging with her cousin, it was not her sharp brain.

"I suppose you'll be staying for breakfast, then," Ivy said. "Still, it will be Sunday, so you can make it in time to confess in church. But enough of all that," she continued. "You are an unattached female and must do what you like. Are you taking Gus? No, I thought not. Anyway, the reason I'm ringing is to warn you that we shall have Miriam Blake looking in on our meeting on Monday. Yes, Miriam Blake. She has a case for us, and Roy, in his wisdom, has decided it is genuine and not another of Miss Blake's alarums and excursions."

"I suppose it is not the vexed question of what to do about Gus's ex-wife," Deirdre said sourly.

"I hope not," Ivy said, and then added that she was sure Deirdre had more titivating to do, so she would see her on Monday at the usual time.

Ivy's next call was to Gus, who was also getting cleaned up to go out, but for him the trip was no farther than next door. Miriam had tempted him once again with a Lancashire hot pot, followed by plum pie and custard.

"Hello, Ivy," he said politely. "How are you, my dear, and Roy, and what can I do to help?"

"A new case for us. Roy thinks it will be interesting and fruitful as far as fees go. Miriam Blake has been to see me and she will explain all when she comes to our meeting at Tawny Wings. Must go. Care assistant knocking at the door to come in and tuck up the old biddy! See you Monday, Augustus."

Roy frowned at Ivy. They were sitting cosily in Ivy's room, with hot chocolate and biscuits on her bedside table. "My dear," he said, "you are certainly not an old biddy. I wonder if this would be a suitable time for me to remind you that we should fix a date when I can do all the tucking up that will be necessary."

* * *

BARRINGTON HALL WAS looking its festive best. Bathed in late sunshine, the golden stone façade welcomed the procession of cars up the long drive. Theo and Deirdre stood in the flower-decked entrance engaging guests in cheerful banter about fox cubs and how many had mysteriously vanished.

Finally the last car had parked, and Theo said why didn't they have a secret snifter in his study before mingling with the throng. Deirdre knew exactly what the snifter would lead to and said she really felt like dancing at the moment. Perhaps later on, when she would be tired and glad of a rest.

Sid and His Swingers were playing with gusto, and with alcoholic drinks flowing and a substantial buffet supper laid out in the dining room, the ball was clearly a success. Before the break for refreshments Deirdre approached Sid to remind him that food for the band would be in the library. As they put down their instruments, the saxophone player, a serious-looking man with a shock of dark hair, came up to her.

"Um, er, hello," he said, and his voice was pleasant, his accent far from what Deirdre would have expected. Eton or Harrow, she thought, and was immediately intrigued. "I wonder if you can help me?" he continued. "A friend from London sent word to say she would be here and we were to look out for one another. Haven't spotted her yet, thank goodness. I am anxious to avoid this meeting, if possible. You know, old flames and all that. No messages, I suppose?"

"If you give me your name, I can make some enquiries. And who is it you are hoping to avoid? I know most people here, so I am sure I can help." Sounds a bit screwy, thought

Deirdre. I bet *he* fixed the meeting and has now thought better of it.

"Her name is Katherine Halfhide," he replied. "I believe her ex-husband lives around here."

Deirdre drew in her breath. "Ah," she said. "I'm afraid you have me there. I have heard of her but never seen her. Perhaps Theo might help. Look, he's over there waving to me. Why don't you try him?"

WHEN DEIRDRE AND Theo finally escaped to his study, she at once asked him about the saxophone player. "What was his name? He dodged my question. Were you able to help?"

"Not really. I knew the chap, of course, son of an old friend. But I have never met Katherine Halfhide, and quite frankly, my dear, I don't give a damn about the ex-wife of my Hangman's Row tenant. She sounds a frightful bore, and a nuisance to poor old Gus. If she's reduced to hiring reluctant saxophone players who look like Rudolph Valentino, then he's well rid of her, I would say. Come on now, my treasure, drink up and we can start to enjoy ourselves."

"And his name?"

"Oh Lord, Deirdre, I've forgotten for the moment. Ask me later. Now, my lovely, forget about Valentino and come to your Theo."

Twelve

THERE HAD BEEN no word from Katherine, and Miriam had wondered about her for a while. Then she decided that Gus's ex-wife was an impulsive woman and had gone back to London. Selfish, too, to leave without explanation. The only recurring thought she had now about her irresponsible guest was relief at her own lucky escape! No wonder Gus was so anxious about her turning up. She saw that two-faced Katherine could easily have been responsible for his original flight to Hangman's Row in search of a hiding place. All the mystery surrounding him was now explained, wasn't it?

"Now we've sorted that out," she said to Whippy, who had come in from next door, hoping for titbits, "we can concentrate on the identity of that poor unfortunate person in the woods."

Whippy rubbed her head against Miriam's leg, and she responded with a biscuit from the cache she kept out of sight of Gus. He was strict with his dog's diet and would not have approved. Miriam stroked her velvety back and reflected that if she couldn't have Gus to stroke, at least she could borrow his dog. She liked Whippy but was hurt by the dog's reaction when on her own territory. Then she would bare her teeth and behave as if Miriam was a dangerous trespasser.

She looked at the kitchen clock and took off her apron. Time to go to Tawny Wings for the meeting with Enquire Within. She asked Rose if she would like to come, too, not expecting her to say yes, and she had refused, saying that David did not want her to be involved unless it was absolutely necessary. They had to think about the little boys and did not want them unduly alarmed.

Miriam had very little hope of police interest and squared her shoulders. It was to be a one-woman campaign, then. All the more reason for employing Enquire Within to take on the donkey work. And she intended to help. She knew she should not be excited about something as frightening as a murder but was quite convinced that this was what the half-hidden hand had meant, and she relished the challenge. The added bonus, she admitted to herself, was that Gus would see how clever she could be, and following on his bad experience with his ex-wife, he would be only too pleased to allow Miriam to look after him on a permanent basis.

She gently pushed Whippy out into the garden and locked her back door. Then, collecting the notebook in which she had detailed the discovery and disappearance of the hand, she set off for Tawny Wings.

THE FOUR TEAM members were settled in Deirdre's upstairs office, and Ivy ran through once more what Miriam had told her and Roy. "If you ask me, it'll all turn out to be a storm in a teacup," she said. "Probably a fallen branch with a twiggy bit showing."

"A *twiggy* bit?" said Roy. "You couldn't mistake twigs for a hand, surely?"

"Depends what the light was like," Gus said. "It is surprising how deceiving things can be in a poor light. Rose saw it first, did you say? She's a lovely girl but a little on the nervous side."

"Well, we shall be able to ask Miriam," Roy said. "I must say I was convinced by her story. There was the ring of truth about it."

"Oh yes," said Ivy, "she undoubtedly thought she was telling the truth. It's not in Miriam Blake's nature to be willing to shell out money unless she really believes in what she's doing. But that doesn't mean it was a real hand, severed or otherwise."

Roy patted her arm, mildly reproving. "Perhaps best not to use that word, dearest, until we've talked to Miriam again."

On cue, there was a firm knock at the front door, and Deirdre went off to admit their client.

"I've never been in your house before," Miriam said chattily as she followed Deirdre upstairs. "It's ever so nice. I know it's not really old, but it looks like it, with all those beams and wood and stuff. You've got the best of both worlds, haven't you?" She laughed. "Olde worlde and all mod con as well!"

Deirdre opened the office door, and said, "Here's Miriam, everybody. You know all these people here, don't you," she added, as Miriam was suddenly struck down with a momentary shyness.

"Oh yes, of course I do," she said.

"Why don't you sit yourself down," Ivy said, "and then Augustus and Deirdre can hear what you have to say. Roy and me have filled them in, but they'd like to hear it in your own words."

"There's more to tell since I saw you, Miss Beasley. Shall I begin at the beginning?"

Ivy looked at Gus and saw miserable apprehension in his face. Worrying about what she's going to say about his ex-wife's confidences, she thought. She decided to forestall Miriam and said would she please start at the point where she and Rose were going for a walk in the woods.

There were inevitable embellishments, and Ivy had more than once to interrupt and guide Miriam back on track. But on the whole, she gave a good, if dramatised, account of what had happened.

"And then, after I came to see you and Mr. Goodman," she addressed Ivy, sensing that she was the boss, "I went in to the Budds, and Rose phoned the police. She was very clear an' that, but it sounded a bit like we'd rehearsed it together, which we hadn't. I always think it's best if evidence is given spontaneously," she said knowledgeably.

"Let's get back to what the police said to Rose," Ivy said.

"Not a lot," Miriam answered. "Just thanked her and said if she saw anything more untoward in the woods, she was to telephone them. In other words," she added, her voice rising to a crescendo, "they ain't going to do nothing!" She sat back in her chair, folded her hands and looked expectantly at the others.

"You can understand their reaction," said Gus quietly. "After all, if there was no trace of a hand, or anything attached to it, there was not a lot more they could do."

"Except," said Miriam, with emphasis, "it *had* been there! You can say what you like about joke hands and silly games, but it was a real hand, a human hand, and that person was dead or I'm a banana."

"Which you clearly are not," said Roy soothingly.

"One thing," said Deirdre. "I know you are certain, Miriam, but can you remember what the light was like in the woods? It was a sunny afternoon, but those big trees can shut out a lot of light."

Miriam frowned. "I couldn't swear to it, but when we were walking along, I remember Rose saying how pretty it all was, with the sun coming through the trees. Dappled sunshine, she said. But it wasn't a shadow, I'm sure of that. We wouldn't both have noticed a hand if it was a shadow, would we?"

"Did you see a wedding ring or anything particular on the hand?" Gus said.

"No, not really. I did look, because I always look to see if people are married," Miriam said uncomfortably. "Not being married myself, an' so on . . ."

"Of course. Naturally," said Roy. "Very well considered, if I may say so."

She looked gratefully at him. "I think that's about all I can tell you. Except for one more thing," she added, as if she had been saving the best until last. They all looked hopefully at her. At this stage, not one of them had a constructive thought how they could begin to investigate.

"On Friday night, around about eleven o'clock, I heard footsteps outside in the lane. I looked out of my bedroom window, and I saw a man. Tallish, with a lot of hair. He was going up towards the woods. Probably nothing, but I thought it was a bit odd. Hangman's Lane is usually deserted after dark."

"This tallish man with lots of hair," said Deirdre, suddenly very interested, "did you see his face?"

"Not really," Miriam said. "It was too dark. But there was moonlight, and I could see what looked like a bright white shirt under a black coat. Made me think it might have been somebody who'd been at the ball."

"Was he carrying anything?" Deirdre asked. "Like a musical instrument or similar."

"He was carrying plastic bags—you know, like supermarket carriers. I couldn't see all that well. The moon went behind a cloud, and as you know, we've got no streetlights in the lane."

Ivy sighed. "Well, that might be of some help," she said, and looked around the others. "Any more questions for Miriam? Or shall we arrange to meet again, when we have considered what steps to take?"

"I can be available more or less any time," Miriam said.

"Not you, not yet," said Ivy firmly. "We have work to do now. We'll be in touch."

"And thank you so much for coming along," said Roy, with a friendly smile. "I'm sure we shall be able to clear things up for you in due course. Good morning, my dear."

After Deirdre had shown her out and come back up to join the team, Ivy said that if anybody asked her, she would say they might as well give up before they started.

"Oh no," said Deirdre. "I think we've something very interesting to investigate. Just listen, Ivy, while I tell you about a man I met at the ball."

Thirteen

AFTER ROY AND Ivy had gone back to Springfields, Gus stayed behind with Deirdre, and they talked some more. "Do you think they really saw a hand, Gus?" Deirdre said. "I reckon they convinced themselves, like people do, after they've had a fright. It could have been anything, perhaps an old rubber glove that had been left behind at blackberry time. I always wear gloves when I go blackberrying. Saves having purple fingers."

Gus thought for a moment, and then said, "That does seem quite likely, sweetie, which is why I asked about a ring on the finger."

"That would have made all the difference," Deirdre answered. "Given us something to get our teeth into."

"Mm," said Gus. "Even so, she was so sure about it being a human hand, and Rose Budd, too. And, knowing Miriam as I know her, it just isn't in character for her to offer to pay fees for us to investigate, if she isn't sure of her facts. The puzzle, as far as I can see, is *why* she is so keen to find out. Most of us would just shrug and say it was easily explained and forget it. We've had at least two good explanations of what it could have been, a shadow or a rubber glove."

"Did either of them touch it? I can't remember Miriam mentioning it."

"No, she didn't, but I can ask her. She's sure to be round to see me later on, with an offer of something tasty."

"Well, I'm still not convinced. But I'll give her the benefit of the doubt and start working on the supposition that it was a murder and the body has been removed."

"Meanwhile, I shall give some more thought as to why Miriam is so keen to pursue an investigation into something so unsupported by evidence."

IVY AND ROY had come to much the same conclusions, except that Ivy's doubts were stronger than Deirdre's. "Still," she said, as she walked beside Roy's vehicle, "if she's prepared to throw good money after bad, then the least we can do is to try and make some sense of what she has told us."

They reached Springfields, and Ivy said she thought she would have a quick nap. "I often think better after a spot of shut-eye," she said, and asked Roy to make sure she was awake in time to go down to lunch.

Stretched flat out on her bed, Ivy closed her eyes and let her thoughts wander. Much of what Miriam had told them this morning they already knew. The only new piece of information was her story of the man walking up Hangman's Lane at eleven o'clock at night. Tallish, with a lot of dark hair, and wearing what sounded like formal evening clothes. But eleven o'clock? Most people stayed at a ball until well after midnight. Deirdre's account of her meeting with a saxophone player not wanting to meet Katherine Halfhide was interesting, but not necessarily connected, though the description sounded the same. And where was he going, up Hangman's Lane with his supermarket shopping? There were no more houses after the Row, and he would soon come to the woods, which stretched on both sides for at least half a mile up the road.

Ivy began to doze. She dreamed she was at the ball, floating round the dance floor in a long evening frock, waltzing in Roy's arms to the strains of Sid and His Boys. The last time she had tapped her foot to their rhythmic beat was when they came to play for an Olde Tyme Evening at Springfields, and she had thought them very polished and professional, considering Sid was a local tax officer and his Swingers had all seen the other side of fifty years old and came from Oakbridge.

Except one, thought Ivy, sitting up with a jerk. There had been one, playing a long curly silver thing with lots of buttons, and he was clearly not a plumber, nor was he any older than forty. He was tallish, with lots of dark hair, and was wearing a very smart dinner jacket, white shirt and black tie, not very appropriate for playing to old folks, half of them asleep, at Springfields.

"Ivy? Are you awake, my love?" It was Roy, of course, and Ivy woke up properly.

"Come in, do," she said. "I am perfectly decent. All I need to do is put on my shoes, and then we can be off downstairs to lunch. There are good smells reaching up here, quite appetising for once."

Roy came into her room, bearing a beautiful red rose, which he handed to her, going down shakily on one knee. "For you, Ivy dearest," he said, and she smiled tenderly.

"You pinched it, out of our gaoler's garden!" she said. "But thanks, anyway," she added, planting a kiss on the top of his head. "I suppose you'd like a hand to get up?"

"I'm afraid so," he said. "I may have been a bit rash, but we can always send for Katya."

"Nonsense!" replied Ivy, putting her arm through his. "Up we come!"

To Roy's amazement, he was hoisted to his feet with a strong lift. Ivy dusted down his trouser knees and said she hoped he would stay upright for any further romantic gestures he might have in mind.

When they were comfortably seated in front of plates of roast chicken and fresh peas, Ivy told Roy about her dream. "What do you think?" she said. "Could it be an omen? I believe in omens, you know. That man in Sid's band answers exactly Miriam's description of the nighttime stroller in Hangman's Lane."

"And there was something else," said Roy, chasing a rolling pea around his plate with a fork. "Miriam mentioned he was holding supermarket carrier bags."

Ivy began to laugh. "He could have been shopping at a late opening supermarket! There is one on the outskirts of Oakbridge. Oh, Roy," she added, "it's going to be hard to take this thing seriously."

"I have a suggestion, my dear," Roy said. "Do you fancy a little walk this afternoon? Down Hangman's Lane, in the direction of the woods? The scene of the supposed crime might at least give us a hint of the direction we should take."

Ivy nodded. She considered how she could tactfully mention that Miriam and Rose had walked into the woods, through bracken and fallen branches, so it would be impossible for Roy to negotiate a path for his vehicle.

But Roy had thought of this and said that he would wait at the edge of the road, and she should venture only as far as it was easy walking. That might be enough to set their imaginations working. And in any case it was a lovely afternoon, and it was a shame not to make the most of it.

IN THE DEEP, dark woods, a man with a woolly hat pulled down over his ears straightened up from his task and stretched his back. It was heavy work, and he thought bitter thoughts about the need to do it. It had taken him longer than he thought, but he was back here today to finish the job. He sat on a tree stump and lit a cigarette, carefully stamping out the match. Years ago, when he had been playing truant from school, one of his fellow cricket dodgers had lit an illicit cigarette and, in a panic of possible discovery, had thrown away the glowing butt end and caused a major fire.

He sighed, and closed his eyes. What a life! Playing in a two-bit band when he had studied at the Royal College of Music and been a star pupil. Women had been his undoing, or so his old father said. The old boy had rather liked the idea of his son romping through London's eligible females, but when it came to bailing him out of debts incurred on his merrymaking adventures, the worm had turned, and paternal disapproval sent him packing.

It was quite a decent mound of earth now, he decided, and began to push two or three holes into it, trying to imitate the badger. He knew badgers cleaned out their tunnels regularly and left the rubbish outside the entrances, so he dragged handfuls of matted dead grass and scattered it around. That would have to do, and he reckoned he would recognise it when the time came. He picked up his spade and turned to leave, when he heard a sound. Fox? Angry badger? He knew it was a human being, when a voice not far away said loudly, "Go away, you nasty creature!" So it was a woman, coming his way. He stayed motionless whilst he decided what to do.

Fourteen

IVY WATCHED AS the snake slithered off into the undergrowth, and she took deep breaths to slow down her pounding heartbeat. Not many things frightened Ivy, but snakes she could not abide. She supposed it was a phobia, and a childhood trip to a zoo had made her tremble with panic at the thought of the reptile house.

She wondered now whether it would be more sensible to go back to Roy. But she had hardly reached the edges of the interior where folk seldom ventured. Sometimes a family would take a picnic and see how far they could penetrate, but they never got very far. She pushed on through the nettles, well protected by good thick stockings, but decided as soon as the brambles thickened she would return to Roy.

Then she saw him. A man, bent double to push through overhanging branches, running away from her. His progress was impeded by the thicket, but he was soon out of sight.

"Hey! Stop! Stop at once!" Ivy was quite restored now and intent on discovering who could be so anxious to get away from her. There was something familiar about him, but he did not turn around for her to see his face.

She began to follow, but even before she had to stop to catch her breath, he had disappeared. A helicopter droned overhead, obscuring any sounds that might tell her which direction he had taken. The sun had gone in, and the woods was dark now, with a thundercloud overhead. Ivy turned to retrace her steps and realised that she had no idea which way to take. She was lost, spots of rain had begun to fall between the trees and even one of her thick stockings now had a large hole.

What to do? Ivy did not panic. She stood quite still and called "Roy!" at the top of her voice. No answer. She tried again, but there was still no reply. Surely she had not gone so far into the woods? She had no position of the sun to guide her, so she set off at random, keeping her eyes open for any landmark she might have noticed as she chased the fugitive.

ROY LOOKED AT his watch. Ivy had been gone half an hour, and he began to worry. He called out, but there was no answer. She had obviously strayed too far away to hear him. He felt spots of rain and worried even more. She had no coat and certainly not an umbrella. It had been such wonderfully dry weather lately that even Ivy had left her brolly in its stand.

He pulled his mobile phone from his pocket and dialled her number. No signal. Well, there wouldn't be a signal in the middle of the woods, would there? He looked up and down the road, but it was empty. No walkers, bikers or cars out for an afternoon drive. He decided to give her ten more minutes, and then go to the Row for help. Someone should be at home there, possibly Miriam Blake, who would be keen to help.

Ten minutes passed, and Roy gave one more shout, as loud as he could make it. Again, no reply, so he set off back towards Hangman's Row. Gus's cottage came first, and then Miriam Blake. He guessed Gus had stayed to lunch with Deirdre but thought it worth a try. There was clearly nobody at home, so he tried knocking on Miriam's door. Each time, as he parked his vehicle, climbed out and made his way up the cottages' short paths, he was aware of time ticking by. With a feeling of relief, he heard steps approaching from within. Miriam opened the door, took one look at him and opened it wider.

"Mr. Goodman! What has happened? You're looking as if disaster has struck!"

"I sincerely hope not, Miss Blake," said Roy. "I am so sorry to trouble you, but I am a little worried about Miss Beasley." He explained Ivy's mysterious disappearance and Miriam took immediate action.

"I know those woods like the back of my hand," she said. "Right from when my dad used to take me with him looking for poachers. I suppose it wasn't very sensible of him, really, but Mum used to say she was glad to get rid of us for a few hours' peace."

Gathering up raincoats and umbrellas, they left the cottage, and until they reached the spot where Roy had parked, Miriam kept up a monologue of inconsequential chatter. Roy was irritated, but consoled himself by seeing that she required no answers or comments. He let her run on, and when they finally came to a halt, so did Miriam's voice.

"She went in over there, through that gap in the hedge,"

Roy said. "I saw her take a left turn, and then she was out of sight. Then I heard her voice yelling at some animal—could have been a snake, because she's terrified of those—and then nothing more."

"How long ago would you say that was?"

"About an hour now," replied Roy, real fear in his voice. "What do you think can have happened?"

"Oh, don't worry, Mr. Goodman! People get lost in these woods all the time. I'll go in now and we'll both be back in two ticks, you'll see."

BEHIND A TREE, the man watched Ivy scrambling along a narrow, sandy path, overgrown with brambles. He felt sorry for her. She must be at least seventy, he reckoned. He wished he could rush out and help her find the way out, but he knew this would be madness.

Then Ivy stumbled and collapsed to the ground gasping with pain. He did not even consider the consequences but rushed forward to help her.

"Oh Lord," he said, "you have taken a tumble! Never mind, my dear, have a moment's rest and then we'll get you up. Meanwhile, let me see your twisted ankle."

Ivy didn't know whether it was the appearance of a man jumping out from behind a tree or the pain shooting through her leg that caused her head to swim and a strong feeling of nausea to overtake her.

"Sick," she muttered, her hand over her eyes.

He leaned over and pulled her into a sitting position, resting her back against his legs. Then he gently moved her head down between her knees as far as it would go and told her to take deep breaths. After several seconds, she whispered that she felt better, and he helped her to sit upright.

"Who are you?" she said, her customary confidence returning.

"The Green Man of the Woods," he said in a mock menacing voice.

"Rubbish," said Ivy. "Here, help me to get up, and then perhaps you can direct me out to the road. Someone is waiting for me there."

He looked around him, smiling. She was a game old thing, he thought. Reminds me of Grandmama, God rest her soul. Have I seen her somewhere before?

"Afraid there are no signposts," he said. "But if you can walk a little, we are bound to come out somewhere useful. There's a golf course runs alongside one of the edges of the woods. Ready? Right, heave-ho, my hearties, and off we go."

MIRIAM, MEANWHILE, WAS walking in the opposite direction. She was following the easiest of the several little paths, which led to where she and Rose had seen the hand. It would be useful, she thought, to take another look. But nothing had changed from the time she and the policemen had investigated. She frowned. It was there, exactly there, she said to herself, and bent down to move the nettles to one side with a stick. Something shiny caught her eye. She picked it up and held her breath. It was a tiny pearl earring, the pearl mounted in gold and a chip of sparkling diamond in the drop.

"Miss Blake! Any sign of her?" she heard Roy shout. For a moment, she had quite forgotten about Ivy Beasley. Now she slipped the earring into her pocket and continued to walk, calling out and blowing a whistle she had thoughtfully collected before they left.

Fifteen

"*THERE* YOU ARE, Miss Beasley!" Miriam was about to retrace her steps and tackle another direction, when she caught sight of the solitary figure thwacking nettles with a stout stick, making her way back through the trees. "We have been terribly worried about you!"

"Who's we?" asked Ivy sharply.

"Why, Mr. Goodman and me, of course! He was so anxious and came to me for help. And you're soaking wet! Here, take this umbrella, and we'll get you back to Springfields as soon as possible. I could call for a taxi on my mobile?"

"Don't be ridiculous, Miss Blake. A little summer rain never hurt anybody. We'll walk back, and I can hold this umbrella over Roy."

"I already gave him one. I've got loads of umbrellas. You never know when you might need them. Like now."

Miriam was beginning to feel miffed. After all, she *had* found Miss Beasley, and there were still several paths to choose from before they reached the road.

Ivy caught the change in her voice and realised she had been unnecessarily short. She knew she had a sharp tongue, and was rather proud of it, but not too proud to admit when she had been mistaken. Also, Miriam Blake was a client.

"It was very thoughtful of you, Miss Blake," she said now. "I can't think how I missed the path. I am usually good at finding my way. But this time, without you spotting me, I could still be roaming the woods and sleeping under leaves when it got dark."

Miriam laughed delightedly. "Oh, very good, Miss Beasley! Babes in the wood, both of us could be, if I wasn't so sure of the way. But here we are, you see, and there's Mr. Goodman waving. Look at his dear old face! He must love you dearly, Miss Beasley. How romantic!"

"Yes, well, that's as may be," said Ivy. "So thank you, Miss Blake."

"Do call me Miriam," her rescuer enthused.

Ivy nodded. She had no intention of reciprocating the suggestion. Then Roy scuppered her and said that he would be delighted if Miriam would call him by his Christian name, and he was sure Ivy would feel the same. After all, they were going to be working together, weren't they?

"And now the sun's coming out again," said Miriam, squinting up at the sky. "So it's a happy ending all round. Do come in with me and dry off, and we'll have a cup of tea, won't you?"

Before Ivy could reply in the negative, Roy said quickly that he couldn't think of anything nicer and left his beloved to follow in what he could only regard as a sulk.

* * *

"I SUPPOSE YOU have to hand it to her," said Ivy, when they were once more on their way back to Springfields. "She does make the best Victoria sponge I've tasted for a long while."

Roy negotiated his vehicle round the considerable hazard of a young woman with twins in a wide pushchair. "She's a really nice person, I'm sure. I'm amazed she hasn't attracted many followers by now."

"She's had her moments," Ivy reminded him. "Anyway, we will do our best to help her. I for one shall be pleased if Gus comes up with a good reason for her being so keen."

Ivy's disappearance had so worried Roy that he had completely forgotten their original reason for visiting the woods. "Oh my goodness, all that went completely out of my mind! Now Ivy, did you by any chance spot any clues as to what Miriam and Rose might have seen in the woods?"

"Let's stop by the seat on the green," Ivy suggested. "The sun's so warm now it's a shame to waste it."

"And you can answer my question?" Roy said with a smile.

"Yes, I'll answer your question," she said, and when they were settled she told him about the man who had run away and then stopped to rescue her. "And then, when he was sure I was on the right path, he ran off again, giving me no time to thank him."

"Did he give you his name?"

"Oh yes. The Green Man of the Woods, he said."

"Ivy, are you making this up?" Roy began to wonder if she was having a reaction to her unpleasant experience. It was not like Ivy to play tricks.

"Of course not," she snapped. "He looked vaguely

familiar, but it was difficult to place him. He had this woolly hat pulled right down. But from what he said, he knew who I was and where I had come from."

"What on earth was he doing in the woods, and why did he run away?"

Ivy paused. She began to feel very tired, but did her best to reply. "He wouldn't answer any questions, Roy. And, to tell the truth, I was feeling too wobbly to ask. All I can tell you is that he was a gentleman. He behaved like a gentleman, and he spoke like one. He obviously did not want to be seen but came to my rescue when he saw I needed help. That's my idea of a gentleman, and I know, dear one, that you would have done exactly the same."

The sun had retreated behind clouds again, and they continued their walk back to Springfields. There they were greeted by a scolding from Mrs. Spurling for being out in the rain. Ivy said that they were not children, and would Mrs. Spurling remember who paid her wages. The least she could do was to have respect. Roy did his best to soften this outburst but saw that Ivy felt a lot better afterward.

MIRIAM WATCHED GUS pass by her window and guessed that he had stayed at Tawny Wings for lunch and most of the afternoon. She sighed. How could she compete with a rich widow, who had not only Gus but also the squire up at the Hall at her beck and call?

She pulled a tray of jam tarts—homemade jam and pastry made with butter—from the oven. They were done to perfection, and she put them to cool on the kitchen table. "The queen of hearts, she made some tarts," she muttered to herself. "That's me, Queen Miriam." Ah well, they say the way to a man's heart is through his stomach. She would call round and ask if he would like to pop in for supper. They could have the tarts for pudding. She had been much cheered by Roy and Ivy, as she now thought of them, agreeing to a cup of tea and being so complimentary about her sponge cake. Roy was such an old charmer, and even Ivy could be pleasant if she really tried! She was sure her cooking would work the same magic with Gus.

As she thought of the afternoon's drama, it occurred to her to wonder what on earth Ivy had been doing in the woods, leaving Roy in the road by himself. Neither of them had wanted to talk about it, and all they had really discussed was the weather. Had their expedition had anything to do with that horrible hand? It was quite possible Ivy had decided to take a look herself. So Enquire Within was already on the case.

Miriam felt in her pocket to check on the earring. She should put it somewhere safe, in case it, too, disappeared. Perhaps she should have mentioned it to Ivy and Roy. After all, it was surely an important piece of evidence. Well, it had slipped her mind in the emergency to be dealt with. She would show it to Gus and ask his advice. A good reason for going next door.

Gus had just switched on the radio for the news when he saw Miriam approach. Oh no, he groaned, not more temptation. This afternoon had gone swimmingly with Deirdre, and he would have been quite happy with a sandwich and something good on the telly. But no, here she was, tapping at his kitchen window.

"Supper, Miriam? Thank you so much, but I had a huge lunch and I think I shall fast for the rest of the day." He began to shut the door, but she put her foot against it. "Well, if you don't want supper, perhaps you'd like to see what I picked up in the woods this afternoon," she blurted out.

"Not another dead hand!" said Gus, and immediately regretted his lapse.

"No joke," she said, backing out. "And I'm sure you can manage a coffee and jam tarts still warm from the oven."

"Fine," said Gus with a sigh. "Five minutes, then."

Sixteen

MIRIAM RETURNED AROUND six o'clock bearing a tray, on which she had placed a plate of jam tarts and a pot of coffee. Gus saw with a sinking heart that there were also neatly cut sandwiches and two mugs, two plates.

"I was feeling a bit lonesome," Miriam said, smiling tentatively at him. "Hope you don't mind a bit of company for an hour or so?"

He thought of saying he minded very much indeed but was disarmed by her anxiously smiling face. "Of course not," he said as kindly as he could manage. "We can't have you feeling lonely. The Budds are out, I suppose?"

"I've got another reason to be here rather than there," Miriam said. "As I said, I have something to show you. Here, look what I found in the woods, just where we saw the hand. Roy asked me to look for Ivy in the woods, and I happened to pass the place, so thought I'd have a quick search. It was under quite a pile of dead leaves, and I should have missed it but for the twinkly stone. Do you think it's a diamond?"

"Could be," said Gus slowly, looking closely at the earring.

Miriam noticed that his usual good colour had gone from his face, and he was now very pale. "Gus? Are you okay?"

He shook his head and handed the earring back to Miriam with a shaking hand.

"What is it? For heaven's sake, Gus, tell me what's the matter? Is it something I said?"

Gus shook his head and shivered. "No, my dear," he said, with obvious effort. "It's just that, well, I gave those earrings to Kath on the eve of our wedding. She wore them on the day and was always very fond of them."

For once, Miriam was at a loss for words. "Oh my God," she said finally. "Does it mean that the hand we saw belonged to . . . Oh no, Gus, don't say that! I don't know whether she was wearing them when she arrived, and I didn't see her at all the morning she vanished again. This could have been an earring belonging to another woman, surely?"

Gus nodded miserably. "I doubt it," he said. "And most unlikely to be in the middle of the woods in darkest Suffolk." He sighed deeply. "Oh dear, Miriam, I'm afraid my appetite's completely gone."

Miriam was having none of this and encouraged him with stories of jewellery that had turned up in the most unlikely places. He managed a couple of sandwiches and two jam tarts and then asked her if she had shown the earring to Roy and Ivy.

"No, I put it in my pocket and then temporarily forgot about it. My first thought was to look after the two dear old things, in case they were suffering from shock."

"Well, do you want me to look after it, or will you keep it with you? We won't do anything until we've told the others. We are having a planning meeting tomorrow at Tawny Wings, and I'm sure the others will want you to bring it along."

"We should tell the police," Miriam said reluctantly.

Gus shook his head. "It will keep another twenty-four hours," he said. "But do look after it carefully."

"I'd be happier if you had it. If that hand was Katherine's, well . . ." She hesitated, and her lip quivered.

"But who on earth would know that you had found it? You didn't tell Ivy or Roy, so there's only me!"

Miriam stared at him. "You? But Gus, why would you not want to tell the police?" Then the full horror of the possibility struck her. Gus had loathed his ex-wife, and her sudden decision to visit could have completely unhinged him. She snatched the earring back from him, picked up her food tray, and left, muttering to herself as she went.

"Oh dear," said Gus to Whippy, who was asleep in her basket. "Looks like I'm suspect number one for a crime that's not necessarily been committed. What next, little dog?"

Whippy opened one eye, wagged her tail and went back to sleep.

NEXT MORNING, IVY was up with the lark, sorting out her clothes for the wash, opening her windows wide to let in the cool breeze, and if anyone had been listening, they would have been surprised to hear her humming a waltz tunelessly as she sorted out sensible knickers, a blouse with soup stains down the front, and a skirt that Tiddles had jumped on with muddy feet.

What am I doing in here? she asked herself, straightening up from putting on comfortable shoes. I am perfectly capable of taking care of myself. I should never have listened to Deirdre. But then, if I had stayed in Ringford, I would never have met Roy.

Dear Roy, he was such a comfort and made her feel wanted and worthwhile. She remembered now her last year in Victoria Villa, where she had sat all day in a rocking chair in the kitchen, old Tiddles on her lap, not bothering to change her underwear or have a bath. Her legs had become almost useless, and she had stopped cooking herself proper meals. The house had lost its pristine shine in spite of the efforts of New Brooms, the cleaning team, chiefly because she had forbidden them to tackle so many precious things that they had given up trying.

Now she heard the breakfast bell and started off downstairs with a light heart. It was summer, Roy would be waiting for her and there was a meeting this morning to discuss their new and possibly difficult case.

"Morning, Ivy dear." Roy was looking his handsome best. He had a fresh shirt and his favourite tie, a cheerful stripe given to him by Ivy, neatly knotted. Never mind his stringy old neck and what was left of his white hair combed carefully over the bald patch! He had his Ivy and the new excitement of his love for her.

"Now," he said, "shall we have porage or porridge?"

Ivy laughed. "Why don't we have a change and have porage?" she asked.

"Good idea," said Roy. "Allow me to help you to sugar."

"No sugar, thanks. Just a pinch of salt, which is always a good thing to take when in doubt."

Roy smiled sweetly at her. "I can see it is going to be a really good morning," he said.

Seventeen

"MORNING, IVY," DEIDRE said, walking into Spring-fields with a brisk step. "Why on earth have you called a meeting for this morning? We met as usual yesterday, and there can't be much new to report."

"All will be revealed," Ivy said. She had thought long and hard after they returned yesterday afternoon, and after discussing the Green Man of the Woods with Roy, she decided to tell the others immediately. Roy had suggested a couple of phone calls, but she thought they should all be together to talk about such an important development. She would ring round and summon them. When she called Gus, he had sounded odd, reluctant even, but she put that down to jealousy of Theo Roussel and his success with Deidre.

Deidre's cleaner was busy in Tawny Wings, and so Ivy had requisitioned Springfield's small conference room for the meeting, where they had in the past played pontoon regularly, until a tragedy involving one of the players had caused them to lose heart. The room, as the three entered, smelled musty and unused. Deirdre crossed to the window and threw it wide open. "Phew! That's better," she said. "Have you ordered coffee from your little Polish friend, Ivy?"

"We must wait for Gus," Roy said mildly. "It would be a shame to start without him."

"Is he bringing Miriam? She's obviously having a great time," said Deirdre sourly. She was very fond of Gus, and although she had no intention of committing herself to him, she objected to anyone else claiming his attentions.

"Don't know," Ivy replied. "She can be quite difficult to shake off. I would rather she did *not* come this morning, but we shall see if Gus is persuaded to bring her along."

In the event, it was more a case of Miriam dragging Gus out of his cottage and on the way to Springfields. "Of course I must come, too, Gus," she said. "After all, I found the earring."

He did not reply, and they walked in complete silence until they reached Springfields, when Gus emerged from dark thoughts and said, "You're unusually quiet this morning, Miriam. Anything up?"

Miriam shook her head mutely, and they checked in with Miss Pinkney, the assistant manager on duty this morning. She, unlike her boss, was a fan of Enquire Within and particularly admired Ivy Beasley for the way she had reorganised aspects of Springfields to suit her requirements. She greeted them warmly and pointed them in the direction of the conference room.

"Ah, there you are, Gus. And Miriam, too?" Ivy's tone was not welcoming.

"Naturally," said Miriam firmly. "It's my enquiry, isn't it?"

"Of course, my dear," said Roy the peacemaker. "But sometimes, you see, we need to discuss other cases on hand, and I'm sure you appreciate that these are confidential, as would your own be, if other clients were present."

"Oh, for goodness' sake, let's get on with it," said Deirdre. "I've got a hairdresser's appointment at midday in Oakbridge."

"I'll open the meeting, then," Ivy said. "Though Gus usually does it, he looks half-asleep. Shall I start, Gus?"

He nodded miserably, and Ivy began to recount what had happened when she was doing a spot of research in the woods.

"You? Did you go into those woods on your own, Ivy?" Deirdre asked. Although Ivy was extremely smart and capable of most things, Deirdre still felt responsible for her, since it was she who had persuaded Ivy to come to Springfields.

"Yes, of course. And Roy was close at hand. I saw this man, and when he saw me he began to run. I followed as quickly as I could until I caught my foot in a bramble and fell. Then he came back and helped me up. He was very pleasant but not at all forthcoming, and as soon as he'd made sure I could walk again, he disappeared through the trees."

"Very succinct, my love," said Roy. "Exactly right. But there was something else, wasn't there? The badgers' sett?"

"The what?" said Miriam.

"Sett, earth, holt," said Ivy impatiently. "You know, the mounds in the woods with holes in them where badgers live."

"No need to be so patronising, Ivy," said Miriam defensively.

"You're a countrywoman, aren't you?" replied Ivy. "Anyway, I was still not sure of the way back to Roy, and luckily he had alerted Miriam, and she quickly spotted me and helped me back to the road. Now, who *was* that man, and what was he doing? He had a spade, and there was a badger's whatsit, like I said. It looked to me to be very fresh soil. Probably to do with badger baiting. He wouldn't give me his name nor answer any questions about himself."

There was a knock at the door, and Gus rose to open it. Katya came in, carrying a tray of coffee and biscuits. "Mrs. Spurling gave instructions for no biscuits," she said with a grin. "But she is out, and Miss Pinkney is a kinder person and found these Jammie Dodgers for you."

Gus laughed, in spite of himself and said that Katya's English got better every day. The others thanked her kindly, and once the coffee was poured, Miriam said they should get back to business.

"I suppose we should," Gus said, and added that Miriam also had a very important piece of information to pass on. "She, too, found an interesting place to investigate," he said, looking at their client, who seemed to have become suddenly dumb.

"The badgers' sett?" said Ivy, surprised that Miriam had not mentioned it yesterday. She must have been going round in circles looking for her.

"No, it was where me and Rose first saw the hand," Miriam finally muttered.

"And?" said Gus. He was beginning to wonder what she was up to.

"And I found an earring," said Miriam. "It was under some leaves, and I picked it up. Showed it to Gus." She paused dramatically and looked at him. "He said it was his ex-wife's, but I knew it wasn't. It was mine, and it dropped out of my pocket while I was moving the mound of leaves to one side. I've only got the one and was hoping to have it copied sometime."

Eighteen

EVERYONE WAITED FOR someone else to break the silence. Miriam was now scarlet, and would not meet Gus's shocked gaze. Ivy looked at Roy, and Roy raised his eyebrows. Deirdre looked at her watch.

"Well, I don't know, I'm sure," she said. "Those dramatic revelations don't seem all that important to me. Ivy met a strange man in the woods and has now, I hope, learnt her lesson. And Miriam lost and found an earring under some leaves. So where's the relevance to our case? Come to think of it, my meeting with a strange, rather nervous man at the other end of a saxophone the other night could be just as important. He was, if you remember, asking about Katherine Halfhide, hoping not to meet her at the ball. If she had been there, I gathered, he would have done a bunk. Isn't that worth some further investigations? If she really had intended to find him at the ball, why didn't she show up?"

Gus found his tongue and said that Deirdre's contribution certainly was interesting, and he, for one, was most anxious to find out what had happened to his ex-wife, if only to, um . . . er . . .

Here he hesitated, looking at Miriam, and Ivy rescued him. "Two strange men?" she said. "Seems likely that it was one and the same man. We don't get all that many tall-ish saxophone-playing men here in Barrington."

"He wasn't playing the saxophone in the street," Miriam said humbly.

Roy had an idea. "If I may suggest a course of action?" he said. "All three of you ladies have heard and seen this man, or these men. Was there any really distinctive thing you remember that would point to him being a sole invader in our village?"

Silence once more, and then Miriam said hesitantly, "When I saw him walk by, the moonlight was bright for a minute, and though I couldn't see much, he definitely had a slight limp with his left leg. Definitely," she said again, gaining confidence.

"I watched him walk over to talk to Theo, and he limped with the right leg," said Deirdre.

"Both legs," said Ivy, fed up with what seemed to her to be unreliable recall and a waste of precious time. She unwittingly released the uncomfortable tension in the room, and the others smiled.

"No, but seriously, Ivy," Deirdre said, "did your man really limp?"

"Yes, he did. It was quite marked, especially when he ran off through the trees."

"There we are then," said Deirdre triumphantly. "Now we're getting somewhere."

* * *

BY THE END of the meeting, they had decided on three
courses of action. Deirdre would concentrate on finding
out more about the saxophonist. Having listened to various
conversations about the brilliant saxophone player at the
ball, she was sure Theo had known him before he had
turned up with Sid and His Swingers. She would get on to
Theo straightaway.

Ivy was to liaise with Deirdre to establish whether the
man in the woods was, in fact, the same person, though Ivy
expressed strong doubts about the likelihood of a visiting
saxophonist, possibly a member of the local toffs' circle,
digging holes in the nearby woods and probably involved
in a badger-baiting ring. "If you ask me," she said, "no kind
of musician is going to risk damaging his hands digging
like a navvy, is he?"

"Good point, Ivy," Roy said. "And I shall help you with
your investigations."

"What about me?" said Gus.

There was a short silence, and then Ivy said baldly that
if he wasn't already answering questions from the police
about the earring, he could approach his onetime gambling
friends to see if they could recollect a saxophone-playing
gamester. "Birds of a feather hang together," she commented enigmatically.

"But Ivy," said Miriam hotly. "I have explained the earring already. It's mine, and I slipped it in my pocket when
I was cleaning round the bedroom the other day. There'll
be no need to contact the police."

"Have you got it with you?" Ivy said. "I think at least we
should take a look at it. Your memory might be playing you
tricks." She had privately thought that she had never seen

anyone so clearly telling fibs as when Miriam first spoke up about owning the earring. And Gus had looked like a frit rabbit when she began to speak. So perhaps the truth was that he *had* recognised it as his ex-wife's, and foolish Miriam was protecting him.

"Sorry, no, I haven't. I've put it in a safe place until I can match it with another the same. You can forget about the earring, Ivy. Afraid it was a red herring, and my fault."

"Describe it for us," said Roy. "Then we can all look out for one to match it. You never know, we might easily spot one in a junk shop."

"Not junk!" said Gus involuntarily.

"Miriam?" Ivy persisted.

"Well, it's got a pearl, sort of dangling and, um, oh yes, a sparkly bit somewhere. Might be a diamond, Gus thought."

"Have you had it long, my dear?" said Roy, perfectly aware of what Ivy was up to.

"Um, several months, yes. It was a present." Miriam couldn't resist an embellishment but immediately regretted it.

Ivy pounced. "Who gave it to you, Miriam?" she said.

Miriam coloured deeply and stuttered that she couldn't quite remember.

"Rubbish, girl!" said Ivy. "It isn't your earring at all, is it? For some silly reason you think you are protecting Gus. Well, I am sure it is quite unnecessary, and in fact you are holding up our investigation. This earring is probably a very important piece of the jigsaw. For heaven's sake, woman, tell us the truth."

At this point, Ivy's cat Tiddles jumped on to Miriam's lap. She buried her face in the cat's fur and burst into tears, at which Tiddles yowled and ran off.

Gus stood up. "I'll go and find Katya and get us some

more coffee. Don't be upset, Miriam—it was a very kind thought."

When Gus had disappeared, Deirdre also stood up and put her hands on Miriam's shaking shoulders. "Come on, girl," she said. "We value your help, and we know this was just an unfortunate blip in our investigations. Let's forget about it." She glared across at Ivy, and added, "We all make mistakes."

They waited for coffee and then slowly relaxed. It was agreed that Miriam should take the earring to the police and explain exactly where and how she found it.

"You also have to tell them it was Kath's," Gus said. He was tired of revolving possible scenarios around in his head, featuring Kath being roughed up by local layabouts and Kath knifed in the dark night and carried lifeless into the woods, there to be buried by a saxophone-playing homicidal maniac.

"If you'll excuse me," he said, "I must be getting home. Whippy has her lunch about now, and I like to keep to a sensible routine for her. She's getting on, you know. I don't know what I'll do when she's gone."

His fading words were so bleak that Deirdre impulsively sprang to her feet and put her arms around him. "Don't worry, Gus dear," she said, "we'll all stand by you."

Not to be outdone, Miriam nodded and said childishly, "And anyway, Ivy Beasley, it could have been my earring." She had no intention of taking it to the police.

Nineteen

EACH DAY SEEMED to Deirdre to be hotter than the last, and she arrived home panting. A swim before lunch, she thought, and went upstairs to change into her swimsuit. Bert had loved the pool in the garden and said it was the best several thousand pounds he had ever spent. In his last weeks, he had found great relief in floating in the warm water, the strain removed from his aching limbs. Now Deirdre thought it should also be a good way of relaxing and thinking clearly about the morning's work.

She brought out a canvas chair and put it beside the pool with the day's newspaper and her spectacles, ready for when she came out of the water. A large gin and tonic and an ice bucket stood on a table by the chair, and she sighed with pleasure at the thought of a pleasant hour on her own.

She swam six lengths, then turned over onto her back and paddled with her feet, moving slowly backwards and looking up at the blue sky. Bliss, she thought. Why don't I do this more often? I could invite Theo or Gus to keep me company when I feel like it. She closed her eyes and felt the heat of the sun on her eyelids. For two pins, she thought, I could go to sleep. But maybe I would sink. Best not to try it.

Somebody cleared his throat loudly.

"Who's that?" Deirdre said sharply, making swiftly for the edge of the pool and looking up at the man who stood there, watching her. His back was to the sun, and she could see only a looming black shape.

"So sorry to interrupt you," he said. "You looked so relaxed and happy."

"I was, until a perfect stranger turned up in my garden. What do you want?"

"To talk to you, if you have time. We met the other night at the ball, where I was one of Sid's Swingers, God help me."

"Oh, you!" Deirdre was too surprised to be frightened, and climbed out of the pool, grabbing a towel and wrapping herself in it defensively. "Well, that's a bit of luck," she added. "I've been wanting to talk to you. But first I shall get dressed. Please wait here. I shan't be long." She felt safer with him out in the garden. Her neighbours were working just over the wooden fence, within call. She supposed he might run off if she left him alone, but that had to be risked. If he really wanted to talk to her, he would wait.

He was still there when she returned, and she noticed her gin was untouched. "Now," she said, "you had better sit down on that bench and tell me what you want. I should point out that I have my mobile phone here, and my friends next door are within earshot."

He stared at her, then burst out laughing. "Good heavens, Mrs. Bloxham, I am not an escaped criminal bent on rape and pillage!"

"I should hope not!" said Deirdre, not in the least discomforted. "So come on, spit it out. I've got a busy afternoon ahead."

"First of all, I must introduce myself. My name is Sebastian Ulph, and I come from Lincolnshire. The family were from Holland centuries ago and came across to drain the fens. Miles and miles of bugger-all, my father used to say, and I do agree. The only redeeming feature is the sky, which is twice as big in fenland as it is anywhere else."

"Except the Utah desert," said Deirdre, who had been there on an adventure holiday with Bert.

"I see you are a much-travelled person, Mrs. Bloxham."

"Yes, well, never mind about that. Just get to the point, Mr. Ulph."

"I am, as you know, a saxophonist and am temporarily playing with Sid and his lot. This is not really my kind of music. I am classically trained and have played in one or two of the best orchestras."

"So what went wrong?"

"Katherine Halfhide went wrong, I'm afraid. And in doing so, she dragged me down with her. You remember I mentioned her to you?"

"For God's sake, don't be so melodramatic! Just say what you have to say, and leave me to get on. As far as I can see, all this has nothing to do with me. If I can help, I will, but you must cut to the point." He was like a dog that has been chastised, his head hanging down and hands limply by his sides. Now, Deirdre, watch what you're doing! She heard Bert's voice as clearly as if he had been beside her.

"So?" she said impatiently.

"I fell in love with her when she was still married. She said she reciprocated my love and took me for every penny I possessed. It was not all that much, admittedly, but all I had. I'm the youngest son of a good but impoverished family, and have to make my way with little support."

Deirdre stood up. "So you want money? Well, the answer's no. So will you please leave now. At once."

"I don't want money, Mrs. Bloxham," he said, not moving. "I understand your late husband was a skilful brass player? Played French horn in the Oakbridge Orchestral Society brass section? Quite a reputation, so I understand from Sid. All I want from you, if at all possible, is an introduction to the orchestra. I think this would give me a very useful platform from which I could proceed to an audition and hopefully a job with prospects."

Deirdre sighed. She was well aware that here in her garden was one of the mysteries she was supposed to investigate. Handed to her on a plate, she thought. Maybe she should pursue him with the promise of help. After all, him being skint was no reason for an orchestra not to employ him. There was more to tell, she was sure. Such as why he did not ask Gus where Katherine was? But then, of course he did not necessarily know that Gus was living in Barrington. And even if he did, he would be very wary of the man whose wife he had stolen.

"Mrs. Bloxham?" He was looking anxiously at her, and she smiled.

"I may be able to help," she said. "I still know some of Bert's chums in the orchestra. Give me your phone number and I will let you know."

He shook his head. "Can't afford a phone," he said.

"An address, then? I'll drop you a note."

"Sorry, but I'm here and there. Best if I call and see you again. Would a week be time enough? I really am grateful, you know."

"That will have to do, then. I am very careful about who

I admit into the house, I'm afraid. So don't be alarmed by bolts and locks before I get the door open. And the bull terrier wouldn't hurt a fly, but don't tell anyone I told you." She paused, as if in thought. "Mind you, there was one time," she added, "when he did take several pieces out of a man who was clearly a bad lot. Otherwise . . ." She left the sentence hanging in the air and could see from his expression that it had had its effect.

After he had gone, she reached for the phone and dialled Gus. She told him everything that had been said, and he said approvingly that she was a bright girl. "But Deirdre," he asked, "since when did you have a bull terrier?"

FOLLOWING DEIRDRE'S CALL, Gus postponed any action he should take for a couple of hours while he thought carefully about her revelations. Sebastian Ulph. It was a name you couldn't forget, and he clearly remembered teasing Kath about her young admirer. That was when they were still happily married, and he had yet to discover just how little she intended to honour her vows, made with such great solemnity at the altar of her mother's church.

Ulph was one of Kath's many attractive young men. She loved to hold court at what she called her soirées, where they would talk about art and life but mostly gossip about their circle of friends, many of them well heeled and idle. There were other women there, of course, but the object of the exercise was a mammoth ego trip for Kath. She was, at that time, rich and beautiful and, as Gus later discovered, ruthless.

If he remembered rightly, Ulph continued to woo her after the divorce, though he had heard no more of him since then.

He did, however, remember hearing of Ulph's determination to see himself through a degree course at the Royal College of Music, playing any kind of music at sundry functions to pay his way. All that was some time ago, of course, and Gus could only guess at the reason for him turning up in a provincial town with Sid and His Swingers. He must have been very curious to know why Gus's fickle ex-wife should show renewed interest in him. Though not curious enough, apparently, to be willing to meet her at the ball. Not the time or the place, possibly. But he might have been keen to see her elsewhere, if he thought she was good for a handout. "If so, Whippy girl, he must be really desperate." And then a terrible thought struck him. How desperate? Desperate enough to silence her mocking voice forever and rob her lifeless body of its jewels, dropping one earring on his flight away from the body? Had it been Ulph who passed Miriam's house in the middle of the night on his way to the woods carrying God knows what in bags?

Gus shook himself. This was ridiculous. He was becoming as overwrought as Miriam Blake! But before he could stop it, he had a vision of Ulph hastily digging a grave in the woods and burying his victim, making it look like a badgers' home. But Ivy had described the freshly turned mound as being some way from where Miriam found the hand. Or imagined a hand?

Gus's brain whirled, and he felt sick. "Come on, Whippy," he said. "Before we do anything else, we'll go for a walk and get some fresh air. The sun's low in the sky now, and it should be cooler. Here, let's put your lead on."

As they walked out of the garden gate into the lane, Gus heard Miriam's voice and cursed. Just when he wanted to be alone to clear his head!

"Going for a walk?" said Miriam chattily. "Mind if I

come along? It's really nice now, in the cool of the evening. Even Whippy looks more lively, don't you, doggy?" She patted the little head. Gus saw the dog's curled lip and hastily shortened the lead and drew her to his other side.

They walked in a reasonably peaceful silence for a short while, and then Gus asked the question he knew he should ask. "Why did you lie about the earring, Miriam? You know it wasn't yours. It was a very silly thing to do. I have a completely clear conscience, so there's no need to worry about me. You had better give it to me to take care of. It will be safer in my strongbox if the new owner of the other one comes looking for it."

Miriam shook her head quickly. "I've lost it," she said flatly. "Sorry. It's gone. I've looked everywhere, but it's gone. Best to forget about it, Gus."

"Miriam! You can't have lost it! It might be a very important piece of evidence."

"Too bad," she said. "Nobody will believe me now. Not them police nor any detective. They didn't believe me about the hand. So stuff them. I'd forgotten about it already, until you said."

"But I saw it, Miriam. And I know where it came from."

"If you don't say nothing, nobody will ever know about it. Except the others, an' we'll tell them it was all a mistake."

"Oh, for heaven's sake!" Gus groaned. He seemed unable to get through to the silly woman. But then, most of his relationships with women were doomed to failure. He could only hope her infatuation with him would fade and enable her to see how necessary it was to tell the truth.

"Don't worry," said Miriam blithely. "Let's enjoy our walk. Maybe we could go up to the woods? Whippy loves it in there."

Twenty

"IF YOU ASK me," said Ivy, "it was a bad day we took on Miriam Blake as a client. You can't trust anything the silly woman says, and it could all very well come to nothing."

She and Roy were sitting comfortably in her room with the window wide open. It was all but dark now, and a couple of hundred yards up the street a security light lit up the front of the village shop. Every now and then, a dark form would walk under the light, and Roy and Ivy amused themselves trying to guess who it was.

"How do you mean, Ivy?" Roy was feeling ready for bed, but his beloved seemed chirpy as ever. He smothered a yawn and smiled at her.

"Well, that ex-wife of Gus's will probably turn up somewhere, with two perfectly good hands, claim the pearl earring she dropped in the woods and vanish again."

"Possibly, Ivy dear. But we still have the missing hand to resolve. After all, Rose Budd supported Miriam on that one," said Roy. "As to Katherine Halfhide, it looks to me that she may well have come to some harm. Her sudden departure from Miriam's cottage was odd, to say the least. I know Miriam irritates you, my love, but no one says clients have to be pleasant."

Ivy made no reply but looked steadily out of the window. "Look, there's that Britwell woman, if I'm not much mistaken," she said. "Going home from the pub, no doubt. She's no better than she should be. Not married, and with all those children. Doesn't need to work, with plenty of child benefit from the state. It's a disgrace, Roy."

He nodded. He knew by now when it was unwise to argue with Ivy and merely said he thought he would toddle off to bed. "And you will need your beauty sleep, my dear, if we are to be off investigating tomorrow."

"Huh!" said Ivy. She helped him to his room and kissed him warmly. "Night, night," she said, softening. "Sleep well, Roy dearest."

She returned to her room, marvelling at how lucky she was. But even when she was safely in bed with the light out and only the soothing sound of hooting owls, she could not sleep.

THEO ROUSSEL HAD retired early to bed and swore when his telephone rang. He had been dozing after a hard day on the golf course and never found it easy to get off to sleep, however tired he was.

"Who is that?" he said sharply.

"Me, Deirdre."

His tone warmed. "Ah, Deirdre, my treasure, how are we?"

"I'm fine," she replied. She could tell from his voice that he was in bed and half-asleep.

"What can I do for you, Deirdre? If there's a problem, why don't you call me in the morning?"

"I need to ask you a question, and then you can go back to sleep."

He sighed. "Fire away, then, if you must."

"It's just this. Do you remember we talked about the saxophonist in Sid and His Swingers? Tallish chap with lots of dark hair?"

"Oh, you mean Sebastian? Yes, of course I remember the name now. It was me that got him the job playing with them. Son of an old chum, you know. Temporarily down on his uppers. His father was older than me, of course, old Donald Ulph. Grew apples somewhere near Boston in Lincolnshire. Interested in rare breed cattle. Dead now. Sebastian was a bit of a lad but good at heart. Excellent musician. Some woman took him for a ride, and I wanted to give him a helping hand." He paused, but Deirdre said nothing. "Is that what you wanted to know?" he continued.

"More or less," said Deirdre. "But one thing puzzles me. If he was such an excellent musician, why couldn't he have got a job with an excellent orchestra? For one thing, the money would be a whole lot better, surely?"

Theo shifted his position in bed and resigned himself to another hour of wakefulness. "You have me there, Deirdre," he said. "Perhaps there was some scandal attached to him, but I don't know of any. Now," he added, "is it in order to ask why you wanted this information so urgently? And are you coming up to help me get off to sleep again?"

"Answer to question one, can't tell you at the moment. Answer to question two, no. Good night, sleep tight and don't let the bugs bite."

Theo grinned. She was a great girl, and he was lucky to be so close to her. If only she would marry him, they could be a great team. Possibly. He sighed, made himself comfortable and went quite quickly to sleep, thinking of all the good times he and Deirdre had had together.

GUS HAD FALLEN asleep in front of the television and was dreaming. He was in the woods, searching frantically for Whippy, who had gone missing. Miriam was with him, and she had run off, saying she knew where the dog would have gone. There was a badgers' holt there, and all dogs made a beeline for that. Then she reappeared, carrying a spade, her hands covered with earth. She was laughing, and saying Whippy would rest easy now. She had buried her comfortably under the trees.

Gus jerked out of the nightmare. "Whippy!" The little dog also woke in surprise and jumped out of her basket. She rubbed her head against his knee, and he picked her up, hugging her tight. Fully awake now, he felt hot tears streaming down his face and knew his grief was for more than a nightmare about his whippet.

Twenty-one

SIDNEY WATSON, CONDUCTOR and music director of the Swingers, sat at his desk in the Inland Revenue office and tried hard to concentrate on an almost illegible tax return from one Augustus Halfhide. Must be a made-up name, he thought. He checked it against the records and found that he was a single man living in Hangman's Row, a terrace of cottages in Hangman's Lane, Barrington. A nice village, Barrington, and Sid and his wife had fancied buying a bungalow there. But it was one of the most desirable villages in the county, only a few miles from Oakbridge and Thornwell, and boasted a grand stately home and ancient church. As a result, its beautiful plastered houses in varying shades of pink, fetched high prices.

His mobile rang, and he saw an unfamiliar name on the screen. Deirdre Bloxham? He thought he remembered the name. Bloxham Car Showrooms were big in the area, not only around Oakbridge but across the county. There had been a Mr. Bloxham, and Sid remembered his obituary. Albert Bloxham had had a whole page to himself.

"Hello? Can I help you?" he said. He had grudgingly caught up with the new policy of being nice to clients of Her Majesty's Revenue and Customs.

"This is Mrs. Deirdre Bloxham here," the pleasant voice said. "I wonder if you could spare me a few moments. No, not to do with income tax," she added hastily. Her financial affairs were handled by her accountant, and she kept a close eye on them herself. "No," she continued, "I wondered if you could help me with a member of your band. Sebastian Ulph? He plays the saxophone."

Sid thought before he answered. Was this why Ulph had left them so suddenly and inconveniently? Said he was off to France or somewhere. "I'm very sorry," he said, "but Sebastian is no longer with the Swingers. He left us after the ball in Barrington. I think he mentioned a trip to France. It was a shame, really. Lots of people had commented on his lovely playing."

"Did he say why he was going?" asked Deirdre. She had felt a shiver of anxiety at the news. He had said he would be here and there. But France? And what was he using for money, if he was as broke as he had said?

"'Fraid not, Mrs. Bloxham. I paid him up-to-date and wished him well. It was inevitable really," he added. "He was much too good to be playing with the Swingers, though I says it as shouldn't. I was hoping to give him an introduction to the town orchestra. They have professional players and a good reputation."

"How long had he been with your band?" She did not tell him that Ulph had requested the same introduction from her.

"Only a month or so. Funny, that. He was quite posh,

but the lads really took to him. Reckoned he was all right. And that was quite a compliment, I can tell you!"

"Well, thanks very much. If you hear from him at all, would you mind asking him to ring me? I might have some good news for him." Deirdre cut off the call and frowned. Curiouser and curiouser, as Alice said.

"I THINK I might take a ride down to Hangman's Row this morning," Roy said to Ivy. "I'd like to have a quiet talk with Miriam Blake."

"You're not going by yourself? I shall come with you, of course."

"Well, actually, my love, I would quite like to see her by myself. Just one to one, as they say. I have a feeling she might be more forthcoming if her only audience was a silly old fool with a trundle and a stick."

"Whatever you like, Roy," Ivy said. "But are you sure you want to be alone with Miriam Blake?"

"Why ever not, dearest? She's not going to seduce an old dodderer who can't remember what day it is."

"Don't be silly! You're the brightest of all of us," she protested. "Still, if you're sure, and promise me you will ring if you need help."

Roy nodded. "If I am helpless in her clutches, I will do my best," he said, grinning. "Now I must put on my hat and be off."

SEBASTIAN ULPH HAD not gone to France. He had had no intention of going anywhere, having decided that Oakbridge and its surrounding countryside was just the place for him to spend time. Sooner or later the police would take a serious interest in the fraudulent activities of Katherine Halfhide, and since she was known to have visited the village of Barrington, they would naturally concentrate first on that area. That would be the time for him to consider leaving. Meanwhile, he had unfinished business with her, when he was ready.

He was pleased with his interview with Deirdre Bloxham. Quite a girl, that one, for her age! A vision of her climbing out of the swimming pool in a mini-bikini had haunted his dreams. But she had seemed serious about getting him a job. Whether he would be able to take it was not certain, however. It would depend on the outcome of his plan. Meanwhile, he became as invisible as possible. Now he had found a cheap bedsit in a back street in Oakbridge and was living a hand-to-mouth existence until the time came for him to follow up messages he had sent to Katherine and act.

He had discovered that his room on the top floor of a three-story house was more or less soundproof, and he was able to practise his saxophone in short bursts so as not to attract attention. His landlady was a kind soul and had several times offered him food left over from her own meals. She said he was starved, and he had looked at himself in the flyblown mirror in his room and seen a hollow-cheeked, wild-haired version of himself. Well, never mind, he had thought, it all adds to the anonymity.

Outside his window, he found he could easily climb out onto the flat roof of a small extension. This evening, the sun was going down over the rooftops of Oakbridge, bathing everything in a spectacular fiery red glow. He climbed out with a rickety chair, and with a large glass of cheap red wine in his hand, he contemplated the sunset, turning over in his mind plan after plan to make sure all details for a deal with Katherine were foolproof.

* * *

IVY PACED AROUND her room, looking out along the high street from time to time. She looked at her watch and rummaged in her handbag for her mobile phone. She dialled Roy's number, heard the message-taking voice, and switched off with a small and inoffensive curse. Where was he? It was half past eight, and he had not been in for supper. Miss Pinkney had come on duty at half past seven, and Ivy had been unable to speak to her. The assistant manager was sitting with a new and agitated resident, who was convinced she had been tricked into coming to Springfields on a long-term basis and was making vigorous efforts to escape.

It was so unlike Roy not to let her know where he was that for the first time in their relationship, she realised how agonising worry could be and how much she relied on his comforting presence.

Just as she had decided to go along to the new resident's room and demand to speak to Miss Pinkney, a tap at her door was followed by Roy's voice, asking to be admitted.

"Roy Goodman! Where on earth have you been? I have been so worried!" Ivy sat down heavily, overcome with relief.

Roy smiled, and there was something foolish about his smile. Ivy remembered her father coming home to her domineering mother, not too steady on his feet and wafting unmistakable alcoholic fumes over her.

"Roy, have you been *drinking*?" she said in shocked tones.

"Only a glass or two of Miriam's beau-beautiful primrose wine," he said, still smiling at her. "She's a lovely person, Ivy dear. We must cultivate her as our friend."

Ivy was speechless. After a minute or so, during which

time she guided him into a chair and put a cushion behind his head, she rallied and said that *nobody* could convince her that Miriam Blake was anything but a self-serving, irritating busybody and the last person in the world she would cultivate as a friend.

"You'll think better of it in the morning, my dearest love," Roy said, and his head drooped forward.

"Roy! Are you asleep?" Ivy was incensed. She poked his arm with her finger. "Roy! Wake up!" But he slept on peacefully, with a seraphic smile on his face.

Ivy heaved a sigh, and decided to let him sleep on. He would probably not wake up until tomorrow morning. Miriam Blake's primrose wine had a reputation that had spread countywide. She had been taught to make it by her wicked old mother, and the recipe was a closely guarded secret. But Ivy had a vague idea that poppies had a soporific effect and had noticed Miriam coming back from the cornfields with bunches of poppies in hand. She feared the worst.

How typical of a man to be taken in so easily by a dreadful woman! Well, he could stay where he was and think up convincing explanations in the morning. She wrapped a rug around his knees, and began to prepare herself for bed, facing squarely the likelihood of trouble for them both.

Her thoughts were interrupted by a sharp tap at her door. "Miss Beasley? Have you seen Mr. Goodman? May I come in?"

"Certainly not!" said Ivy loudly. "He's probably staying at his niece's overnight. Now please go away. I'm in bed and going to sleep. Good night."

Twenty-two

WHEN IVY AWOKE, for a couple of seconds she forgot that she had had a nighttime companion in her room. Then the fog of deep sleep cleared away and she sat up with a jerk, looking across at the armchair where she had tucked up Roy, asleep in his alcoholic stupor. She blinked when she saw the chair was empty.

"So the bird has flown!" she said aloud, and then startled at the sound of her voice sounding exactly like her mother's, she frowned and got slowly out of the bed. Sunlight already filled her room, and for several minutes she stared out of the window, seeing nothing of the lovely morning but lost in memories of her poor father, turned out of the house to sleep in the shed and followed out there by a shrill diatribe from her shrieking mother.

"Am I turning into my mother?" she muttered. This thought was not a comfortable one. She had never noticed it before, but then she had only once before had a man in her life. By the time she had washed and dressed ready for breakfast, she had considered the whole matter seriously and decided to surprise Roy with tolerant understanding. He should see that she was quite capable of handling any such situation with broad-mindedness and humour. She had even practised her opening words. "And how's my beloved this morning?" This she would say with a warm, amused smile.

Roy was already at the breakfast table, nursing a sore head and dreading the appearance of Ivy. He had been woken in the middle of the night by a care assistant who had put her hand over his mouth to prevent him protesting as she led him silently out of Ivy's room and back to his own. He had sobered up with the hideous memory of himself lurching in and disturbing Ivy with eulogies on the subject of Miriam's primrose wine. Oh, dear God, how could he face his beloved this morning?

"Ah, so there you are!" Ivy sat down at the table, cleared her throat and said sharply that if anyone asked her, she would say that the demon drink was responsible for many things but that only a fool would be witless enough to allow a silly woman to ply him with that primrose stuff!

This was more or less what Roy was expecting, and he was never to know what good intentions Ivy had nurtured but not fulfilled. He apologised profusely, said that she was exactly right, that he *was* a fool, and was now paying for it with the mother and father of a headache.

"The sins of the father!" said Ivy, and although Roy was not quite sure of the aptness of this quotation, he once more apologised and said that she should never again see him in that parlous state. Would she give him another chance?

Ivy subsided sadly, and told herself that although her mother no longer spoke to her in her head, the old ghost was still in control. She reached out and took Roy's trembling hand. "You shall have as many chances as you like," she said. "For better, for worse, that's how I intend our marriage shall be." So buzz off, Mother, she added in her head.

When equilibrium was restored, Roy gave her a sober account of what had happened with his Miriam Blake interview. "She was very cheerful, Ivy, and thoroughly enjoying the whole prospect of being a detective. I questioned her closely about the hand she saw and the earring, which she claims she had picked up but then lost, and was, in any case, her own. I have to say, my dear, that your assessment of Miriam's character is probably very near the truth. Her story varies according to her mood, it seemed to me. The hand, once that of a small and defenceless woman, now appears to have been possibly that of a small man and has adopted a faded whitish, yellowish colour."

"There you are, then," said Ivy. "The woman is ridiculous. Time to be firm with her. We should say that it is Enquire Within policy to carry out investigations without the client present. A report will be made to her as and when we have fresh information."

"I got the impression that Gus was feeling like barring his doors against her, poor man. I suppose we could abandon the case?"

"Certainly not," said Ivy. "There has been a crime. I am convinced of that. But what it is and who's involved is still a mystery. What we need is some hard evidence."

"Such as what, dearest?" said Roy admiringly.

"A body," said Ivy flatly. "More toast?"

BY MIDDAY, THUNDERCLOUDS were gathering, and Deirdre rushed out to bring garden chairs into the conservatory. As the first drops of rain began to fall, she heard her phone ringing and ran through to answer it.

"Hello? Oh, Gus, how are you doing? There's going to be a storm, I'm afraid. What did you say? Oh, that was a hell of a clap! A meeting? What, this afternoon? Well, I suppose it would be all right if the storm clears away. Have you spoken to Ivy and Roy?"

Gus said that he hadn't, wanting to clear it with her first. He explained that he was considering going away for a week and he wondered what the others would think. The Miriam Blake case seemed to have ground to a halt, and he was not at all sure that it was worth pursuing. They really needed to have a discussion, with all present.

"Going away? What for? And where?"

"Can't tell you, I'm afraid. One of those things that come up now and then."

Deirdre sighed. "Oh, Gus, not that old thing! I thought we'd left Gus the Secret Agent behind us now. It's much more likely that you don't want to have anything more to do with a case involving your ex-wife. That's quite understandable, you daft old thing! No need to go away. Just leave the rest to me and the two oldies. Anyway, I'll give Ivy and Roy a buzz and see if they're free. Be here at two o'clock, unless you hear to the contrary."

AROUND TWO, THE skies cleared, and the air was fresh, washed clean by the sudden storm. It was cooler, and Ivy and Roy set out from Springfields in a much happier mood. Deirdre had given them no details about this meeting, apart from saying that Gus had called it.

As they walked up the drive to Tawny Wings, Ivy remarked that it was looking its best after the rain. The tall hollyhocks had withstood the heavy shower and stood unbowed by the front door. Deirdre was there to welcome them, and Gus hovered in the background, looking worried.

"Come on in," Deirdre said. "Can you manage the stairs again, Roy?"

He was tempted to answer that given a shot of Miriam's primrose wine, he could leap over the moon. But, glancing at Ivy's stern face beside him, he thought better of it.

When they were settled, Gus cleared his throat and began to speak. "Sorry about the short notice, folks, and thanks a lot for coming along. The thing is, I am feeling in need of a break."

"I thought you had a top-secret mission," Deirdre said.

"That too," said Gus. "And to continue, as we seem to be getting nowhere on Miriam Blake's case, I am planning a week or so away from the village. A long way away. I wanted you all to know now so that any lingering difficulties regarding the missing hand and the lost earring can be dealt with before I go."

There was a shocked silence, and then Ivy spoke. "When do you propose to go, and where can we get hold of you if something urgent comes up?"

Gus replied that he planned to travel on Monday, and asked how likely was it that something urgent would come up? As far as he could see, they had no reliable facts to investigate. And where was the crime? Originally, Miriam had wanted the missing hand investigated, but she herself had muddied the water there. Was it actually in the woods in the first place, and given that Rose Budd had seen something, had it been a severed hand from a dead body? And then it had disappeared, and every time Miriam talked about it, it assumed a different description. Severed or not? A deathly white or a faded yellowish colour?

"But what about your wife, Gus? I don't wish to be alarmist," said Deirdre mildly, "but she does seem to have disappeared without a word. And why did she come here in the first place, when she knew she would not be welcome. And again, what did Miriam Blake say to her to cause her to do a bunk, if that is what she has done?"

Gus hung his head. "Kath was always doing things for no reason at all," he muttered. "I don't think there's much for us to investigate there."

Another silence, then Deirdre continued. "Gus, why did you go rushing home and then back again on that day I asked you to lunch? Did you go to see Kath? And wasn't it the day she disappeared?"

"Of course not!" he replied crossly. "The less I saw of her, the better. I thought you all realised that. I went home to feed Whippy. What are you suggesting, Deirdre? That I went home, strangled Kath and buried her in the woods, dropped her earring and got back here in time for lunch?"

His face was red and angry, and he got to his feet.

"Sit down, Gus!" said Ivy, in a new, powerful voice. "Deirdre is only suggesting what others, meaning the law, might come up with. There is obviously much more to discuss, and I suggest we break for a cup of tea. Will you oblige, Deirdre? And Gus, you might like to take a turn round the garden. But be back in here in ten minutes."

Deirdre and Gus left the room, and Roy turned to Ivy. "Has our Deirdre loosed a cat among the pigeons, my dear?" he said. "This will take a bit of sorting out."

Twenty-three

WHEN THE MEETING reconvened, Gus found himself at the receiving end of a barrage of awkward questions. These mostly came from Deirdre and were on the subject of his relationship with his ex-wife, Kath. He protested that his private life was his own affair, but Deirdre would not leave it there. She said that since Kath's disappearance and failure to reestablish contact, it was now very important for Gus to think carefully about his conversations with her and prepare an accurate account of his movements since she vanished.

"Why?" said Gus, desperately trying to avoid Ivy's gimlet eyes. "I had very little to do with her. She stayed with Miriam. And anyway, why does it matter? She's probably somewhere miles away, living in the lap of luxury at someone else's expense and giving no thought to any of us. She obviously made a quick getaway before poor Miriam could ask for her lodging money. She didn't pay her, you know."

"The reason, Augustus," said Ivy, in measured tones, "why you need to listen to Deirdre, is that Kath might turn up at any minute, not living in the lap of luxury and possibly not living at all. In plain English, the woman might be dead. Her earring was found in the woods, and who knows, there may be a hoard in there, buried out of sight until it could be collected."

"So?" said Gus defiantly.

"So, you are known to have hated her and equally well known to be hard up. You returned to the Row, supposedly to feed Whippy, around the time when she could have been abducted, hidden away or"—she hesitated—"murdered."

The others were speechless, and Gus stood up, shoving his chair back with a thump. "How dare you, Ivy!" he said. "I have had more than enough of this. I thought I was among friends who trusted me, but I see I was mistaken. I hereby resign from Enquire Within. I have personal things to sort out and shall be out of reach as from Monday. Do not try to get in touch."

Ivy shrugged her shoulders and said she had merely pointed out a few facts and would say no more.

It was Roy who came to the rescue, as he had a number of times in the past. He reached out his hand and took hold of Gus's sleeve. "Sit down, old chap," he said. "I am sure Ivy meant no harm and may even have intended to help you by pointing out a dangerous situation that could occur in the future, for which it would be prudent to be prepared. Please sit down, do, dear man. We are all your friends here, and friends stick together. And if Kath does turn out to be alive and well, we shall all be delighted."

"Well said, Roy," said Deirdre. "Whatever happens, Gus, we shall support you in every way we can."

Gus took a deep breath. "I haven't bloody well *done*

anything!" he exploded. Then he sat down and wiped his hand across his eyes. "Anyway," he said in a calmer voice, "thanks, Roy, for your vote of confidence, if that's what it was. Ivy?"

Ivy nodded. "Never had any doubts," she said.

"Deirdre?"

"Of course, you old silly."

"And Roy," said Gus. "You are a boon and a blessing to men. Thanks, my friend."

Twenty-four

GUS WALKED TOWARDS home, head down and lost in thought. He pondered ruefully on the fact that of all the tight situations he had been in, this last meeting at Tawny Wings was the worst. He had been right, he realised, to have chosen Ivy Beasley to be his ally in forming Enquire Within, but little had he thought she would turn against him. Not that she had done so now, not completely. But her old face was severe with suspicion, and it had not entirely cleared when the meeting ended.

"Penny for 'em, Gus!" It was his darts chum, James from the shop, delivering groceries on an old-fashioned errand-boy bike. He had announced to the village that this was part of his contribution to the battle against global warming. Everyone would have noticed, he had added, how much healthier he had been from the exercise and fresh air. "Oh no, no thoughts worth a penny, really," said Gus. "Just considering the never-ending puzzle of womankind."

"Blimey, that sounds serious! Has our Deirdre given you the boot?" It was well known in the village that Deirdre Bloxham entertained two close friends, and one of them was Gus.

"Don't even suggest it," said Gus, with a smile. "I am persona non grata with my colleagues at the moment. So much so that I am planning a week or so's holiday to escape."

Naturally James thought he was joking, but there was truth in Gus's words. He had been developing a theory about what had happened to Kath, but it was too unsupported at present and might easily come to nothing. He intended to keep it from the others. It was this theory that involved going away, and he had already made plans to follow it up.

The one big snag was Whippy. He could not take her with him, and he was unwilling to allow Miriam to have her for two weeks. The last thing he wanted was to be beholden to Miriam Blake and submit himself to her questioning. It might have to be boarding kennels, but first, he could not afford the exorbitant charges, and second, he hated to think of Whippy in a small concrete cell, released for a run twice a day in a bare enclosure with assorted fellow boarders.

He could not believe his luck when he heard James's next question. "What are you going to do with Whippy? Is Miriam having her? If not, you know I am only too pleased to look after her. She can help the cat hunt for mice in the storeroom and come with me on my twice-a-day runs. How about it, Gus?"

This was such a wonderful offer, coupled with no need to answer any of James's questions except the last, and Gus grabbed at the opportunity. He agreed that he would bring

Whippy round to the shop in due course, together with her bed and baggage.

They parted amicably, and Gus strode home with his head held high. He would book a taxi to get him to Thornwell for the earliest train to London on Monday morning. He had a small qualm about deserting Ivy and Roy, and Deirdre, but then he remembered their unfriendly questioning and cheered up. Let them stew, and see how they could get on without him!

IVY HAD TRIED but failed to put the drama of the meeting behind her and told Roy she was going for a stroll on her own to do some serious thinking. He was concerned and suggested he could accompany her in total silence, if necessary. Then, if some mishap occurred, he would be beside her. "What do you mean by mishap? I am perfectly capable of dealing with anything likely to threaten me on a stroll around the village. And when you are with me, I just cannot think of anything else but how much I love you."

Roy gasped, and sat up very straight in his chair in Springfields lounge. "Oh, Ivy!" he said. "Do you really mean that?"

"No, not really, my dear one, but it is the only way I can think of getting you to agree to my going out alone."

Roy recognised stalemate and was relieved to see Miss Pinkney coming towards them, bearing Tiddles, Ivy's small black cat.

"Ah, Miss Beasley, would you take Tiddles to your room? We have a new prospective resident coming in to have a look at us, and she is bringing a cat-eating dog. Her words! I am sure we shall be able to arrange something, should she decide to come here, but meantime I cannot be responsible for the safety of Tiddles." She deposited a squirming cat on Ivy's lap and departed quickly.

"Well!" expostulated Ivy. "Tiddles was here first, and I shall have to consider my position very carefully if a cat-eating dog is allowed!"

"So you won't be going out, then?" Roy looked hopefully at her.

"Yes, of course I shall. You can sit in my room and guard Tiddles. Much better than guarding me from imagined disasters!"

So Roy sat in Ivy's room and watched her determined figure walk purposefully down the High Street and vanish into the village shop.

"GOOD AFTERNOON, MISS Beasley. How are you today?" James was not always pleased to see Ivy, as more often than not she had a complaint, but it was near the end of the afternoon and the shop was empty.

"As well as can be expected from someone threatened by a cat-eating dog," she said sharply.

"Not Tiddles!" said James, duly shocked.

"Not yet," said Ivy, pursing her lips. "A possible resident with dog coming to Springfields," she said.

"Not fond of dogs, Miss Beasley?"

"In their place, dogs are bearable. But I could not tolerate having to be constantly vigilant with my Tiddles."

"I suppose you are used to a kind, gentle sort of dog like Whippy? Gus is never seen without her."

"Huh! Even Whippy can be smelly at times." Ivy sniffed. "The man is quite besotted with her."

"Well, he's leaving her with me for a week. As you will

know, he is holidaying where he can't take her, so he's entrusting her to me."

Ivy thought rapidly. "Of course, yes," she said. "Now, let me think, where is it he is going? France, is it?"

James shook his head, well aware that Ivy was fishing for information. "I don't think he told me where, exactly. I expect it is abroad, hence leaving Whippy with me. Now, Miss Beasley, what can I get you? Your usual chocs?"

IVY LEFT THE shop and headed on towards the church. She had checked with the parish magazine and knew that it was Rose Budd's turn to do the flowers. It would be the ideal quiet time to ask her a few questions.

Sure enough, Rose was surrounded by greenery and cut flowers, happily arranging them in the font, on the stand by the altar, on windowsills and anywhere else she could fit in a posy. She loved flowers and was never happier than when arranging them. The Women's Institute always chose her as its representative in countywide competitions, and Rose had a shelf full of cups and trophies as reward.

"Good afternoon," Ivy called from the church door. "Am I intruding, Mrs. Budd?"

Yes, you are, Rose wanted to say, but she was a nice girl and instead welcomed Miss Beasley with warmth. "Lovely afternoon for a walk," she said. "How is Mr. Goodman?"

Ivy sat down in the front pew and placed her shopping beside her. "He's cross with me at the moment," she said cheerfully. "He is a dear and always wants to be with me, but sometimes a person needs to be alone, don't you think?"

Rose said a heartfelt yes and turned away to anchor an unruly chrysanthemum.

"How are your family? Quite recovered from all that t'do about a severed hand in the woods? Your neighbour, Miss Blake, has a fertile imagination, as I am sure you've discovered."

Rose turned back to look at the black-clad figure in the pew. She's like an old crow, she thought. "Oh no," she said. "The hand was there, all right. I saw it myself. Horrible, it was, at the time. We didn't stop for a second look and beat it out of the woods as soon as possible! O'course, as you no doubt know, when Miriam went back, it had gone. Fox took it, probably. My David says they are like magpies and take things. Mind you, I never heard that before, and I reckon he made it up to set my mind at rest. So, yes, we have forgotten all about it. When you have two young sons to look after, there isn't much time for dwelling on such things!"

My, thought Ivy, that was a long speech. Did young Mrs. Budd have something to hide?

"And now," continued Rose, "if you'll excuse me, I must get on with these flowers. It's a benefice service on Sunday with all those people from other parishes coming over and criticising my arrangements and dropping hints about their own superiority! Some folk!" she added finally, and walked away.

Dismissed, thought Ivy, and rose to her feet. She walked slowly to the door, opened it quietly, and left Rose to her flowers.

Twenty-five

THE GOOD WEATHER lasted for the next two days, and Sebastian Ulph sat drinking red wine from an unwashed glass on his improvised rooftop terrace. The sun was hot, and church bells were ringing, reminding the people of Thornwell that it was the Sabbath. He felt happily secure from interruption. It was unlikely that his brief appearance in Barrington woods would still be remembered. Old people's short-term memories were often unreliable. By old people he meant Miss Beasley, whom he had later recalled as an old lady living in Springfields, where the band had played to entertain the residents. He guessed she might have recounted her experience to friends, but he was sure they would have considered him a poacher and dismissed him from their thoughts.

But what friends? There had been talk among fellow musicians of an enquiry agency in Barrington. During their refreshment break at the hunt ball, they had, as usual, discussed the likely female talent, including the blonde debs who all looked alike to Sebastian. The exception had been the squire's lady, one Deirdre Bloxham, and all had agreed that she was very tasty. She was, they had heard, part of the enquiry agency team based in an old folks' home in the village. Old folks? Just coincidence, surely.

Well, he could do without enquiry agents of any age on his track, although under other circumstances he would certainly have pursued the attractive rich widow he had admired emerging from her pool. He had put in some spadework there, mentioning an introduction to the town band. Now he had to lie low, let time pass, and wait for his opportunity to collect from Katherine. His current priority was to work out and rehearse until he was word perfect what he would say to her. She had always been able to out-argue him, but this time he meant to win.

GUS, BUSY WITH organising his trip, was growing more hopeful about finding his ex-wife, certain that until she was found, he would be suspect number one in whatever had happened to her. He had bought his ticket to Aberdeen and packed Whippy's bed, blanket and supply of dog food, ready to take her to the shop. He had also put in a moth-eaten soft toy to which she was devoted. With that beside her in her bed, she would not miss him too much, he hoped.

To occupy the hours he had left before tomorrow morning, he planned to engineer an invitation from Miriam to supper—not a difficult assignment! He knew she would open her heart to him, and all he had to do was saunter into his garden and sniff the air. He opened his back door and stepped out into the tiny backyard.

"Morning, Gus! Nice to see you out in the sunshine,"

chirruped Miriam. "You men are much too inclined to slump in front of the telly!"

"Good morning, Miriam," said Gus, his voice much more friendly than of late. "Are you off to church as usual? I do admire your devotion, you know. Only wish I could share it," he added humbly.

"But you could, Gus! All you have to do is go and get your jacket and walk alongside me. You know I'd be really pleased."

He shook his head. "Can't teach an old dog new tricks," he said. "Confirmed heathen, that's me."

"Never too late, as they say. Still, if I can't persuade you to come to church, how about supper this evening? We haven't had a nice long chat for ages, and I've a juicy piece of sirloin that is far too big for me. Shall I expect you about half past six?"

Not wishing to appear too eager and rouse her suspicions, he hesitated. "Oh, well, if you're sure," he began, "I would be very grateful. I'm off up north tomorrow and have no time to cook myself more than a boiled egg this evening!" Oops, he thought. Now she'll ask me about Whippy.

"Taking Whippy, are you?"

He shook his head. "No, it was fortunate that James asked me if he could borrow her for a few days. Overrun with mice in his storerooms apparently. Too many for one cat, he said. I expect you know that, anyway, from working there!" he added jovially.

Miriam's face fell. "Um, well, I do see his point. But I love having her, so any other time, don't forget me." The church bells had stopped, all but one, which was ringing a final reminder. "Must dash," she said, "but I'll see you this evening. Bye for now."

Gus returned to the cottage and sat down with pen and

paper, intending to make a list of questions he would ask Miriam. Kath had, after all, stayed with her overnight, and they must have talked for at least an hour or two. Miriam was an expert at worming trivial facts out of people, and Kath, being new to the village, might well have let slip some clue to the reason for her visit. He had thought long and hard about this and was convinced it was not an accident that her arrival had coincided with the annual hunt ball up at Roussel's place.

Deirdre had mentioned in passing that Theo Roussel was now on his way to Scotland, staying with friends in a draughty old castle and pursuing little birds over the moors in order to shoot them. It was entirely possible that Kath had departed in the same direction. She had friends on a grand estate near Aberdeen, and a reason to go there.

Questions for Miriam, then. What had the two of them talked about? Had Kath mentioned their marriage? And if so, what had she told Miriam about their friends and acquaintances? Had any of them figured in any explanation of why she was in Barrington, or did she stick to an unlikely wish to see her ex-husband? Had she talked about what she was planning to do next? Did they talk about dogs?

This last was not an idle question. Kath, usually an urban person to her painted fingertips, was passionate about hunting and hounds and especially fond of an old hunt terrier that had been retired after being stepped on by a horse. She had left old Jack with her Scottish friends and might well have told Miriam she was returning to collect him.

With a deep sigh, Gus put down his pen. No doubt other questions would occur to him during supper. Right now, he was sleepy, and leaving the back door open for the warm sun to fill his damp cottage, he stretched out on the sagging sofa and began to tackle the newspaper.

* * *

"WE COULD GO to evensong if you like, Roy," Ivy said. They had arisen too late to go to the morning service and were sitting in an empty dining room lingering over last cups of coffee, to the annoyance of Mrs. Spurling. It was Miss Pinkney's turn for weekend duty, but she had gone down with a severe cold and so her chief had reluctantly taken over.

"Now then," she said, marching up to the lingering pair, "are we all finished? Good, then let me help you up, Mr. Goodman."

"Leave him be!" said Ivy sharply. "We're not finished yet. Another five minutes, and we'll be out of here under our own steam. I'm sure you have better things to do than chivvy residents from room to room."

I shall murder her one of these days, thought Mrs. Spurling, forcing back an angry reply. I shall put my hands round her skinny old neck and squeeze. But she nodded and stalked off. She would go out into the garden and cool off. Her ex-husband, when being particularly unpleasant to her, used to tell her to go out into the garden and eat worms. One of these days she would do exactly that and then return indoors with them half-eaten and dangling from her mouth. That would fix Miss Beasley!

As Roy watched her leave, he put out his hand and touched Ivy on her arm. "Don't be too unkind, dearest. The poor woman has a difficult job to do, and we should try to help her out on bad days like today."

"Bad days? Today is another beautiful day! Just look out of that window. A perfect sky, blue with puffy white clouds, birds singing in leafy trees and a gentle breeze to keep us cool."

"And Gus Halfhide coming up the path with an anxious

look on his face," answered Roy, smiling broadly. "Let's go and see just how bad he can make our day."

"They are still in the dining room," said Mrs. Spurling huffily as she met Gus coming in. "Go straight through. If you can unseat them and take them into the lounge, you will earn my undying gratitude."

"Good gracious, is it that bad?" said Gus, twinkling at her. "Right. Here goes." He went through to the lounge and met Roy and Ivy on their way. "Ah! There you are," he said. "I was warned."

"Warned of what?" said Ivy, frowning. "I assume you have spoken to Mrs. Spurling?"

Gus nodded and suggested they all repair to Ivy's room, as he had some confidential details to tell them about his trip north. He had more or less recovered from his furious reaction to what seemed to him like accusations and decided it would be more sensible to tell them when and where he was going. *Why* was another matter. If they guessed, fair enough, but he had no wish to tell them of suspicions that were still vague and unsubstantiated. When he came back, he would hopefully be able to be more precise.

"To Scotland?" Ivy raised her eyebrows and looked at Roy.

"Needing a break, are you, Gus old chap?"

"Exactly. I shall take a train very early tomorrow morning and be away for probably a week or so. You can always ring me if there's anything urgent."

"Well done," said Roy. "You deserve a break. Vanishing ex-wives are not in the normal run of things, and we've seen that you are a bit shaken up. Go right away and forget about all of us. That's my advice."

"And mine," said Ivy, "is to keep your eyes and ears open at all times. Now," she added, "if you two would excuse me, I have to go out for ten minutes or so. Have a good break, Gus, and a productive one, if you can."

"No flies on Ivy," said Roy, after she had left the room. He looked at Gus's glum face and smiled. "Take no notice, lad, and just have a good time. Shooting?"

"Possibly," said Gus. "It's not really in my line, but the friends I shall look up are very much the huntin', shootin' and fishin' gang. So, when in Rome, and all that."

"Bring me back a plump pheasant, then. Haven't had a decent roast pheasant since I've been here. And dear Ivy likes them, too. Smooth the way, Gus, smooth the way."

After this, they discussed shooting prospects, and Roy remembered days when he and his friends had bagged a good number of birds and duly celebrated at the farm afterwards. Gus confessed that he was against blood sports, but a nice little partridge on toast was very difficult to refuse.

Finally, feeling much restored, Gus got up to go, and as he did so, the door opened and Ivy returned. "My goodness!" she said. "You two still gossiping? Do you know that old song about Gossip Joan? Should've been Gossip Jack! On your way, are you, Augustus? Off you go, then. Take care of yourself and be nice to your ex-wife."

Gus fled.

Twenty-six

ULPH WAS FEELING claustrophobic, confined as he was to one room, with only a small roof terrace for a breath of air. The room was very hot, his gammy leg ached, and he was longing for a cool dip in a pool somewhere. Perhaps he could find the town leisure centre and go for a swim. He sighed. There were two reasons why he could not: first, he had no swimming trunks, and second, he had no money for a ticket. Then he remembered the last time he had seen a tempting, shimmering pool, with a water nymph climbing out of it. Oh God, he was feeling light-headed with the heat. Why shouldn't he drop in on Mrs. Bloxham? He had said he would be back to see her about the town band.

Before he could allow himself to remember all the reasons he had for choosing to stay hidden, he left his room, went downstairs and asked Mrs. Feather if she had trunks to lend him. She disappeared upstairs and returned with a pair of red and white striped trunks smelling strongly of mothballs. "He loved swimming, my hubby," she said, and Ulph accepted them gratefully.

HIS LUCK WAS definitely in, he told himself, as a truck driver stopped for him not more than ten minutes after he had set out along the road. "Barrington, mate? We'll be there in twenty minutes. Visiting a friend, are you?"

Ulph chatted away, speaking about nothing much and answering none of the driver's questions, which could have identified him. They agreed that it was a boiling hot day, and the best solution would be a refreshing dip in an outdoor pool.

"Thanks a lot," Ulph said, as he waved to the truck driver, who continued on his air-conditioned way, not noticing until he was ten miles away that there was a plastic carrier bag on the floor where his passenger's feet had been. He drew into a lay-by, and had a look in it, pulling out a pair of very large swimming trunks. "He'd have had a job keeping these up!" he said, laughing loudly, and decided there would be no need to make an effort to return them.

"MR. ULPH!" SAID Deirdre. "You're soon back! I'm afraid I have not yet had time to talk to my musician friend. In any case, I was told you had gone to France?"

Ulph shook his head. "Had to postpone the trip," he said. "My reason for coming is not to do with playing the saxophone. I was wondering whether you could possibly allow me to swim in your pool. I have this trouble with my knee and am supposed to swim daily. I confess I cannot afford to use the public pool at the present, and thought I might as well ask. You can set the bull terrier on me if you like, but all you need to do is say no and I shall go quietly." He smiled his most winning smile and saw her soften.

"But where are your things?" she asked.

He looked down at his empty hands and swore. "Must have left them in the truck cab," he said. "I hitched a lift to get here."

Deirdre hesitated. Careful! said Bert's voice in her ear. But surely she could lend him a pair of Bert's trunks and allow him a short swim? After all, she would not let him into the house.

They were standing in the front drive, yards away from the house door, and she said, "Wait here. Don't move. I'll fetch a pair of my late husband's trunks. Then you can go round to the pool and have a swim. After that, please leave. And this is a one-off. No more swims after this."

She disappeared into the house, and Ulph stood as instructed without moving. His thoughts were on how he was going to replace the late Mr. Feather's trunks, and he began to regret his foolish expedition. He could easily have had a cold shower and rested instead on the terrace in the shade of the chimney stack. Ah well, too late to go back now. He would have his swim and then scarper.

Twenty-seven

ULPH'S DECISION TO swim and flee was scuppered by
Deirdre, who halfway up the stairs had remembered that
for at least a week she would have neither Gus nor Theo to
amuse her, now reappeared with black swimming trunks
and a small tray bearing two twinkling, ice-filled glasses.

"Here," she said, "you'd be better cooling off a bit before
swimming. I find a gin and tonic is just the thing. Sit down
and try this." She pointed to a chair by the pool and handed
him a glass. Then she sat beside him and smiled. She had
changed into a swimsuit and presumably intended to
plunge in with him. He took a deep swig of the gin and said
to himself that since he clearly could not escape in the way
he had planned, he might as well enjoy himself.

"Here's to autumn," said Deirdre. " 'Season of mists and
mellow fruitfulness.' "

" 'And beaded bubbles winking at the brim'?" he suggested.

"Quite right. Keats. But isn't there something about 'close-bosomed something or other' in there somewhere?"

Blimey, she was a quick worker. Ulph could not help his eyes lingering on her decidedly close bosoms as she leaned towards him, offering him a small plate. "Have a nibble," she said. Not at all what he had expected and quite a change of heart from what she had said at first. He hadn't had much experience of middle-aged widows, but this one was decidedly frisky, and he began to feel a whole lot more cheerful.

The drinks went quickly, and Deirdre said they might as well have fill-ups, since the evening was so fine. "Best part of the day," she said happily.

They chatted easily, Deirdre telling him all about her life with Bert and motorcars, and Ulph saying nothing very much about himself. By the time they thought of taking a dip, dusk was beginning to fall. "I know what we'll do, now the light's going," said Deirdre. "You needn't put on these things of Bert's. Just go over there in the summerhouse and strip off. I'll do the same, and we can jump into the pool quite discreetly. Nothing like swimming in the nip!" she added, and laughed uproariously.

Ulph had lost count of the gins but realised he was more than a little squiffy as he stumbled up the summerhouse steps. Not a good idea to swim when drunk, he told himself. But not drunk, just a bit tiddly. He took off his hot, confining clothes, and feeling ready for anything, he ran to the pool and dived in.

He knew he had misjudged his dive the minute his head came into contact with soft flesh. He surfaced and saw Deirdre shrieking with laughter. "Oops!" she shouted. "Mind me close bosoms!"

At this point, struck dumb by what confronted him, Gus Halfhide walked around the corner of the house.

Ulph sank beneath the water, but Deirdre waved a hand. "Hi, Gus!" she yelled. "Come on in. The water's fine!"

"I THOUGHT YOU were having supper with Miriam?" Deirdre said meekly. She had managed to persuade Gus to stay, asking him to wait in the house. Then she ordered Ulph out of the pool to dress and get going as soon as possible. She had grabbed a bathrobe and made strong coffee in the kitchen before joining Gus and taking a seat opposite him in what was always Bert's chair. Perhaps his spirit would stand by her in her hour of need.

Gus looked across at her. He had felt a bit of a heel, ringing Miriam to duck out of her beef sirloin, especially when she was pleasant and understanding. And now here was wicked Deirdre, reminding him of a small girl who has been found stealing sweets. He had a strong urge to laugh at her antics but didn't, deciding that she should be punished for such wantonness. "I don't understand, Deirdre," he said. "Who was that man, and why were you . . ." His voice tailed off as a sudden vision of the pair of them splashing about like a couple of porpoises was too much for him. He spluttered and then burst into roars of uncontrolled mirth.

"Oh, Deirdre," he said finally, "if you could have seen yourselves!"

Deirdre frowned. She expected disapproval but was not prepared for mockery.

"It was just a bit of fun," she said defensively. "That man had a bad leg, and . . ."

At this, Gus became helpless with laughter once more. "Oh, don't explain," he gasped. "No need to explain."

Deirdre sniffed. "Here, drink your coffee," she said.

"Personally, I don't see what's so funny. Surely what I do in my own back garden is entirely a private affair. Anyway, what do you want?"

"A four-course meal was what was on offer from my neighbour," said Gus. "But a couple of eggs and bacon will do. I nipped up here just to check one or two things before tomorrow. But if you're up to it now, we could discuss Sebastian Ulph. It was him, wasn't it?"

"Yes, it was, and I don't intend to have anything more to do with him. If he turns up here again, I shall threaten him with the police."

"Don't do that. You can always set the bull terrier on him. Anyway, we need to keep him in our sights, and I have certainly not finished with him yet."

EARLY NEXT MORNING, as planned, Gus took the train to Scotland, and it was much more pleasant than he had been expecting. The train was swift and comfortable, and he had a snack lunch in the restaurant car. He read the *Times* from cover to cover, and after changing trains in Edinburgh he settled down for a light snooze.

He was woken by the train slowing almost to a stop, and then crawling along at a snail's pace. He looked out of the window but could see nothing but a landscape of fertile fields and the occasional farmhouse. Then, with a whooshing roar, a train passed going south, and in that instant he thought he saw the familiar face of his ex-wife, Katherine.

There was no chance of a second look, and he told himself he had imagined it. After all, he was only half-awake, and the train had gone by at speed. How could he possibly have been right? No, she was on his mind, and it played its usual tricks on him. After their divorce, he had seen her face a dozen times a day, walking down streets, sitting on park benches, in office lifts and at his door every time he opened it. He thought those days had gone for good, and now he was convinced that there had been no real Kath. He felt unaccountably sad.

When the train finally reached Aberdeen, he stood up and found his legs reluctant to work after sitting for so long. Maybe he should have walked up and down the train more often. Wasn't there a risk of thrombosis? He must remember on the return journey.

He checked in at the small lodging house and asked where he could get a bus in the morning that would take him past Granfield Hall. His landlady was helpful and suggested he take a picnic lunch, as the weather was so fine.

It was still broad daylight, and he decided to have a walk around the streets, aiming for nowhere in particular, until he found somewhere to eat, and then return for an early night. He had a great deal to do in the morning.

Twenty-eight

KATHERINE HALFHIDE WAS bored. She was bored with people who had too much money and too little to say that interested her. Her host had been one of her beaux in their young, dizzy days of parties in London and stately homes in the country, but now he was a solid, respectable citizen with a position of responsibility for his estate and household. His ruddy face told of tramping around moors and imbibing large glasses of whisky, and his girth was steadily widening.

The other guests were stalking some unfortunate animal out in the wind and rain, and she sat alone by a log fire smouldering in the draughty drawing room, wondering what to do next. Her dear old dog, which she had come to collect, had been parked out for quite a while with her host but had died, and he had carelessly forgotten to tell her. It was difficult to believe she had left the south in warm sun, and yet here inside the baronial house it was cold and dank.

Increasingly, she thought of Gus. At least he had had tales of adventure and a ready wit that had kept her amused.

Perhaps she had been hasty in leaving Barrington, but her reason for going there had come to nothing. She had recently confided to a close friend her suspicion that Ulph had stolen her jewellery. Predictably, she had received a frivolous reply, suggesting that he had probably buried it in the deep, dark woods, where nobody would find it and where he could collect it at his leisure. It had been too much like a nursery story to be taken seriously at the time.

But later she had brooded on the likelihood of this. It seemed as good a theory as any other, and she remembered Ulph's connection with the Roussels at Barrington, where Gus had holed up. Information from her social network told her that Ulph had been seen playing in a dance band in and around the town of Oakbridge, and she had decided to start with Barrington woods, confident that she could persuade Gus to put her up for a night or two. As to the search, surely freshly turned earth would be easy enough to find? It was worth a try, but she had succeeded only in losing from her pocket her one remaining pair of earrings as she grubbed around in the undergrowth and brambles. She had quickly given up.

But then, the more she thought of it, the more she became convinced that her ex-lover *was* the culprit. In their friendlier days, he had been in and out of the flat and her bedroom several times a week. He had seen her dress for smart occasions and must have noted where she kept her jewellery box.

And, rashly, she had given him a key to the flat.

When they split up, she had asked him to return it but could not now remember if he had handed it back to her. She sank lower into her chair and closed her eyes. What a muddle! So what should she do now? Stay put, Kath, and wait for a while. She had a comfortable billet here in Scotland—well, fairly comfortable—and here she could plan her next attempt at retrieving her property. Perhaps a wider search in those tangled woods?

She felt a little guilty about deceiving Miriam Blake into thinking she was still resting in her comfortable bed, but no doubt a humble apology would be kindly received.

GUS HAD WOKEN early and decided the best thing he could do for the job in hand would be to hire a motorbike. He hadn't ridden one since he had careened, Buchan-like, around the roads of Slovenia, mostly on the wrong side of the road. He had no idea where to go, but his landlady had suggested McDougall's Car Hire, just around the corner. She had never heard of hiring motorbikes from there but knew the proprietor had one of his own and thought it worthwhile for Gus to enquire.

"Enquiring is what I'm good at!" he had replied jovially, and set off in a good mood. Unfortunately this was soon dashed by the receptionist at McDougall's saying they had no motorbikes for hire, only cars.

But then the boss appeared. "A biker, are you, sir? If you are an experienced rider, then I could lend you my own bike and some gear. Have to charge you, of course. Just in case of damage."

Gus agreed and paid up. The minute he mounted the bike, he felt a different man. Something about having a powerful beast beneath you, he said to himself, and proceeded noisily out of town and on the road towards Granfield Hall. He had precise directions from Mr. McDougall, and when the sun finally came out from behind heavy clouds, his spirits rose.

The Granfield estate was around thirty miles from Aberdeen, and the bike roared along at a satisfactory speed. It seemed no time at all before Gus slowed down outside the big wrought-iron gates of the Hall. A large brown dog with unfriendly eyes looked at him and barked fiercely. A woman appeared from the small lodge house by the gates and said something, which he could not hear. He switched off the bike's engine and asked her politely what she had said.

"Can I help you?" she replied shortly. Black leather–clad bikers were obviously not welcome at the Hall, and Gus thought too late that maybe he should have turned up in tweeds and brogues. He took off his helmet and smiled charmingly at her.

"Do forgive me for disturbing you," he said. "I am looking for Granfield Hall and wonder if you could direct me?"

"This is it," said the woman. "What do you want? There's a tradesmen's entrance about half a mile farther on."

Put firmly in his place, Gus thanked her and said he would go along and find it. But she still seemed deeply suspicious.

"What's your business, anyway?" she asked.

"It is rather personal," he said. "But I assure you I am not about to commit burglary at the ancestral home. Lovely morning now, isn't it? And thank you for your help."

He started the bike and rode off in an undignified wobble. Half a mile farther on, the unfriendly woman had said. He went slowly, looking for the tradesmen's entrance, and in due course he saw an unmarked lane leading off to the right. He took it, hoping this would lead him to the Hall and to his elusive ex-wife, Katherine.

BACK IN BARRINGTON, the sun shone in a cloudless sky, and Ivy found herself wishing for at least a thunderstorm. "Too much sunshine can be bad for you, Roy," she had said last evening, when he had insisted on sitting outside in the twilight.

"But it is beautifully cool now, beloved," he had said. "The strength of the sun has gone, and there's a lovely sunset over there, beyond the woods."

There had indeed been a spectacular sunset, and Ivy had said that unfortunately a red sky at night meant shepherd's delight, and it would be yet another boiling hot day tomorrow.

She was right, and now she and Roy lingered in the cool dining room, speculating about what Gus might be doing, whether he would find Katherine, and if so, what he was plotting to do with her.

"Best be off upstairs before we go to Tawny Wings," Ivy said. "I always say coffee goes straight through, missing out all the usual routes. I'll meet you in reception in half an hour. That should give us plenty of time. It'll be a funny sort of meeting without Augustus, though." She stood up, kissed Roy lightly on the top of his head, and walked slowly out of the dining room.

Deirdre was also thinking about Gus. She had had a disturbed night, with the most ridiculous dream. She woke early with a feeling of relief, only to fall asleep again and continue the same stupid dream. She had conjured up Ulph and in her sleep had faced him with a challenge. He was to agree to a duel with Gus, weapons being tennis racquets and decided by a fight to the death. Both had agreed, and she had stipulated the duel must be poolside in her garden. Before a grisly conclusion could be reached, she had woken up once more, terrified, and certain that Ulph had cheated, knocking Gus into the water with a hefty clout from his tennis racquet. Gus had sunk to the bottom and not resurfaced.

It was with the gloom of the dream still hanging around her that she drove into Thornwell for her early hair appointment but with the certain hope of flattery and personal attention.

"Ah, there you are, Mrs. Bloxham! And how are we this fine morning?"

Deirdre relaxed. She smiled and agreed to a new hair colour, which cost a small fortune. Things were certainly looking up. When she had got rid of Ivy and Roy, she planned to ring Theo's mobile and see when he planned to return. He was bound to be jolly after a break from the cares of his estate, and he might very well have something more to tell her about the mysterious Ulph.

Twenty-nine

IN A SMALL café in a narrow backstreet of Aberdeen, with grey granite buildings looming all around them, Gus and Katherine sat drinking scalding coffee. He had found her easily, first asking the housekeeper if she was a guest and then being led straight into the baronial Hall. There Katherine had jumped up and hugged him and begged him to take her away from all this. She had hopped onto the back of the bike with glee and had ridden back into Aberdeen, arms around Gus's waist, laughing and shouting in high spirits.

Now they were talking seriously about the theft of valuable jewellery from their London flat, and Katherine had said she was convinced the thief was Sebastian Ulph. She felt a bit of a fool about her brief and impulsive search in Barrington woods and had already decided to keep it to herself.

Gus was a little sorry for Katherine, but more than that,

most of the jewellery had belonged to his mother, and it had held many warm memories for him. Katherine, typically, had seldom worn any, saying it was old-fashioned, and anyway she did not like wearing a dead woman's jewellery.

"It was a terrific surprise when you appeared this morning," she said now. "How did you know where I was?"

"Guesswork," Gus said. "I remembered you were sweet on Hamish Granfield before we were married. I thought he was going to carry you off before I could screw up enough courage to pop the question myself. I know his wife left him a couple of years ago, and I knew you often came up to commiserate."

Kath was silent for a minute and then said she had become something of a rolling stone and had thought a lot lately about settling down into a more steady way of life. Gus heard alarm bells ringing and said hastily that he had more or less done that himself and had decided he was happier living alone. "Some people should never marry, don't you think?" he said hopefully.

"Depends *who* they marry," Katherine said sadly. "But you're right, Gus, I reckon I am not the marrying kind. Living with you was the nearest I got to being a faithful wifey but not near enough."

"So," replied Gus, relief palpable in his voice, "having got that out of the way, how did you know Ulph was in Oakbridge, and what do you propose to do about him? He's a slippery fish, and having said he was going to France, he clearly remained locally, turning up only when I accidentally ran into him at a friend's swimming pool."

"The lovely Deirdre? Was she the friend?" asked Katherine, ignoring his questions.

"None of your business. What matters is what exactly

Ulph is doing hanging around Oakbridge and Barrington. I know he had a job with Sid and His Swingers, but now he's resigned from that, ostensibly to go abroad. He turned up at my friend's house, asking for help getting a place in the town band. Before she had a chance to do anything about it, he appeared again, asking to use her pool, pleading a damaged leg. What is he up to, Kath? You know him better than I do. In fact, very well. Isn't that so?"

He had debated whether to tell her about Ivy's encounter with a man sounding very like Ulph, lurking in the woods and apparently burying somebody or something under the trees. But this, and the pearl earring, was Enquire Within business, and confidentiality was important. After all, that man could have been a poacher, burying game until he was able to fetch it safely. Or a desperate farmer, convinced badgers were spreading tuberculosis amongst his cattle, or even a badger baiter sussing out territory. And he was not keen for Kath to claim the earring until he was ready.

"Yoo-hoo! Where have you gone?" Katherine asked, snapping her fingers in front of him.

"Sorry. Thinking. So, anyway, why did you say you think he's still around?" He reminded himself that he could not rely on Katherine's telling him the truth about anything.

"He'll have hidden it—the jewellery, I mean—and is aiming to sell it through some local contact. The fact is, Gus, he has got me over a barrel. He knows I have had one or two not entirely straight insurance claims and is using this to get me to hand over some cash in return for giving back the jewellery. Unfortunately, I am somewhat strapped for cash at the moment. On the good side, I do have some information about his dealings, which he would not like spread abroad."

"But what brought him to Barrington? I know his father

was a friend of Theo Roussel's up at the Hall, but it's a pretty tenuous connection."

Katherine pounced. "There you are, then!" she said. "It's obvious! *That's* why he came to Oakbridge. He left me ridiculous Boy Scout messages in what amounted to a code for finding him, which I have cracked a lot sooner than he would have expected. Suffolk, he said. Blowing his own trumpet, he said. *Hunt* the *ball* was his last instruction! I mean, I ask you, when is he going to grow up? I reckon he's hidden the jewellery—and there was a lot of mine as well as your mother's—somewhere on the Roussel estate, and if I don't agree to do what he wants, the squire will help him to get rid of it. On commission, most likely. Another impoverished aristocrat there, I imagine."

Gus gazed at her in astonishment. "You aren't serious, are you?" he said. "I am sure you couldn't be further from the truth. Theo may be a bit of a fool, but he's straight as a die. I am sure of that." How am I so sure? he asked himself. Because Deirdre is sharp as a pin and would not associate with anyone she suspected of being a crook.

But now he began to think again of the man digging in the badger sett. Possibly hiding something. And the missing hand? He looked across at Katherine. Well, at least it wasn't hers. She was using two perfectly good hands to eat a large toasted bun.

THEO ROUSSEL, BLISSFULLY unaware that he was suspected of receiving stolen goods, felt his mobile phone vibrate in his pocket. He was not far out of Aberdeen, having just boarded a train heading south.

"Hello? Who is that? You'll have to speak up. I'm on the train."

"It's me. Deirdre."

"*Deirdre*? Is that you?"

"I just said it was. Can't you hear me?"

"I can now. What can I do for you, my dear? I'm on my way home. Fed up with wet feet and cold hands. Heading for home."

"Oh, that's great! Just wanted to know when you'd be back. Are you coming straight on to Barrington? I could go and put some flowers in the hall, ready for your return."

"Yes, I'll be back late this evening. Never mind about flowers. Why don't you come along and warm up my bed?"

"No chance. I'll be up to see you tomorrow, anyway. I want to ask you some questions. No, nothing alarming! And I'll put a hot water bottle in your bed this evening. You won't be back until the wee small hours. Bye, you old weakling!"

Theo grinned fondly and looked happily out of the window at the receding empty landscape, stretching out as far as the eye could see.

"DO YOU THINK Gus will let us know if he finds Katherine?" Ivy said.

"I am sure he will tell us, if he has time, my love," said Roy. "We have his mobile number, if you want to ring him. But I don't advise it. He may be concentrating hard on picking up a scent. Aberdeen, did he say? Cold place. Very forbidding, with all that granite."

"Doesn't sound a likely place for our Katherine, then! But you never know. If you ask me, she's stuffed in a cupboard somewhere, minus her left hand. Her sort usually end up dead. Playing one man off against another, I shouldn't wonder. Well, we shall see."

She and Roy were sitting in her room, drinking hot chocolate and eating half a digestive biscuit each. "Not a good idea to eat too much before bedtime," Ivy had pronounced.

"I think I might risk another half," Roy said, helping himself. "And by the way, have you had any more jolly thoughts about when we shall be leaping into one large bed together? Sometimes I think of nothing else."

"Naughty old thing!" said Ivy. "Of course I've given it thought. Sometime next spring, do you think?"

"How about next week?" said Roy.

Thirty

"THE THING IS, Kath," said Gus, as they perched on bar stools in the city's best hotel, "I really do need a few days' break. Finding you so soon has been a bonus, but I left Barrington walking wounded. Misunderstandings with my colleagues, false accusations, all of that.

"What colleagues?"

"You know perfectly well. My fellow investigators in Enquire Within."

"Well, I don't see that it's any business of theirs where you go and what you do in what I thought was a week's holiday. Holidays are for getting away from everyday life, aren't they?"

"This is not a holiday. I had an assignment. My purpose in coming to Scotland was to find a missing piece in a jigsaw."

"What missing piece?"

"You."

Katherine was silent. "I had no idea I was part of a jigsaw," she said finally. "Are you still nosing about with—what was it?—Enquire Within? Honestly, Gus, I never thought to see you wasting time with a couple of old fogies and a merry widow! After all the things you have done!"

"Death is death, wherever you find it. And there is a possibility that all the apparently unconnected things we have discovered actually add up to a death, could be a murder."

"So was I the possible victim? The missing jigsaw piece? Just because I left Barrington without telling anybody?" Not telling was Katherine's speciality, and among other things, she had no intention of mentioning her morning's search before she left, nor her realisation that to have any chance of success in finding her jewels, she would need to search a great deal longer. It was all her fault, all that cloak-and-dagger rubbish, pretending to Gus that she was in danger. She had come to her senses and decided to get right away and do some constructive thinking about what to do next. Retrieving old Jack had been the perfect excuse. "So do I fit the puzzle?" she asked.

"Got it in one," said Gus, smiling at her. "Would you care to join the team?"

"Don't be ridiculous. But now there has been no murder nor any other kind of violence, I still don't see why we can't have a few days back in your cottage, reminiscing about good times. We should stay in touch, anyway. It would be nice to be friends."

It was Gus's turn to be silent. He could not deny he had enjoyed the few hours he had just spent with Kath, riding about on the motorbike, walking the streets of Aberdeen and admiring the grandeur of the place. She was cheerful and affectionate, and he was reminded that when in this mood, she could be irresistible. He weakened but reminded himself that it would be better for him if he kept her away from Barrington at all costs.

"Supposing we check in somewhere along the coast, a small fishing village, maybe, and spend a couple of days walking and talking or just doing nothing?"

"Sounds a good compromise," said Katherine. "And then I promise to go back to London and try dealing with my stolen jewellery from there. Funds are a bit short at the moment, but the insurance on the stuff—if I can't find it— would be very useful."

Gus, only too familiar with her promises, did not believe a word of it.

EARDPORT WAS A tiny village not far from Aberdeen, with a few houses, a school, a church and an excellent pub with fish restaurant, perched on steep cliffs which dropped down to a rocky beach and a noisy colony of seals.

Gus and Kath were welcomed warmly and, without questions asked, given a double room. It was perfectly private and, they agreed, exactly what they wanted.

"Double bed," said Gus, looking around.

"Naturally. We signed in as man and wife."

"Oh well."

"Come on, Augustus," said Kath, laughing, "cheer up! I'm not going to seduce you against your will."

"You won't have to try very hard," Gus said gloomily, looking at her across the bed. She was glowing with the excitement of an adventure.

"If anyone had told me I would be hiding in a small village in the north of Scotland with my miserable ex-husband, I would not have believed them." Katherine walked across to Gus and planted a quick kiss on his cheek. "Let's go roaming in the gloaming," she said. "It's a lovely evening, and we can look at the seals and then come back for a drink and supper. And after that, well, we'll take a vote."

NEXT MORNING, DEIRDRE awoke from another dream about Gus. He was missing, and she was desperately trying to wade through a sea of treacle to rescue him from a sinking ship, when she was woken by her telephone ringing persistently on her bedside table. She reached sleepily across and lifted the receiver.

"Gus? Is that you?"

"Certainly not!" said a deep voice.

"Theo! You silly old sod! It's very early, and I was fast asleep. Aren't you exhausted by your long journey?"

"No, just disappointed to find only a hot water bottle in my bed."

"Oh, for God's sake! It's much too early for that silliness. Can I ring you back in an hour or three?"

"Of course. Just wanted to thank you for the flowers. Lovely welcome to a weary traveller. May I take you out to lunch? So much to tell. About twelve? Sleep on, then, lovely Deirdre."

In spite of herself, Deirdre smiled. She had been worrying about Gus and now remembered he was hundreds of miles away. Never mind, Theo was a good substitute, and usually found a pleasant place to eat. Perhaps they would go to Foxley Park, a beautiful Elizabeth mansion, now a luxury hotel. I was born to be rich, Deirdre thought, and thanks to dear old Bert, I am in my rightful element.

She was drifting back to sleep when her telephone rang again.

"Hello, Deirdre. Gus here."

"Gus! How are you? Have you found anything—anybody?"

"Yes. I have found what I came for and shall be back soon. Must go now. Love to Whippy. Bye."

"Wait, Gus! What have you—" But he had ended the call, and now cross and wide awake, she decided to get up and shower. A bad start to the morning, but she refused to be downcast. Lunch with Theo would cheer her up, and maybe Gus would phone again later. She was sure she had heard a woman's voice in the room with him, just before he signed off. So he had found Katherine.

GUS FACED HIS ex-wife and waited until she had finished shrieking at him. "You couldn't wait, could you!" she yelled. "As soon as I was out of the room you're on the phone to the rich widow! Well, you can stuff your couple of days by the sea. I'm off!"

"How?" said Gus, stunned by this outburst.

"There must be taxis in this godforsaken place! I'll get one to the nearest station and take the next train. And don't try to follow me! This is the last you'll see of me, Gus Half-hide." And with that, she picked up her bag and stormed out of the room.

Gus sat on the bed and tried to restore some sanity to the situation. But leopards don't change their spots. Katherine had always had sudden blind rages and closed her ears to any appeals to reason. The sweet, friendly person she had been for the last twenty-four hours had gone. He should have remembered but had been blinded by her skilful manoeuvring. She had avoided all further mention of Ulph, had skirted round Gus's suggestion that she should go to the police about her jewellery and refused to talk about anything but past good times they had had together.

What a fool! He had forgotten, too, about her savage jealousy. And now she had relapsed into the old ferocious Katherine at the mere suggestion that Gus had another woman in his life.

He walked to the cliff edge and stared out to sea. It was a grey morning, and the beach looked rocky and uninviting. It was still early, and he would skip breakfast. All thoughts of a holiday break now seemed to him to be ridiculous. No, he would speed back to Aberdeen and splash out on a plane ticket to London, and thence to Barrington and Whippy as soon as possible.

He was lucky to catch a plane directly, and as he checked in, he was reminded of something Katherine had said about insurance on stolen jewellery. Would she ever tell him the whole truth?

Thirty-one

"SO GUS IS coming back," Deirdre said. She had enjoyed her lunch with Theo and now, much later, was sitting with Ivy and Roy at Springfields on her way to the shop to stock up on her supply of gin. Thank goodness the shop was a late opener! Theo had dropped her off at home and had come in for several snifters and a bit of fun, and she was in need of a stiff hair of the dog. She had no qualms of conscience. Gus had found Katherine and was probably enjoying her company, else why would he be staying on for a couple of days? Well, two could play at that game.

"What exactly did he say this morning?" Ivy could see that Deirdre was put out by his call, but so far could not see why.

"He said he had found what he was looking for and would be back soon. That's all. Oh, except that I could hear a woman's voice in the background. She was shouting, and I heard her say his name, so she must have been talking to him."

"Katherine," said Ivy.

"Exactly," said Deirdre. "He cut off the call before I could ask him any questions. Honestly, Ivy, I do get a bit fed up with his mystery Gus act."

"I shouldn't worry," said Roy comfortingly. "It doesn't sound as if the pair of them were getting on too well. Let's just be grateful that he found her and that she's not dead in a cupboard somewhere, minus her left hand."

"Roy! Private joke?" Deirdre was shocked to see both he and Ivy smiling conspiratorially.

"Anyway," he continued, shaking his head, "now we know that Katherine is alive, we can get back to poor Miriam's encounter with a severed hand and the disappearing earring."

"I don't think we've heard the last of Katherine, whatever she may have said to Gus. That Ulph fellow is still around, isn't he, Deirdre? And he and Katherine have unfinished business." Ivy's tone was serious.

"But that's nothing to do with us," said Deirdre, who had had quite enough of Gus for the moment.

"Maybe not," Ivy said. "But it almost certainly has lots to do with Gus, and he is still our colleague, as far as we know. Yes, we know Katherine is not buried with the badgers, but it could be somebody else."

"Minus the left hand," all three chorused.

"Perhaps we should excavate the mound?" Deirdre did not fancy the job herself but thought they might persuade Gus on his return.

"Don't be ridiculous!" said Ivy. "Those woods are private property, and although villagers walk through them, it is with the squire's permission. But on no account would he allow anyone to go digging great holes on his property!"

THE SHOP STAYED open until seven thirty this evening to catch the return of commuters, and Miriam Blake was on late duty when she heard an anguished howl from the stockroom. She left a mother and child hovering over the sweets and rushed out.

"Whippy! What on earth is the matter? Did you see a rat? Oh Lord, I hope there's not rats! Come here. There, there, Miriam's here. Don't be frightened. All gone now."

"Miss Blake!" The child had made her choice, and Miriam returned to the shop, apologising for the noise and for deserting them. "It's Mr. Halfhide's dog," she explained. "James is looking after him while he is away. Now, is that all? Thank you very much."

She went back into the stockroom and saw that Whippy was still shivering and whimpering. The cat sat high up on a stack of boxes looking smug. No wonder Whippy was unhappy, poor little thing, Miriam thought, shut up here all by herself. This was not strictly true, as James took her out at least twice a day, but Miriam still smarted at not having been asked to have Whippy while Gus was away. She opened the back door for the dog to go out into the garden, where like a swift grey shadow it scuttled round the side of the shop and out into the road.

Cursing the deliveryman for leaving the side gate open, Miriam dashed back into the shop. Then she heard frantic, delighted barking. Going to the open doorway, she saw to her great relief a familiar figure coming along the street.

"Gus!" she shouted. "You're back!"

"Good evening Miriam. All going well? I can see Whippy has been well looked after."

"It wasn't me that left the gate open," Miriam said. "The deliveryman was here earlier on. I would've caught up with her, anyway."

"Don't apologise!" Gus said. He realised that for the first time since he moved to Barrington, he was glad to be home, that he actually thought of Hangman's Row as home. It had been worth his long and tiring journey. "I just need a few supplies—"

"You must come to supper with me," interrupted Miriam. "I got a lovely piece of salmon from the fish van and shall be cooking it with white wine and herbs. Does that appeal?"

"Rather!" said Gus happily. He turned to fasten Whippy to the dog hook outside the shop and saw a familiar car coasting along the street. Deirdre. Ah, well, he might as well face her now as later. He was well aware that he had been very abrupt on the phone, cutting her off midsentence.

The car slowed and stopped, and the door opened. Deirdre got out and slammed the door behind her. She stood perfectly still and stared at Gus. "Well, fancy seeing you!" she said loudly.

"Evening, Deirdre," he said. "How have you been? Not too lonely, I hope."

He should have known that this would be red rag to the bull, and she charged. "Of course I haven't been lonely! Just what do you think you are doing, saying one thing and doing another, coming and going and leaving enigmatic messages and then coming back sooner than you said, striding about as if nothing had happened! Well, nothing has happened to us, me and Ivy and Roy, but what the hell have you been up to?"

All this was said at the top of her voice, and Miriam was agape at the shop door. Gus took Deirdre's hand and guided her gently to the seat beside the bus stop. "Here, shall we calm down for a few minutes?" he whispered.

"I'm perfectly calm," yelled Deirdre, and then looked behind her at Miriam staring at them in fascination. "All right, then," she said in a more normal voice, "start talking, and you'd better make it good."

He said nothing for a minute or two, until he felt her relax, and then he said quietly that he was very sorry for cutting off the call, but if she would let him explain, in a strange way it had been a good thing, saving him from taking some very foolish steps towards reconciliation with his ex-wife.

AFTER THEIR CONVERSATION with Deirdre, Ivy and Roy had agreed that she was getting herself in a foolish tangle with her two men friends but must be left to sort out her double life by herself.

"It's time she decided on one or other of them," Ivy said now, as they sat in the cool of the evening. I don't know what her father would have said! I knew her parents well, of course," she added. "We used to drive over to see them two or three times a year. Very decent people, they were, and her father was quite strict. Not as strict as mine, of course! But they believed in a godly, righteous and sober life, as the saying goes."

"And Bert, her husband, what would he have said?"

"I know what he'd have *done*," said Ivy with a smile. "He would have put her over his knee and given her a good smack bottom!"

Roy chuckled. He looked at Ivy, cheeks flushed with indignation and her eyes sparkling behind her glasses.

"Now then, Ivy Beasley," he said. "Tomorrow we are going out on the town. I shall order our taxi, and when we get into Thornwell . . . No, not Thornwell. That's no treat! We shall go to Oakbridge and I shall buy you a present to show how much I love you. You can choose anything you like, anything at all. What d'you say?"

"What I say is," Ivy began, smiling at him lovingly, "that I need some new hairnets, and it's almost impossible to get them anywhere else but in that old-fashioned haberdasher's in town. So hairnets will be very acceptable, thank you."

Thirty-two

ROY AND IVY were on the road in their special taxi by ten o'clock next morning. With the sun shining from a clear blue sky, and efficient air-conditioning to keep them pleasantly cool, they were in a cheery mood.

"I thought," said Ivy, after a short pause in the conversation, "that we might go into that new coffee place and treat ourselves to scones with jam and cream. Breakfast was a bit meagre this morning, wasn't it?"

"Good idea, my love," said Roy. He took her hand and kissed it.

Ivy caught sight of the taxi driver looking at them in his driving mirror and grinning to himself. She drew back the small window and said to him, "What is your name, young man?"

"Elvis, missus," he said.

"Never heard that name before," Roy said, squeezing Ivy's hand.

"What? Never heard of Elvis? You must've, sir, you ain't that old!"

Ivy looked at Roy, and he winked. "I am very old, and my memory is short. What's in a name, anyway! We are very satisfied with your service, and that's all that matters."

"Fancy never heard of Elvis," the driver muttered to himself. They were approaching Oakbridge, and he asked them where they would like to be dropped.

"That good shoe shop over there, please," Roy said. The driver gave Ivy his hand, and she stepped neatly onto the pavement, then he turned to help Roy in his trundle.

"Oops! Be careful, young man," Roy warned, teetering on the edge, "I'd hate to run over your blue suede shoes . . ."

The driver directed him safely onto the pavement and then looked at him, frowning. "There we are, sir, safe and sound. We don't want you all shook up!" he said.

Delighted, Roy patted him on the arm and agreed that they would see him around twelve thirty.

"What was all that about?" said Ivy.

"Nothing at all," he replied. "Just an old fool having fun."

"Not an old fool!" said Ivy, taking his hand again. She stopped outside the shoe shop and whispered in his ear, "Have I told you lately that I love you?"

THE NEW COSTA coffee shop was now doing a roaring trade in premises that had once sold knitting wools, embroidery silks and knicker elastic.

"Haberdashery shops are almost gone," Ivy said as they settled in a window seat. "The big do-it-all supermarkets have driven them out of business, more's the pity. Katya was telling me she went all round one of those huge places looking for a packet of pins, and there wasn't one to be had. Mind you, I think those assistants, most of them look about twelve, and don't know where to—Oh! That's him!" she said suddenly, craning her neck to look up the street.

"Who?"

"The Green Man of the Woods! I am sure it was him. Perhaps he'll come back this way, and I'll point him out to you."

"What, him that was digging for badgers?"

"Well, digging for something. I'd know him anywhere, with that funny walk."

"You had a good look at him, then!" Roy smiled. "You said he limped, I remember. Did he by any chance have his empty left sleeve tucked in his pocket?"

"Couldn't see," Ivy said seriously. "And don't mock. I think our Green Man may be a very important part of the Miriam Blake investigation."

At this point, large, fluffy scones with lots of jam and cream were put in front of them, and they tucked in. The conversation changed to the likelihood of Deirdre ever getting married again, and Ivy said that if anyone asked her, she would say her cousin had enough sense to see that neither Theo Roussel nor Gus Halfhide would be good husbands. One was after her money, and the other clearly would be better staying a bachelor.

Fascinating as this was, Ivy's eyes kept flicking back to the street outside. She and Roy had moved on to discussing Katya's decision not to work up at the Hall when Ivy suddenly stiffened. "There he is!" she hissed.

"Don't look now, but he's coming in," Roy said.

"So he is. I shall wave him over," Ivy announced firmly. She half rose from her seat and called, "Yoo-hoo!" The busy restaurant stared at her, and the Green Man turned in alarm.

"Oh goodness, it's my forlorn little maid," he said without thinking, and approached their table.

"I *beg* your pardon?" Roy struggled to his feet, but Ivy took his arm and reseated him.

"Do join us," she said. "And please allow me to treat you to a creamy jammy scone. I have never been able to thank you properly for rescuing me in the woods. Do you live in Oakbridge?"

"In and around," he replied. "It is very nice to see you again. And this is?"

"Mr. Roy Goodman, my fiancé," said Ivy. "We both live at Springfields, a residential prison in Barrington."

"Did you say *prison*? Surely . . ."

Roy rescued him. "My beloved's little joke," he said kindly. "We are both able enough to escape into the outside world once or twice a week. You can have no idea how depressing it can be, cooped up like a couple of chickens, day after day."

Ulph, who owing to rash bets on sure losers, had come close to the debtors' prison himself once or twice, said that he had every sympathy and how pleased he was that they were able to live a relatively free life.

"And you, Mr. er . . . er? What is your work?"

"He's a musician, aren't you?" said Ivy, watching him closely. His reaction was interesting. He coloured, cleared his throat, and said she must be mistaken. He couldn't play a penny whistle. "Tone deaf, I'm afraid," he said.

"Ah, sorry," she replied blandly. "I could've sworn you were playing at Springfields with Sid and His Swingers. Olde Tyme Evening, I think it was?"

"If only!" Ulph said heartily. "Could do with a few bawbees at the moment. Difficult to find work in my line of business."

"Which is?" persisted Roy.

"Oh my goodness! Just look at that gorgeous confection!" Ulph said, gratefully receiving a plate of scones. "Well, here's to the escaped prisoners," he added, and lifted a fork piled high with whipped cream.

The conversation continued easily, especially when Ulph was discovered to have an enthusiasm for rare breeds of cattle. "My late father grew apples, mostly, but he also had a herd of Dexters," he confided, studiously avoiding any more questions from Ivy. "Had to give them up, of course, when he got ill. I've always thought I'd like to take up farming when all else fails!"

"Couldn't do better," Roy said. "Hard work, not much profit, but great satisfaction," he said, with a notable sadness in his voice. "I had some Belted Galloways in my day. Won first prize at the Dairy Show for years."

Ivy was bored. Herds of cows were all very well, but they weren't getting much in the way of useful information out of the Green Man. So far, they still did not know his name or where he lived.

"Well," she said, looking obviously at her watch, "if we're going to get everything done, we must be on our way."

"Where are you heading?" Ulph said. He had really taken to this nice old man. It was a long time since he had had a pleasant conversation about farming.

"Up to the one remaining haberdasher's," Ivy said. "I need new hairnets, though I suppose you are too young to have seen such things, Mr. er . . . er . . . ?"

"Nonsense! I remember my grandmother putting on her hairnet before retiring to bed. Made her look like a football in a string bag!"

Roy laughed. "My dear Ivy looks even lovelier in hers," he said loyally. "Are you going our way?"

"Part of the way," he said. "Now, will you let me settle the bill?"

"Certainly not," said Ivy. "My treat, Mr. . . . er . . . ? Off we go, then."

But Ulph was already on his feet. The pavement was too narrow for all three to walk abreast, so Roy and Ulph went in front, still chatting about pasture and the relative merits of cattle feeds, and Ivy followed behind. Ulph was carrying a briefcase, and she peered more closely to see the name label as they walked.

As they approached an adjoining road going off to the right, Ulph stopped. "I'll say good-bye then. Perhaps we'll meet again, Roy, and you can show me photos of your prize winners! Good-bye, Maid Marian." He touched his forelock and was soon lost among crowds in the street leading to the market.

"Wasn't that interesting, Ivy? What a nice fellow. Hey, wait a minute, Ivy, that's not the way to the haberdasher's! Wait for me, dearest. . . ."

Thirty-three

IVY HAD SET off at such a pace that Roy had great difficulty in keeping up with her, even though his trundle was capable of more than four miles per hour. He had to stop frequently at first. More than once a young mother laden with shopping and children warned him crossly to watch where he was going.

For her part, Ivy had completely forgotten that Roy might have trouble. Full of zeal for what seemed to her like a golden opportunity to find out where Ulph lived, she stepped out, skilfully avoiding prams and pushchairs and, when forced into the road, waving a stern arm at oncoming cars. When she finally caught sight of the easily recognisable hairy-headed, limping figure in front of her, she stopped. A young boy crashed into her from behind, and to her annoyance said, "Look out, Granny!" in a loud voice.

Without taking her eyes off Ulph's retreating back, she

set off more slowly, staying close to the kerb. Reminded of Roy, she took a quick glance behind her and saw him steadily approaching as the crowds now parted like the Red Sea in front of him. She matched her pace to Ulph's, and proceeded carefully, pulling her black straw hat over her forehead in case he should look round.

The marketplace was tricky, and it was clear Ulph was not going to linger. Ivy took a deep breath and followed him, and Roy did his best to keep up. They found themselves in a narrow street of four-story houses, shabby and uninviting. Ulph stopped outside one of these and fumbled in his pocket. Ivy and Roy waited fifty yards back, their faces turned away. At last, their quarry found the key and let himself into the house, closing the door behind him.

"Ivy Beasley," said Roy as they arrived outside Ulph's house and he struggled to get out of his trundle, "you are to sit down here at once while I give you a stern lecture."

"I am perfectly all right, thank you," said Ivy, but nevertheless perched on the seat and adjusted her skirt. "First time I've tried one of these," she said. "Very comfortable, aren't they? Go on, then, speak up."

Roy looked at her, sitting like Queen Victoria in her favourite dogcart. "I can't think of anything to say," he said with a sigh. "In the face of your triumphant expression, I can only think that your mission is accomplished. And if it is at all possible, my love, to give me a little more warning when you next decide to chase a known criminal through the streets of Oakbridge, then I shall be grateful."

"He is not a known criminal! Not yet, anyway. And I was merely walking briskly in the same direction as Mr. Sebastian Ulph."

"How do you know that is his name?" Roy frowned and

leaned against an overflowing rubbish bin. Without a word Ivy eased herself off the trundle and motioned him to sit in it again.

"It's on his briefcase. A travel label. Just as well I had my new glasses, though it was quite easy to read as you walked along."

"I might have known it," said Roy. "And now, if you'll accept a piece of advice from an old man, I think we should clear out of here pronto, before he comes out again and shoves a gun against your ribs."

ELVIS STOOD BESIDE his vehicle, looking anxiously up and down the busy street. He checked his watch. A quarter to one. There was no sighting of his passengers. Had he been too late turning up? No, he had noted the time, and he had arrived at the meeting place at twenty past twelve. There had been no sign of them then, and there was still no sign.

"Now then, sir, you can't park here," said a uniformed parking attendant.

"Can't you see I'm a taxi? Meeting a couple of elderly people, one in a shopping trolley thing, and they are late."

"Sorry, but that won't do. Still, as I can see you're worried about them, I'll give you another five minutes, and then you'll have to move on."

"Right. Thanks, mate. I'll do the same for—Oh, there they are! Thank God for that."

"Friends of yours, are they?"

"Um, yeah, I suppose they are. Anyway, cheers, mate. I'll get the ramp down."

Roy apologised profusely, and Ivy slipped a five-pound note into the driver's pocket. "My fault, Elvis," she said. "I got too interested in the market. Right, are we ready, Roy? Off we go to face a grilling from La Spurling."

"Did you get all you wanted?" said the driver.

"No," said Roy.

"Oh yes," Ivy said at the same time. "More than we expected, didn't we, Roy?"

"If you say so, dearest, if you say so."

ULPH, MEANWHILE, WAS thinking about his encounter. His daily craving for a cup of real coffee with cream and brown sugar had led him into dangerous waters. They had been a very nice old couple, Ivy and Roy. And what a chance meeting it had been with Ivy, his maid from the woods! He wished he had been able to answer with his own details, but he could not risk it. It seemed unlikely that two old pensioners would relay such information back anywhere that would do him harm. But if, by some extraordinary coincidence, his name and address filtered through to Katherine too soon, she would be only too anxious to do him harm.

But would she? She would want her jewels back, of course, and he was quite prepared to return them. At a price. He knew almost certainly that she would not go to the police, because of information he held about her claims for insurance. But Katherine Halfhide had always had access to some pretty shady characters. He would not put it past her to enlist the aid of one of her thugs to wrest her jewels back by force, not caring tuppence what happened to him in the process. And anyway, he was almost ready to confront her now. He had decided exactly what he would say to her and intended to learn it like a script, word for word, so she could not defeat him in argument. She would see the sense of his proposal, and that would be an end to it.

So he had done the right thing with Ivy and Roy. In a way, he wished he had been able to arrange to meet them again. It had been so nice talking to the old fellow about rare breeds and his father's Dexters. He should have stuck to farming, instead of playing the saxophone. How happy old Pa would have been!

"Mr. Ulph, can I offer you a bite of lunch?" It was his landlady, and not for the first time he wished he had had the presence of mind to give her a false name. With luck, that would have thwarted Kath's network of contacts for as long as he needed.

"Not just now, thanks," he said. "I've got a sandwich and some coffee. I'll be fine. And once again, I'm sorry about the swimming trunks."

Her face creased into a smile. "Don't you worry about those. I'm not likely to be needing them, am I?" She disappeared, shutting the door quietly behind her.

Another nice person I am deceiving, he thought. Oh, what a tangled web, his grandmother would have said. His leg was hurting again, probably from hurrying over hard pavements. Maybe he should have a shot at cadging another swim with Mrs. Bloxham? He sighed. No, his life was fraught enough already. The best thing would be to take his sandwich and coffee out onto the rooftop and watch the birds.

It was hot now, and there was no shade, except for the small rectangle cast by a chimney. He positioned his chair and thought about the sandwich. It was yesterday's, and curling at the edges, and he was sick of instant coffee. He went back inside, poured himself a large glass of cheap red wine, and returned to the sun. After several gulps, he saw the doves returning, smiled, and closed his eyes.

Thirty-four

"THAT WAS DELICIOUS, Miriam," Gus said, wiping his mouth with a paper table napkin decorated unseasonably with holly berries.

"Jolly good!" she replied, gathering up the plates. "Now, do you fancy peach melba for pud? One of my best, though I says it as shouldn't."

"Oh my, I've scarcely room for anything more! Well, just a spoonful, then."

"And can you finish up the primrose wine with a sliver of mature cheddar?"

By the time Gus had managed all Miriam's goodies, he felt so sleepy that he was not sure he could make it back to his cottage next door.

"Come and sit over here," Miriam said, patting the seat next to her on the sofa. "Black or white coffee? And a chocky to round off the meal?"

"Good heavens, Miriam, do you always live like this? I wonder you're not too roly-poly to get through the door!"

"Of course I don't. Only when I have very special guests . . ." She looked sideways at him and smiled indulgently. His eyes had closed, and when she touched his hand, it was limp and relaxed. Bless him! He had obviously had a lousy time up in Scotland with that awful wife of his. Why on earth did he marry her? She was quite goodlooking but nothing special. And that earring. Of course it was hers, given to her by Gus when he was her husband and the marriage just about to begin. She must have loved him then, surely? Fancy losing such a lovely present. The mystery of finding it in the woods still nagged at her, though she intended to persist with her story that it was hers.

She stood up, carefully avoiding the slumbering figure. She looked at herself in the mirror and smiled. I'd marry him with or without jewels, she thought. He needs someone to look after him. A pair of fake pearls off the market would be enough for me!

Gus heard none of the clatter of clearing dishes and washing up. And when Miriam gently covered him with a fluffy rug, he slept on, whiffling rhythmically. "Night night, Gus," Miriam whispered. She would keep her bedroom door open, just in case.

NEXT MORNING, DEIRDRE had decided to rise early and bully Gus into coming with her to sign on at the local golf club. He was looking decidedly peaky on his return. Added to that, she had begun to think the occasional swim in her pool was not enough exercise to keep a middle-aged widow in trim. Too much lardy cake and ice cream. She had risen at once when her alarm went off and had a lukewarm shower. Soon, she said to herself, in my new regime, I shall take a cold one.

Probably have a heart attack, said Bert's photo on the dressing table.

Deirdre laughed. It was so good that Bert's voice came back to her so often. It meant he was not really dead, at least not to her. Was that life after death? Living in someone's memory?

After a piece of dry toast and a black coffee, she put on casual trousers and walking shoes and set off for Hangman's Row. As she approached the cottages, she stopped in her tracks. Miriam Blake's door was opening, and the wretched woman, clad only in a flimsy nightie, was waving good-bye to, yes, it was Gus, and to add insult to injury, she was blowing him a kiss!

"Gus! Wait!" He stopped and looked round with a furtive expression. Deirdre walked smartly up to him and said sternly that they should go inside. She had important things to say to him.

"Oh God," muttered Gus. "Can't we stay out here for a bit, just to clear my head?"

"If we must," said Deirdre. "And it's nothing to me where you spend the night. I have a proposition to put to you."

"But—"

"But nothing. I expect you'll be wanting to have a bath and change. I can wait. The thing is this. I have made an appointment for the two of us at the golf club. You and I are both in our middle years and need fresh air and exercise to keep ourselves fit. Muscles get weak, and then the flab takes over. I loathe exercise classes, and I can't see you doing press-ups in the gym. So, rather than go alone, I thought you might come with me, and we could be rabbits together. What do you say?"

"I say," Gus replied, with some gusto, "that it's all very well for you, but how do you think I am going to find hundreds of pounds for a year's subscription to Thornwell Golf Club? And then buying new drivers and irons and putters to play with and drinks in the bar afterwards? Besides which," he added, "I used to play with Katherine, and don't particularly want to be reminded of those days. And anyway, I sold my clubs."

"Rubbish! It won't be like that at all. We'll just go up and practise and then come home. I haven't a clue, and you can help me along. Mind you, I used to be good at tennis, and I don't suppose there's much difference. It all comes down to hitting a ball with a bat, surely?"

"And I suppose now you're going to offer to pay for me? Well, Deirdre, I have had quite enough of being beholden to rich women, so don't even try."

Deirdre coloured and bit her lip. Then she walked up to him and slapped him hard across his lean cheek. "I shall be home later, if you wish to apologise," she said, and stalked off.

BEHIND HER LACE curtains, Miriam had watched the whole scene, and though she couldn't hear what they were saying, she saw the slap and chortled. "Poor old Gus," she said aloud, and planned to make a chocolate sponge for his tea.

"Women!" said Gus to Whippy, who jumped all over him as if he had been away for weeks instead of nights. "Now the lovely Deirdre has taken the huff, and I shall have to eat humble pie in large quantities to crawl back into her favour."

Whippy rolled over onto her back, and Gus tickled her. If only it were that easy with women! Just roll them over and tickle their tummies. . . . Well, he supposed it was worth a try and went to take a shower, ready to walk athletically up to Tawny Wings.

ROY AND IVY had hidden themselves in the summerhouse, away from the bright morning sun, and Mrs. Spurling's strictures. "If she reminds me once more about punctuality," said Ivy, "I shall give in my notice and find another more congenial prison."

"Shall I be included?" Roy said.

"Of course. You and me are one, aren't we?"

"Not yet," said Roy. "But soon."

"Tomorrow," said Ivy, and Roy brightened hopefully.

"Tomorrow," repeated Ivy, "we will fix a date. We'll have a guess at when this particular enquiry will be sewn up, and then we will book the church."

"Wonderful," said Roy, taking her hand. "Let's put all our energies into solving the case of the severed hand at once."

"And don't forget the disappearing earring," Ivy said, smiling. "Now, when are we going to tell Gus and Deirdre that we have useful background information on Mr. Sebastian Ulph, who resides at number seven Folgate Street, Oakbridge?"

"As soon as possible, if our wedding date hangs on solving the case."

"Very well. I shall telephone them, and ask them to come here for a meeting this afternoon. Remind me to ask Katya to bake some cakes to put Gus in a good mood."

"Me, too. That young lady has a rare talent. Cakes as

light as a feather are not easy to come by. Please God she never again thinks of taking up Roussel's offer to join him, not in matrimony nor as housekeeper at the Hall."

"No fear of that," said Ivy cheerfully. "I believe she has a new boyfriend. Came to call for her yesterday. Nice looking young chap of her own age."

"Perhaps we could have a double wedding at Christmastime?" suggested Roy. "What a wonderful celebration that would be!"

"Calm down, dear," said Ivy. "The lad is a law student, and it takes half a lifetime to become a barrister, which is apparently what he plans to be."

"Ah, well, never mind. Come to think of it, I don't want to share our day of days with anyone but you, Ivy Olive Beasley."

They hugged, and Mrs. Spurling, coming around the corner to summon them for coffee, for once had the sensitivity to retreat quietly back into the house.

Thirty-five

"I'VE ASKED KATYA to bring our tea out here," said Ivy. She and Roy had again taken up residence in the summerhouse, which, with tall sycamores shading it most of the day, was pleasantly cool.

Deirdre subsided gratefully into a canvas garden chair, and fanned herself with her straw hat. "It's not British," she said. "We just aren't used to long periods of hot weather in the summer. I shall be glad when it rains again. Proper rain, not just a quick storm with the blackbirds and thrushes singing their hearts out as if we'd had a good soaking."

"Poor Deirdre!" said Roy. "Would you like some iced tea?"

"As a matter of fact," said Ivy, smiling, "I have already asked Katya to bring us iced tea this afternoon, with cream cakes for a change."

"Ivy! And just when I have started a new diet!"

"Don't be ridiculous, girl," said Ivy. "Why do you think you've got so many admirers? Nice, plump widow—"

"With a nice fat bank balance," finished Deirdre, laughing. "But how comforting you are, Ivy. I can't wait for our treat."

When Gus had arrived, also complaining of the heat, Katya appeared with a tray of tea and cakes as instructed. "I hope you will enjoy this," she said proudly. "Bill thinks I make the best cakes in the world."

"Who is Bill?" Gus said sharply. "Not your pet name for him up at the Hall, I trust?"

"No, no. Bill is my boyfriend. He is studying the law and is very serious and nice. Mrs. Spurling approves and says I can go off duty now to meet him in town. His parents are visiting, and he wishes to introduce me."

When she had gone, Ivy said that it was clear love was in the air, what with Katya and Bill and she and Roy, and Deirdre and sundry admirers.

"And me?" asked Gus.

"We really must get on," said Deirdre. "Now, Ivy, are you going to tell us what is so important? Gus and I are all ears."

Ivy started the story at the point where she hailed Ulph as he walked into the coffee shop. "He looked surprised but came and sat with us. We talked generally, but it was obvious he was not going to give us any details about himself. Roy and he got on like a house on fire, talking mostly about cows."

"His father bred Dexters," explained Roy. "He was a nice chap, I thought, but sad. I don't know what was wrong, but he talked nostalgically about his days on the farm. Didn't want to talk about music, though, and actually denied being the man who had played with Sid at Springfields. Silly, really, since Ivy remembered him clearly, not only playing the saxophone but also helping her in the woods."

"Did he admit to the woods?" asked Gus.

"Oh yes. He teased Ivy, calling her Maid Marian."

"So he was definitely your Green Man?" Deirdre said.

Ivy nodded. "Brightened up a lot when we talked about that. Mind you, he wouldn't answer any direct questions. But when it was time to go, he walked along with us until we reached Market Street, then he turned down there and we lost him for a minute."

"Ah, but tell them what you did next, Ivy," said Roy.

"I followed him. Well, we both did. We kept out of sight among the market crowds and finally caught up with him where he'd let himself into one of those tall houses in Folgate Street. Number seven, it was, and quite dingy-looking. Then we walked back to our taxi driver, and he was worried because we were late, and when we got here, our luck was in. La Spurling was off duty, and Pinkers was waiting for us with a beaming smile and plates of ham salad."

"So, as you see, we now know that the Green Man, the saxophonist and Deirdre's swimming pal are one and the same man. We still have to identify the man with supermarket bags outside Hangman's Row late at night, but since that was our Miriam's evidence, well, you know, moonlight and all that." Roy sat back in his chair and folded his hands across his stomach. "And that, Ivy Beasley, was the best afternoon tea I have ever tasted."

"Well done, you two," said Deirdre admiringly. "So I suppose you had a good talk with him over coffee? Did he give you any clues about why he is living here? Or why he gave up playing with Sid? Did he explain why he said he was going to France and then didn't go?"

Ivy bristled. "I have already told you, Deirdre, that he was very cagey about giving information. The minute we tried to ask him personal questions, he clammed up or changed the subject."

"He was quite forthcoming about his father, though," Roy interposed. "He's now dead but was a gentleman farmer and very keen on rare breeds. I got the impression that being a musician was not his father's idea of a proper job."

"So what next, Ivy?" Gus could not quite concentrate as he should on the meeting. He had received a message on his phone, apparently left the evening before, and his mind repeatedly returned to it. Kath had said in her haughtiest voice that she meant all the things she had said but needed to complete something she had started in Oakbridge and Barrington. He was to take no notice if he saw her. As far as she was concerned, they were complete strangers and would remain so. She did not know how long she would be in the village. He had already decided not to mention it to the others, wanting nothing more than to get Kath out of his life for good.

"Gus? What did you say?" Ivy leaned towards him. "You're muttering again. Speak up."

"Sorry, Ivy. I asked what we were to do next."

"Visit Mr. Ulph, and continue our friendly chat. Me and Roy have phoned the coffee shop and asked the waitress to give him a message this morning, saying we'd like to call on him next time we're in town. He goes there most days, apparently, and they confirmed what we already knew about where he lived. We shall root him out to have coffee with us. We've thought of a good excuse. Roy's got a book about rare breed cattle, and we'll give it to him. Then we'll ask him to come with us to the café for a chat about it. That should do the trick."

"But why are *we* so interested in him?" Gus said.

"Think, lad!" said Roy. "It all happened in the woods. Miriam and friend saw the hand, and I believe they *did* see something like a hand, buried in the leaves. Ivy saw Ulph the Green Man with a spade. Though *we* can't start digging on private land, he obviously could. Or didn't care about trespassing. It could have been to do with badgers but, then again, might have been something more sinister. Miriam found a valuable earring near where they saw the hand. It doesn't take too much savvy, old chap, to see why we need clarification from Mr. Sebastian Ulph, does it?"

There was silence for a minute or so, and then Deirdre cleared her throat. "I think I might be able to help," she said, and the others looked at her with relief. "As you know, Theo Roussel is a friend of mine."

Gus spluttered ice cream into his saucer in an attempt to resist commenting.

"He was also a friend of Ulph's late father," continued Deirdre. "I don't know how much he can tell us about Sebastian as a young man, but it will be worth asking. He might come up with something. And it is always possible that Sebastian might appear again for a swim, in which case I shall be ready for him. When he's in the pool, I could steal his clothes and refuse to return them until he tells me what on earth he's up to around here." And then she looked expectantly at Gus.

"And you, Gus, what will you do?" she said in a distinctly cool voice.

"Bide my time, Deirdre love. I have a feeling trouble is on its way to me, so I do not intend to go looking for it."

Thirty-six

AFTER TEA, IVY and Roy retired to Ivy's room to plan their Oakbridge visit in order to beard Ulph in his den. They had decided to waste no time but booked a taxi for tomorrow morning, giving themselves plenty of time to walk through the marketplace to Folgate Street.

The phone rang, disturbing a pleasant moment's silence. "Yes?" said Ivy. "Who is it?"

"I am sorry to bother you, Miss Beasley, but there is a call for you from Mrs. Rose Budd. Do you wish to take it?" Katya's precise English always made Ivy smile, and she said that yes, she would certainly take the call. She wondered why Rose could be calling her. Something to do with the missing hand?

"Hello, Miss Beasley. Sorry to disturb you. Do hope you weren't having a little snooze?"

"Good gracious me, no!" answered Ivy. "I don't believe

in wasting time sleeping during the day. Now, what can I do for you?"

"I was hoping I could pop up and see you for a few minutes. I have something to show you, and it is rather confidential."

"Come now, at once," said Ivy briskly. "No time like the present. See you in ten minutes?"

"Oh, thank you! That will give us time to have a chat before I fetch the boys from their friend's house."

Ivy replaced the phone and smiled at Roy. "Guess who?" she said.

"Rose Budd," said Roy. "I'm telepathic."

"No you're not, you just eavesdropped, you awful man. Well, anyway," Ivy continued, "it was indeed Rosebud, and she is coming up here to see us. Should be here any minute."

"Did she say what she wanted?"

"No. Just said it was confidential. So we must wait and hope it has something to do with our enquiry."

Mrs. Spurling was back on duty in the office when Rose appeared, asking for Miss Beasley. "Is she expecting you?" Mrs. Spurling said. "Miss Beasley and Mr. Goodman have retired for a quiet time after tea. I like all my residents to have this opportunity for rest without being disturbed."

"She's expecting me," said Rose flatly. Who was this old bag and what did she think Springfields was? A royal residence?

A figure appeared at the top of the stairs. Ivy had heard their voices and now smiled warmly at Rose and said she was to come up straightaway. Mrs. Spurling managed a small sentence of welcome, and then accompanied Rose to the foot of the stairs.

"We shall all be requiring a glass of sherry as soon as possible, thank you, Mrs. Spurling," Ivy said, and, taking

Rose's hand, disappeared into her room, shutting the door firmly behind her.

Roy struggled to his feet and shook the hand that Ivy relinquished. "How nice to see you, my dear," he said in his kindly way.

Rose relaxed and could not remember why she had been so nervous. She sat down as instructed, asked polite questions about the health of Ivy and Roy and then began to fumble in her handbag. She produced a small package of tissue paper and slowly unwrapped it.

"I found this in the woods, when I took the boys for an adventure at the weekend. We often go there and I tell them the *Babes in the Wood* story. They love it, until we come to the bit about the gingerbread house and the witch, and then I have to make sure we're in a sunny clearing or on the way home. Otherwise they see witches behind every tree! I must say I had a fit of the shivers when I realized we were near where we found the hand. But I believe in laying ghosts, and banishing bad memories."

By now she had finished unwrapping, and Ivy saw an earring. As Rose held it up, she saw a pearl drop and a tiny stone that she was sure was a diamond. The sparkling fire in it was unmistakable.

"Good heavens, where did you find it? I mean, whereabouts in the woods?" Ivy was already sure that this must be the pair to the one Miriam found and claimed she had lost.

"Well, funnily enough, it was where that horrible hand turned up. I am sure this wasn't there when me and Miriam first saw the hand. But you know what it's like in the woods. Animals turn the leaves over, looking for insects and things. Actually, it was my son who spotted it. He wanted to keep it, but I made him put it in my pocket, and then luckily he forgot all about it."

"Didn't you think of giving it to Miriam? We understood that you wished to have nothing more to do with the mystery." Roy spoke very gently and saw the colour rise in Rose's face.

"That's true," she said. "But this looks to me like a valuable earring, and, well, I wasn't sure what Miriam would do. I decided she would more than likely go to the police, and David would be very cross if they came poking around again. So I thought you would be more sensible, Miss Beasley, and deal with it without that happening. At least, I thought it was best. Miriam is quite an impulsive person," she added.

"Quite right," Ivy said. "So now, Roy, what do you think we should do."

"I suspect you have already decided, beloved," he said, and winked at Rose.

"Well, yes, of course. I would say leave it with us, Rose. We won't mention your name unless we have to. The thing is, I think we know where the other one is. Your son's sharp eyes may very well have found something valuable. So thank you, dear, for bringing it here. You did the right thing, didn't she, Roy?"

Roy said that, as usual, Ivy had talked a lot of good sense.

"SO, SHALL WE tell Gus that we've found the matching earring?" Ivy said, after Rose had gone. "I am certain Miriam still has the first one. Silly woman thinks she is protecting Gus from suspicion. But now we know Katherine is safe and well, that lets him off the hook, doesn't it?"

"Depends what happens when we winkle out Ulph and find out what he was burying in the woods," Roy said. "A pity we can't just take a digging party and look for ourselves.

But with so little hard evidence, I think we'd get short shrift if we asked permission from Roussel, or David Budd, come to that. I suppose we could ask Gus to do a little surreptitious investigating? He has permission to take Whippy into woods and around other parts of the estate. He needn't dig deep. If there *is* anything, it'll have to be near the surface to be collected again. Possibly by Ulph. I think Ulph is a very worried and unhappy chap, and he may well come out with the whole story to us."

"You mean because he thinks we are a daft old couple and wish him well?"

Roy frowned. "That is ticklish, Ivy," he said. "I really took to Sebastian Ulph and believe that he may have done something stupid but not necessarily criminal. I should feel bad if our investigations resulted in some undeserved punishment for him."

"It sounds as if the really tough person in all this is Gus's Katherine. He certainly hurried back from Scotland in a funny mood. He's bound to know more than he's telling us. Maybe Deirdre can entertain him with food and strong drink and get something useful out of him."

Roy sighed. "It is unfortunate that Enquire Within should be investigating one of our own team," he said.

"Well, we're not, are we? Gus is one of us, and he may know a few things he's not telling us, but I suspect he plans to do so when he has sorted out his relationship with that woman. And by 'that woman,' I mean Katherine."

"So shall we ask Gus to come up on his own, show him the earring, and see what he suggests? I have a hunch that it might encourage him to be more forthcoming."

Ivy blew him a kiss, and smiled broadly. "I love your hunches, Roy Goodman," she said.

Thirty-seven

IVY AND ROY decided to walk down to Hangman's Row in the cool of the evening and see if Gus was at home. They had had an excellent early supper and now moved along at a steady pace through the village.

"I always liked this time of day in Ringford," Ivy said as they passed the shop, its blinds just being pulled down, and the sandwich board stowed away in case of theft. "There was not much traffic, and people came out for an airing after their high tea. We used to sit on a bench under the trees and watch the children playing on the green."

"Who was 'we,' dearest?" Roy was curious about Ivy's past life, and though she did not dwell on her many years in Round Ringford, every so often she would release a snippet of memory that illuminated her character.

"Me, Doris and Ellen, of course. We knew we were referred to as The Three Graces in the village but reckoned it could be a lot worse and so we put up with it."

"A very nice name, Ivy. And very appropriate, if I may say so."

"Oops! Look out, Roy. Looks like a boy drunk in charge of a scooter!"

With great dexterity, Roy avoided the young lad, who wove his way between the two of them, and disappeared, shouting "Sorry!" as he went.

"Would you like to have a rest at the bus stop seat?" Roy suggested.

"No, no. We must get on. Gus might well be going to the pub later on. He is apparently a very able darts player, among his many other skills."

"Right-o. Let's forge ahead."

They passed Rose's cottage, but she was not to be seen.

"Getting the boys to bed, I expect," said Ivy. "And here's Miriam, hovering on her doorstep. Say nothing," she added.

"Good evening! Lovely evening, isn't it?" Miriam was, of course, interested to see these two heading down Hangman's Row, not a frequent occurrence. "Are you calling on Gus? He is at home. I spoke to him only a few minutes ago."

"Mind your own business," muttered Ivy, so that only Roy could hear.

"Thank you, Miss Blake," said Roy. "We are really just taking the air. So pleasant in the evening, don't you think?"

"Roy!" Ivy frowned and walked on, up to Gus's door, where she rang the bell.

"Bell doesn't work!" yelled Miriam. "Use the knocker!"

Gus came to the door, looking alarmed. "Ivy? Roy? Is everything all right?"

"As all right as it will ever be," said Ivy, giving Roy a hand to climb out of his trundle. "We've come to call. Have you got a free half hour?"

Gus took a deep breath and said he was delighted to see them. They must come in and have a glass of wine. Whippy loved visitors and would be so pleased.

WITH TWO GLASSES of cold white wine inside them, Ivy and Roy relaxed as much as was possible in Gus's uncomfortable chairs.

"There's a spring gone in this one," Ivy said, giggling a little, and bouncing up and down in the shabby chair. She had been persuaded against her better judgement by Roy to try the wine. Gus said it had a low alcohol content, but as she felt the pleasant fizzy feeling in her head, she began to doubt him. Anyway, she told herself, if I'm to enter the man's world with my Roy, I must get used to the odd glass or two.

"So have you got the earring with you?" Gus asked. He had been given a very succinct account of Rose's discovery and felt a rising excitement that they were really making headway.

"And now, Augustus," said Ivy, not answering, "I want you to do something that neither of us can do. You remember that I saw Ulph—we now know that it was him—in the woods, carrying a spade covered with fresh soil? Some of us imagined a body buried dramatically at the dead of night, possibly in the light of a full moon. By some of us, I mean, of course, me. I dismissed it at the time as fanciful. Like Miriam's severed hand. And now we have no body and no missing person. At least, not that we know of. So what else? Do we take into account that a pair of earrings had possibly been dropped in a rush to conceal treasure, or to hunt for it, and that in the mound there could be other valuables, hurriedly buried by Ulph in a shallow grave?

Have we given up the idea of murder but instead are left with a b-bungled burglary?"

Wow, that wine was a good idea, thought Gus. He had never known Ivy so loquacious and so perceptive in her reasoning. Roy also was looking at her in admiration.

"So we would like you to find this mound," Ivy continued. "I can give you a rough idea of its whereabouts. And take a spade with you to dig for worms. No, not worms! Just my joke, though you might find some of those as well."

Gus looked at Roy, who nodded approvingly. Then Gus made a decision and cleared his throat, as if to preface an important announcement. He had thought long and hard about Katherine, about their past lives together and apart and had searched his memory for what he had heard about others of her long list of lovers, each one ruthlessly milked and then ditched. He remembered hints she herself had given him in Scotland about being hard up and Ulph using bad things he knew about her to extract money.

"I think I can save myself the job you so vividly describe, Ivy. The fact is, I reckon I know what's in the mound. It is almost certain to be Kath's jewellery, hidden by Ulph. She may even have connived with him, so that she could claim insurance money. I doubt it, and if I am wrong, and Ulph has genuinely stolen it, then his motive is likely to be blackmail. He is probably offering, at a price, to return the stuff. Those earrings are hers. I designed and gave them to her. That much is fact. The rest is surmise but extremely likely. Poor bloke probably had no money left after she had finished with him. Former lovers have thought of other means of revenge, most not so foolish. But Ulph has a reputation for boyish pranks. Other swains concentrated on skilfully damaging her reputation."

"She can't have much of one left," said Ivy sourly.

Gus shook his head sadly. "No, you are quite right. And neither has Ulph, amongst those circles. So he turned up here, where Theo Roussel, a friend of his late father, lives. But I reckon that before he could make a considered approach to him for help, maybe in finding buyers for the jewels if she refuses to play ball, she came looking for him. She has her spies, I'm afraid. Distributes her favours according to how well they serve her."

An absolute silence from Ivy and Roy greeted these revelations. Ivy spoke first. "Why on earth didn't you tell us all this before," she said.

Roy sighed. "Of course he couldn't, dearest," he said. "He said himself that the only thing he was sure of was that an earring had been found in the woods, similar to the ones he gave Katherine. The rest, as he just said, was surmise. But I am afraid, Gus, that Ivy's plan still needs to be considered. She saw Ulph with a spade by the mound, and if you now find the rest of the jewellery there, you will be the one to recognise it as Katherine's. Or not, as the case may be."

"May I think about it?" Gus said. "I do see your point, but I don't fancy being nicked for digging in the woods by a prowling David Budd. Especially if I had just turned up the jewellery. You can see that if he finds me with the stuff, that might well return me to the spotlight, and then I'd have no chance of seeing this whole business out. He would not hesitate to inform the police or, at the very least, his employer, Roussel. It would be more than his job's worth to ignore it."

"Very well," said Ivy, beginning to feel a nagging headache over one eye. Perhaps wine on top of sherry had been a bad idea. "We shall be in Oakbridge tomorrow, hopefully finding Ulph, and with many questions to ask him."

"With considerable tact, of course," added Roy. "We can't go in there with all guns blazing."

"And we will contact you directly, when we return," said Ivy.

Gus frowned. "It rather looks as if I, as a member of Enquire Within, am more trouble than I'm worth," he said.

"Don't be ridiculous!" retorted Ivy. "And buck up, Augustus. The end is, I suspect, in sight."

Thirty-eight

ULPH'S LONG EXPOSURE to the sun, combined with more than one bottle of cheap red wine, had taken its toll. He had spent the last twenty-four hours in bed, alternately sweating and freezing, and in between lurid dreams had shouted through his locked door to Mrs. Feather that he was fine, just tired. And no thank you, he did not need any food at the moment, just rest.

Now it was early morning, and his thirst was overwhelming. He put one foot down to the floor, and the room spun round crazily. He waited, trying to breathe deeply to stop himself fainting into darkness. He felt sick, but his stomach was empty, and all he could do was retch. At last the room steadied, and he very tentatively put down the other foot and tried standing. So far, so good. Now he must reach the hand basin on the other side of the room, so that he could fill his tooth mug with water and take a long drink.

Feeling desperately unsteady, he reached the basin, drank two mugs of water and looked at his watch, still lying where he had left it on the ledge above. It had stopped. Flat battery, he supposed, and caught sight of himself in the shaving mirror. He groaned and shielded his eyes from the sun streaming through the window. The chair and bottle still stood where he had left them outside. Well, never mind. He would bring them in when the sun had moved round. Now, back to bed and sleep, more peacefully now, he hoped.

He was halfway across what seemed an enormous distance between the basin and his bed, when a sharp knock on his door stopped him.

"I'm fine, Mrs. Feather," he said, as loudly as he could manage.

"It's not Mrs. Feather. She's gone to see a neighbour. Told me to let myself out in due course. It's me, Katherine. Open this door at once."

Ulph swayed on his feet. Katherine! How had she found him so soon? Was it soon? He had lost count of days as he lay in a fever. Oh God, why did he send those silly coded messages? He should have known they would be child's play to someone as clever and quick as Katherine. He reached for the end of the bed, and said, "I'm ill, Kath. You must go away and come back later."

In his present condition he would be totally unable to carry out his plan to strike a deal with her. He could scarcely remember a word of his prepared speech. He knew only too well he would need to muster all his strength of mind and body to out-argue Katherine. He dreaded her next words.

"Rubbish! Don't be such a juvenile idiot! Either you open the door, or I go down and find Mrs. Feather next door and tell her all I know about you. I can guarantee she'll have you out of her house in minutes. I'll count to ten. One . . . two . . ."

He clung on to the bedpost and said that she must give him time to get to the door. Then he would open it and she could see that he was telling the truth.

THE MARKET PLACE was now familiar to Ivy and Roy and they threaded their way through throngs of shoppers. When they arrived at number seven Folgate Street, Mrs. Feather answered the door, and said they were lucky that she had just arrived back from next door. She was sure Mr. Ulph was at home, because he had been very tired and had refused food.

"Come in, won't you," she said, noting that this was a very respectable-looking old couple, one of them clearly disabled, who probably needed to sit down. "Take a seat, and I'll just go up and ask if he's feeling well enough to see you. He did have a visitor earlier, though whether she stayed I couldn't say. I was a little concerned because, as you see, my hallway and stairs are very dark. O'course, I can go up and down with my eyes shut, but strangers, well . . . I kept asking my husband to fix the light, but he never got round to it. Useless in that way, he was. All I can say is that it was a woman, and she had a nice voice. Now, what name shall I say to Mr. Ulph?"

"Miss Beasley and Mr. Goodman," said Ivy firmly. "We met him recently. He will remember us."

It was a matter of minutes before the landlady was back again. "He is not answering his door so may have gone to sleep again," she said. "Or he could have gone out, I suppose, if he was feeling better. I've been round chatting to my neighbour, and you know how long that can take! What would you like to do? I could make you a cup of tea, as you've come specially?"

She paused to draw breath, and Ivy looked at Roy for support.

"I think we'll accept your offer and then try again in a few minutes," he said. "If he still doesn't answer, we'll leave it to another day. Thank you, Mrs. Feather. It's a hot day for tramping round the streets, and we have, as you say, come specially."

Ivy and Roy drank their tea in silence. They had a tacit understanding that it would be best not to say much more at present. Finally, Ivy said conversationally, "Nice lace curtains, Roy. My mother had some just like that. Must be quite important to shield the window from prying eyes, what with the house being right on the pavement."

"I'm sure you're right, dearest," he said. "Though I must say this house is a bit too dark for my taste."

Ivy could tell he was not concentrating on lace curtains and looked at her watch. "I suppose we should think of going soon. Let's ask the landlady to try once more, and this time I'll go up with her."

"It may be too steep for you," Roy said anxiously.

"Stairs don't bother me," Ivy said. "Now, you wait here, and I'll call her."

When Ivy suggested accompanying her, Mrs. Feather was not happy. "He's on the second floor, my dear," she said. "Those old stairs are very narrow."

"I've always lived in old houses," Ivy replied blandly. "Up we go now. He might recognise my voice."

After one or two pauses for Ivy to get her breath back, they arrived outside Ulph's door and Mrs. Feather knocked once more. Silence. Ivy put her hand on the door handle and turned. Then she opened it wide enough to peep in, and at the same time said, "Mr. Ulph? Are you there?" Silence. Ivy pushed the door wide and walked in.

"You'd better come in, Mrs. Feather . . ." she said. "The bird has apparently flown."

Mrs. Feather looked in. "My goodness," she said, wrinkling her nose. "It's very stale in here. No, you're right. He must have gone out with his visitor."

Ivy walked over to the window, which was open, and said, "What's out there?"

"It's a flat roof, and Mr. Ulph used to get out of the window and sit in the sun. You can see his chair. I told him not to sit in the full sun, and I think that's what made him poorly."

"Not too poorly to walk off with his woman visitor," said Ivy, smiling.

"Huh, men!" said Mrs. Feather, returning her smile.

"What's that down by the chair?"

"Oh, that'll be an empty wine bottle. I'm afraid he did indulge himself. Still, he didn't seem to have any other pleasures, and anyway, it's none of my business so long as he behaved himself and paid the rent."

"And he did that?"

"Oh yes, he was a real gentleman, you know. But anyway, you would know that, being his friends."

Ivy nodded, and looked again at the window. "I could get out there, couldn't I?" she said. "The sill is very close to the floor and close to the roof outside. Not much more than stepping over a cat!"

"That's right," said Mrs. Feather. "It was very convenient for him."

Before the landlady could stop her, Ivy had pushed up the sash window to its full extent and neatly climbed out onto the flat roof.

"Miss Beasley! Are you safe out there?"

"Perfectly safe, thank you," she said, and walked over to the edge. She looked down into next door's concrete yard, full of old lawn mowers and piles of wood. And she spotted something else. A man, wearing what looked like pyjamas, lay spread-eagled on the concrete, and even from the height of the roof Ivy could see his limbs were awkwardly bent. She peered over again and saw a familiar head of thick black hair.

"Mrs. Feather!" she called. "Can you come here?"

"Oh dear, no, I have no head for heights, I'm afraid."

"Don't worry, I'll hold your hand," Ivy reassured her. "I just need you to see something, before it disappears. That's it, dear, you'll be quite safe with me."

Thirty-nine

ROY WAITED ANXIOUSLY for Ivy and Mrs. Feather to return, and he supposed they must have found Ulph. They were probably encouraging him to come down, so that they could all have a good talk. Thank goodness the poor fellow was feeling better. He had seemed such a nice chap, though clearly unhappy and worried. Perhaps Ivy was just what he needed. She was famous for putting things right!

Now he could hear footsteps on the stairs, and stood up, holding on to his chair.

"Ah, there you are, my dear," he said. "And is the invalid receiving visitors now?"

The two women looked at each other. Ivy said, "You go and telephone," and then walked across to Roy to suggest he should sit down again for a moment. Mrs. Feather, meanwhile, went out to the hallway, and Roy could hear her telephoning.

"What's to do, Ivy?" he said. "You look quite pale. Those stairs were too much for you, though I don't expect you to admit it!"

"No, it's not the stairs. Looks like Sebastian Ulph is past receiving visitors. There's a flat roof outside the window in his room, and he must have gone out there with a chair and a bottle of wine. We looked around but no sign of him. There was no safety fence or anything, and when I looked over the edge—"

"You did *what*, Ivy?" interrupted Roy.

"Oh, I don't mind heights. Anyway, there he was. Flat out on the concrete yard below. More or less dead, I suspect. His arms and legs were all anyhow. Mrs. Feather is phoning the police, so we'll have to stay here a bit longer."

Roy was confused for a few minutes. The baldness of the news was almost too much to take in, but his main concern was Ivy herself. "You must sit down, too, my love. There, in the chair next to me. Take it easy, and we'll try to unravel what has happened."

"The police and ambulance are coming straightaway," said Mrs. Feather, returning to the room. "I'll go and put the kettle on. We all need a good strong cup of tea with sugar. And don't worry, Mr. Goodman, the police will sort it all out."

DEIRDRE WAS WEEDING in the garden when she heard the telephone. She rushed back inside, kicking off her gardening shoes, and lifted the receiver.

"Hello? Ivy, is that you? No, I'm not busy. Of course I'm alone! What's up?"

After a minute or so, Deirdre pulled up a stool and sat

down heavily. "Oh my God! How on earth did that happen? What did you say? The signal's not too good."

"I said, it is a clear case of 'did he fall or was he pushed?' Anyway, the reason I'm ringing you, is that we have dismissed our taxi and shall need a lift back home when the police have finished with us. Can you come? Oh, good, thanks Deirdre. I'll let you know when we're ready. Oh, here they come. Bye."

Deirdre was trembling. That poor man, with his bad leg. He had been so polite, and she had not been very nice to him. And now he was dead. It was hard to believe, and yet there had been something doomed about him. She told herself she was being ridiculous. But the memory of his pale face and dark eyes returned as she poured a large whisky and began to drink.

When she was calmer, she decided to ring Gus. His phone rang for a long time, and eventually the mechanical voice clicked in. She left no message. The best thing she could do was have a shower and walk down to Hangman's Row. He should be back by then, and if not, a walk would do her good.

But then what about fetching Ivy and Roy? And how was she going to get Roy's trundle in her car? Perhaps Ivy had been too shocked to have thought of this. She rang her on her mobile, and Ivy agreed that they would order the special taxi instead. Apparently a sympathetic policeman had told them he wouldn't keep them any longer than was necessary.

It was midafternoon when Deirdre finally set off for Gus's cottage. The sun was still high, and the warmth was comforting as she walked at a steady pace through the village. When she turned into the lane, she could see Miriam

Blake in her front garden, chatting to Rose Budd over the low wall dividing the cottages. They turned to watch her approach, and before she got to Gus's, they hailed her with a cheery wave.

"'Mad dogs and Englishmen go out in the midday sun!'" quoted Miriam with a smile. "We were just saying that we should soon be seeing signs of autumn. How are you, Mrs. Bloxham?"

"Very well, thank you, and not mad, I hope," Deirdre replied. "I'm on my way to see Mr. Halfhide."

"Not there, I'm afraid," said Rose. "I saw him go off quite early this morning, and he hasn't come back yet, so far as I know."

"True," said Miriam, not to be outdone. "I heard Whippy whining and went round to let her out into the garden. Gave her fresh water, too, poor little thing. Funny, that. Gus usually asks me to keep an eye on her if he's going to be gone long. "

"Ah, well. I'll give him a ring later. Thanks, anyway." Deirdre turned to go back home, and saw a tall figure approaching. "Oh, look!" she said, relieved. "There he is, just coming down the lane." She waved, and walked to meet him.

"Hello, Deirdre," he said, frowning. "What brings you down here?"

"You, you silly chump!" she replied. "I came to call but found you were nowhere to be seen. Miriam and Rose said you'd gone out, so I was going home. But now you can give me a cup of tea. I've got news for you, but not nice news, I'm afraid."

GUS'S RECEPTION OF the news was oddly calm. He said that as his cottage was so dreary and depressing, he would walk back with her to Tawny Wings and would stay while they talked over the distressing news.

"I expect Ivy and Roy will be back by now," Deirdre said as they walked past Springfields. "We won't disturb them. They must have had quite a shock, and even though Ivy sometimes seems bombproof, they are probably both feeling a bit shaken up."

Gus agreed, and they walked on, waving to Theo Roussel as he drove past them in his Land Rover.

"I was going to see him today," Deirdre said. "But I think I'll leave it until we find out more about Ulph. Things have changed a lot since we last talked. And, by the way, were you out investigating today? Miriam said you hadn't left a note for her to mind Whippy, so she was doing it anyway."

Gus scowled. "That woman is altogether too nosey!" he said. "I try to creep out without her seeing, but it's impossible. No, I didn't tell her I would be out, and Whippy was perfectly happy for an hour or two. Now, here we are, Deirdre. One of your ice-cold pink gins would be just the ticket, don't you think?"

In the shade of the spreading mulberry tree in Deirdre's garden, they drank in silence for a while. Then Gus said he had a lot to consider, but had she had any thoughts about who might have wanted to get Ulph permanently out of the way? When she talked to her friend Sid, had he told her any personal details about his best saxophone player?

"Not really. Sid was sad to see him go. But I didn't speak to him for long. I did get the impression, though, that Ulph had been very private and hadn't made close friends with any of the band. They all liked him, but he kept his distance."

Gus was quiet again, and Deirdre got up to refill their

glasses. "Would you like to stay for supper?" she said. "I don't fancy being on my own this evening."

"That would be nice, Deirdre. But I think I should perhaps go back to the cottage, in case Whippy has had enough of Miriam."

"She'll be fine," Deirdre said. "Dogs don't mind nosey women, just so long as they stroke their ears and give them bones. I'll go and look in the freezer and see if there's something delicious for us. I don't know about you, but I'm not really hungry yet."

She went off, carrying their glasses, and Gus watched her go. What a lovely girl! But now things had changed, and maybe for the worse. He was haunted by Kath's phone call yesterday. What had she said? Not to acknowledge her if he met her around locally? She didn't say when she was coming, but it had sounded like soon.

Forty

"DON'T YOU THINK you should ring her?" Deirdre said. She and Gus were sitting on the terrace at Tawny Wings, digesting their supper and sipping iced coffee. She had been asking questions about Katherine, trying to find out tactfully the nature of their relationship now, and he had told her about the latest call.

"I've tried," he said. "I tried her mobile when you were cooking. No answer, so I left a message for her to ring me. I am afraid it's what I expected. She seldom answers, unless it's someone she wants to talk to."

"Won't she want to talk to you?"

"No."

Deirdre shrugged. "More coffee?" she offered.

Gus shook his head, and leaned back in his chair. He closed his eyes. Deirdre wondered if he had gone to sleep, poor chap. But he began to talk, almost as if to himself.

"I don't know how I was so blind about Kath. After all,

my former job was information gathering. Once or twice in the past I had to confront danger face on, but more often I lurked in the shadows."

"Lurking in the shadows is dangerous, isn't it?" Deirdre spoke softly, and his eyes remained closed.

"Sometimes, yes. Depends on the enemy. If he is clever and ruthless, it can be very dangerous."

"Or she?" Deirdre said. "Is Katherine clever and ruthless?"

"Yes," said Gus. He opened his eyes and smiled at Deirdre. "Shall we have a swim?" he suggested. "No need for cozzies. We're not overlooked. Then I must go home."

"Let's skip the swim, shall we? If you've got another hour or so . . ." All unpleasantness forgotten, they went hand in hand upstairs.

IVY AND ROY were very tired by the time they arrived back at Springfields. Miss Pinkney was waiting for them and ushered them into the now empty lounge.

"All the other residents have retired to their rooms, so we can have a peaceful hot drink. Come along, my dears, it is all ready for you. I really don't think the police should have kept you so long without food."

"It wasn't them," Roy explained. "We were ready much earlier, and Mrs. Feather made us a sandwich. But our special taxi was out on another job, and we had to wait until he could come for us."

"Never mind, you're home now. Katya insisted on staying late and baking these cookies for you. She's a good girl. I do hope she stays with us, though her boyfriend seems very attentive!"

"He's still a student, so they won't be thinking about marriage yet," said Roy.

Ivy had said very little, and he wondered if she was feeling all right. Just tired, maybe. She drank her Horlicks and ate a couple of cookies and then said she was ready for bed. "I'll see you both in the morning," she said, and bent to kiss Roy's cheek. "Night night, my love. You were a good ole boy. Night, Pinkers."

She walked slowly away and up the stairs. Roy and Miss Pinkney watched her in silence. Then, when she was safely in her room, Miss Pinkney began to gather the crocks on a tray.

"Just a minute, Miss Pinkney," Roy said. "Have you time for a little talk?"

She sat down. "Of course, Mr. Goodman. How can I help?"

"I am a little worried about Ivy. She looked so tired, didn't she? The afternoon's events must have been a great strain for her. She had to go over the whole story with the police, finding Ulph's body and coping with Mrs. Feather. Mind you, that one was very tough. Seemed mostly concerned with the bad publicity for her lodging house."

"And I suppose suspicion could have fallen on her? The landlady, I mean?"

Roy stared at her. "Oh, I don't think so!" he said. It was then that he realised that if Ulph had not fallen as a result of weakness and too much alcohol, then a number of people could be suspected of pushing him over the edge of the roof. Yes, the landlady for a start. Then there was Sid or any one of his band harbouring grudges. Or Deirdre, fed up with him and his bad leg.

"You're smiling, Mr. Goodman," Miss Pinkney said

gently. "Not too worried about Ivy, then? I am sure that after a good night's sleep, she will be her old feisty self. I don't know what we'd do without her at Springfields!"

"Let's hope we won't have to, not for many years to come. And once I am her husband, I shall be very firm."

At this, Miss Pinkney chuckled heartily. "That will be the day!" she said, and offered to help Roy up to his room. "You must be very tired, too," she said, and patted him affectionately on his shoulder.

IN DEIRDRE'S BEDROOM at Tawny Wings, she stretched out and composed herself for sleep. What a day! And poor old Gus, now whiffling quietly by her side—what secrets was he hiding from her now? Sleep would not come, and she reviewed in her mind the day's events. Fancy Ivy and Roy being caught up in what could easily be a murder enquiry! And not as investigators but as witnesses to the result of the crime. So who could have killed Ulph? First of all, person or persons unknown. They really knew nothing about the man, and the snippets he had told her by the pool could easily have been a pack of lies.

Oh my God! Suppose they think I could have done it!

Deirdre felt an overpowering need to wake Gus and tell him she hadn't done it. But then she calmed herself, and thought back over times during the day when she had been alone long enough to have been able to get to Oakbridge and do the deed. And then home again in time to receive Ivy's call for help with transport. No, not possible, thank God.

She propped herself up on one elbow and looked at Gus. He was nice-looking when asleep. That hunted look had gone, and his fine features were very attractive in repose.

She smiled. Funny old thing, he was. Where had he gone to all day?

Oh! She caught her breath and collapsed back on the pillow. Where *had* he been all day? He'd gone out early, Rose Budd said, and it must have been four o'clock by the time she met him coming home down the lane. Plenty of time to get to Oakbridge and . . . Oh, Deirdre Bloxham, don't be so ridiculous! She turned her back on him and, after quite a long time, drifted off into a troubled sleep.

Forty-one

MRS. FEATHER HAD locked up her house and gone to spend the night with her neighbour. She had no other lodgers at the moment, and now that Mr. Ulph was gone, there was no reason for her to stay overnight by herself. The thought of a man possibly murdered in her second-floor back bedroom had temporarily unhinged her, and she had shouted at the police, telling them to go and park somewhere else. "You can take your sirens and winking lights and zebra stripes somewhere else!" she had yelled. "And if that's the ambulance, get poor Mr. Ulph out of the yard and away to wherever you take dead people as soon as possible!"

And then she had muttered to herself that all kinds of harm had already been done to her bed-and-breakfast business. There were nosey parkers everywhere, out in the street and behind lace curtains. Who would want to come and stay in number seven now? At last the police had gone, and eventually that nice old couple had been collected and taken home, and now, after little sleep, she was sitting in her neighbour's back kitchen, drinking strong tea and trying to get yesterday's horrible events into some sort of order.

"I tell you, this will be the finish of me. I shall have to sell up and go into the workhouse. You will come and visit me, won't you."

"Don't be so daft!" her neighbour said, laughing. "It'll all blow over in a couple of days. Hey, do you think the wind could have blown him over the edge? There were some strong gusts now and then, and you said he'd been poorly."

"Now who's being daft? Of course he wasn't blown over. Anyway, the police will find out all the details. They're brilliant these days, with genes an' that. He probably did fall, now I think about it. He hadn't eaten for ages, and he lifted the elbow more than most. It seems a hard thing to say, but I reckon I'm well rid of him."

"And you needn't worry about the newspapers. There's been a big fire over at the shoe factory. Still burning, apparently. That'll fill the front pages, you can bet your life. No, it'll all be forgotten in a few days. Perhaps a few more questions to answer, and then it will be finished. He had a funny name, didn't he? What kind of a name is Ulph? Perhaps he was foreign, and all his relatives are dead. You should go to the funeral, out of respect, and then put the whole thing behind you. I'll come with you, if you like."

Mrs. Feather knew very well that this was not the act of kindness it appeared to be. Her neighbour was extremely fond of funerals, and here was an excuse to attend another one.

"We'll see," she said. "I might just close up for a couple of weeks and go to my sister's in Brighton. Then I can come back and make a new start."

"Always supposing the police will give you permission to leave town," was the worrying reply.

IN BARRINGTON, THE centre of the village was very quiet, as though the death of Sebastian Ulph had spread gloom countywide. Even Hangman's Row was quiet, where usually neighbours gossiped over the wall most mornings. All doors were shut and gardens empty. Only Miriam Blake was to be seen, hurrying from her backyard to Gus's with an important question.

"Any luck?" she said as she popped in to offer Gus a home-cooked fish-and-chip lunch.

"Any luck with what, Miriam?" Gus had been miles away. He had come home early from Tawny Wings, and was thinking about the time when Sebastian Ulph had been a regular visitor to the house where he and Kath lived in relative harmony. She had a good explanation, as always, for the periodic attentions of young men, whom she described as her "swains," as if referring to them in Olde English made the whole thing innocent. Which, of course, it was not. He knew that now, and it still hurt him. She had been so beautiful in those days, and he was well aware at the time that he was considered lucky to have married her. Luck, however, did not feature in Katherine's plans.

So why *did* she marry him? Because he was good-looking, confident, and mysterious. He had the glamorous aura of being an undercover agent. Life with him promised the excitement of danger. Katherine loved danger, particularly when it involved someone else, and all her instincts were tuned to making sure she survived.

"Hi, Gus, I'm still here!" said Miriam, perching herself on the edge of his rickety sofa. "What I meant was, have you had any luck getting hold of Kath? I remember you saying she had been a friend of that man who was found dead in an Oakbridge backyard. It was on the local radio. Terrible thing, that. Do you think he was pushed?"

Gus stiffened. "How should I know, Miriam? And I don't remember telling you anything about Katherine. She must have told you herself, that night she stayed in your house. And no, I have not had any luck telephoning her, and what is more, I do not intend to try again."

"Okay, okay! Keep your hair on, Gussy!"

"And for God's sake don't call me Gussy!" he shouted at her.

Miriam was surprised, but not squashed. She had had parents who shouted at each other all the time and was inured to it. "Forget it, my dear," she said soothingly. "I just came in to see if you fancied fish-and-chips for lunch? I suppose it should be a roast for Sunday, but I've got two nice pieces of plaice. It's very fresh, and there's plenty for two."

She never gives up, thought Gus, and then he smiled. There was something steadfast about Miriam, and he accepted gratefully.

"About twelve then? We can have a glass of primrose wine before lunch. And yes, of course you can bring Whippy. She loves me, don't you, doggie?"

Whippy, ears down and teeth bared, crept behind Gus's legs, and he said, "Typical woman! Fickle little creature. When *you've* been looking after her, she gives *me* the brush-off! Thanks. See you later." He turned back to his desk, and she left quietly.

"NOW WE SHALL never know if it *was* Ulph that night," said Miriam, as they sat at lunch. She placed a new jar of tartar sauce in front of Gus. "You know that time I heard footsteps going up the lane late at night. Didn't one of your agency say it could've been him?"

"I must confess I have forgotten, Miriam. My goodness, this fish looks good and still smells of the sea! You're a dab hand with cooking!"

"Do you know," confided Miriam, forgetting about the night prowler, "that reminds of a holiday we took once at the seaside. There was a small fishing boat that came in and set up a stall by the slipway. They had these small flat fish called dabs, and Mum would buy three and cook them for our supper. We were renting a cottage, and it was the only holiday I can remember as a child."

"Were you an only child?"

Miriam nodded. "My dad spoilt me rotten. I think Mum was jealous, in a way. When she got old, she didn't seem to like me much. Hurtful, really. Still, I manage okay now, especially since you moved in next door!"

Gus saw the warning light flashing and hastily changed the subject. They talked about childhood and their parents. But mostly Miriam talked and Gus listened, guiding her every so often away from the subject of Sebastian Ulph.

After they had finished, Miriam suggested Gus have a rest on the sofa while she washed up the dishes. "Then we can relax. I bought a new CD last week you might like to listen to," she said, and handed it to him. He was alarmed to see it was *Sweet Listening for Lovers*, and he handed it back, saying he really only liked Bach, and perhaps he should be going now.

But Miriam insisted, and he sat hunched up on the sofa, waiting for her to join him from the kitchen.

"I meant to ask you," she said, drying her hands and

taking off her apron, "where did you get to yesterday? I kept popping round from time to time to check on Whippy, but you seemed to have been out all day, until Mrs. Bloxham came down. Of course, I don't want to pry! I know how you hate that. But if there is anything I can do to help, you must say."

Gus got to his feet. "Are you perhaps wondering if I went early into Oakbridge, visited the hapless Sebastian Ulph, quarrelled with him, and in the heat of the moment shoved him off the edge of his flat roof? Maybe we should cook up an alibi for me? I'm sure you would oblige, Miriam. Well, fortunately my trip to Oakbridge had nothing to do with that poor fellow. I was visiting the hospital. Piles, Miriam. Very embarrassing and very uncomfortable. There now, you have the whole story. I must go. Thank you for a lovely meal," he added, very much as an afterthought. And then he was gone.

For a few minutes, Miriam wondered if she should have a good cry and get Augustus Halfhide out of her system. Then she remembered his angry face and faced the fact that she had been thinking exactly what he suspected. She could call to mind word for word what he had said. He knew Ulph had a flat roof to go out onto. How did he know that? From the local news on telly, of course. But surely piles could be dealt with by a doctor at the surgery?

She went upstairs feeling a little wobbly, and decided to have an afternoon snooze. When only half ready, she went to her dressing table drawer and took out the little parcel containing the pearl and diamond earring. Poor Gus. He must have suffered a great deal when he split up from Katherine.

She replaced the earring and checked under the bed, as

always, fearful of possible intruders. It was well after three
o'clock before she finally drifted off to sleep, still brooding
about the flash of real anger she had witnessed in Gus. It
was quickly over but full of restrained violence. Or so she
imagined.

Forty-two

THE LAW HAD gone immediately into action as soon as the police had been summoned to Folgate Street. Areas cordoned off, witnesses identified and questioned, Ulph's room guarded while any trace of him and his mysterious lady visitor had been taken and recorded. As expected, Mrs. Feather was asked to postpone her visit to her sister, and at Springfields, Mrs. Spurling had difficulty in overcoming an irrational atmosphere of alarm and suspicion.

Ivy was unmoved. "Stupid old things think the murderer will come here in search of us, Roy," she said, and laughed.

"Have you noticed how everybody assumes he was murdered?" Roy replied seriously. "But I can quite imagine him walking over to the edge to take a look and having a dizzy turn. It wouldn't have taken more than seconds. Poor young man. From what Mrs. Feather said, he was far from strong and didn't eat enough. Didn't Deirdre say he had a bad leg? That could easily have let him down."

"She'll be coming in to see us after evening service. We'll ask her then."

At this point, they were surprised to see Deirdre entering the lounge. "Evening, you two," she said, without her usual smile.

"I thought you were—"

"Coming in after church," Deirdre interrupted. "I was, Ivy, but then I thought perhaps I should come with you and say a prayer for poor Sebastian Ulph. Is that all right?"

"Of course, my dear," said Roy. "There's just time for a quick coffee before we go."

"And by the way, Deirdre," said Ivy, "did he have a permanently bad leg?"

"I honestly can't remember," Deirdre said. "But I have a vague idea it was something to do with a skiing accident."

THE BELLS HAD stopped ringing by the time the three arrived at the church porch, and the churchwarden was about to shut the door.

"Oh, sorry! Good evening, Miss Beasley. And Mr. Goodman, let me help you with your vehicle. *And* Mrs. Bloxham! How nice to see you!"

"No need to warn the entire congregation," muttered Deirdre, acutely aware that she had not darkened the door of the church since the day of Bert's funeral. Her discomfort was increased by Ivy determinedly marching to sit in the front pew.

The vicar looked around, saw the usual handful of worshippers, and sighed. "Good evening, everyone," he said. "May I say how lovely to see you all here this evening." He looked at the old lady at the front, still on her knees and saying goodness knows how many preliminary prayers. Oh well, the fall of a sparrow and all that.

They began with the first hymn, and the order of service soon came back to Deirdre. She had been a faithful church-goer with her parents at the parish church in her youth, and there was not much difference between then and now. She stood up when Ivy stood, and sat down when Ivy sat. The hymn tunes were traditional, and she had no problem in singing in a good soprano voice. Every so often, if she lost her place in the service book, Roy would lean across and find it for her. The peace and quiet of the ancient church gradually worked its magic, and she relaxed. The vicar's sermon was incomprehensible, so she gave up trying and thought back to when Ulph had first appeared at her door.

So far, she guessed, nobody had actually mentioned suicide. But it was a very real possibility. He had clearly been an unhappy man, up against mysterious forces and confused about what his future should be. He had left one job, petitioned for another, disappeared and then turned up again. There was his conversation with Ivy and Roy in the café. Roy had obviously taken to him, but he had resisted even their tactful enquiries into his private life.

And then Ivy and Roy had found out where he lived. Did he realise they had followed him, marked him down? Was there something so awful that he could not risk exposure and had taken the only way out? For all his anxious contradictions and conversations, she had not reckoned him a candidate for suicide.

"And our last hymn," said the vicar, looking at his watch, "is number one hundred and twenty-five. Thank you, Mrs. er . . ." But the organist was not to be hurried, and she set off at her customary slow and solemn pace.

It was while they were filing out, ready to shake hands and have a chat, that Deirdre finally allowed herself to think the unthinkable. Was it possible? She shuddered and pushed it to the back of her mind. But then it surfaced again, and as they reached the gates of Springfields, she blurted out, "I suppose you haven't thought of Gus and Katherine? They both had reason to dislike Ulph and could have acted together."

Ivy, who was, as usual, marching ahead, stopped dead, and was almost run over by her beloved. "Deirdre!" she said. "What an appalling thought! Dislike is no reason for murder, for heaven's sake. I think we had better forget that you even thought such a terrible thing."

Leaving Deirdre to walk back to Tawny Wings, the others made their way into the dining room, where the rest of the residents were already tucking into their supper. The latecomers were seated and their food brought in under silver covers. Ivy took one bite and pronounced it stone cold.

"If you ask me," she said, "we pay enough money to this place to ensure piping hot Sunday suppers."

Mrs. Spurling was summoned and a certain amount of acrimonious dispute ensued. Fresh plates were brought, and they finally settled to eat. They had finished their first course before Ivy spoke again.

"She could be right," she said.

"Deirdre?" asked Roy, knowing at once who Ivy meant. "But surely, my love, it is extremely unlikely?"

"More likely than anyone else we've thought of . . . so far . . ."

"I am sure Gus could produce a perfectly satisfactory alibi, and as for Katherine, I was certain we had seen the last of her. Surely Gus has severed all contact?"

* * *

GUS HAD BEEN late collecting his Sunday paper from James at the side door of the shop when the churchgoers went by and wondered at Deirdre accompanying them. He was hoping to contact her later, to suggest another evening of unparalleled delight, but now had a thought that perhaps she had been going to church to confess her sins.

He walked slowly home, relishing the evening sun warming his narrow frame. He passed the pub, stopped and went back, and ordered a pint of Jones Best. There were several locals propping up the bar, and he sat down at a table nearby. Their conversation was inevitably about the rooftop murder. The red tops seemed to have decided without question that it had been a crime of vengeance.

"The silly bugger should never have been out on that roof with no safeguards," said the chairman of the parish council. His view was always sought first, and he was only too ready to give it. "Anyway," he continued, "it looks like he were a foreigner, with a name like Ulph. Probably sent over from some terrorist organisation to plant bombs, an' that, and some of our lot got to him first."

"They didn't say nothing about a terrorist." This timid suggestion was made by a freelance gardener, who earned a decent wage doing rough jobs for old ladies and busy incomers. He was reckoned by the others at the bar to be a bit of a wet, and they scoffed. What did he mean by "they"? Without waiting for his answer, they ignored him and ordered more drinks.

Gus opened his paper and decided to start on the quick crossword. He could usually finish it in the time it took to down a pint, and he read the first clue.

One across: Guilty conscience (5), he read. He sighed. Could it be a coincidence or a message from above? Or was he already getting paranoid? He took up his pen and filled in the five squares—SHAME—then downed his pint in two deep draughts and stalked out of the pub.

Forty-three

THE THOUGHT OF yet more speculation from his colleagues had been too much for Gus, and he had spent the rest of the evening at home on his own. He could not have said exactly what had been on television, though it had blared at him until he retired miserably to bed.

Now, this Monday morning, with a meeting at Tawny Wings at eleven, he had to make an important decision. Once more, he went over in his mind that last phone message from Kath. The only possible explanation she could have had for coming back to Barrington and Oakbridge was to find Ulph. She no doubt intended once and for all to retrieve her jewellery by threatening him with the police. He had probably planned to retaliate with similar threats, including exposing her insurance scams. Supposing she *had* come to see him on Saturday. It could have been stalemate between them. She could have known where the jewels were likely to be—a word dropped by mistake in a telephone call?—and if he had won their argument, she could have gone down into the woods to find them before he got there himself.

So, had it all gone wrong? What if she had found Ulph in Folgate Street? Had there been a preliminary drink out on that terrace and then the conversation had gone sour? Kath was quite capable of driving him over the edge, physically as well as metaphorically. She was a big strong girl, and he was incapacitated by illness and hunger.

"Oh God," Gus moaned. "I can't keep all this to myself." And along with telling the others about his suspicions, he had to abandon any lingering feelings he might still have for his ex-wife. Could he deliberately shop her to the police?

"Yoo-hoo!" Miriam had passed by Gus's window and seen him with his head in his hands. She feared the worst. He was ill and was too proud to call for her help. She knocked at his door and then walked in.

"Morning, Gus! Are you okay? Can I come in?" It was a rhetorical question, since she was already close to him, looking concerned.

He sighed, and stood up. "Morning, Miriam. Nice of you to look in. No, I'm fine. Got up late, and still feeling sleepy."

"Watched television too late last night?" she said. "I can hear it through the wall, you know. We are that close together!"

"Ah, yes. Well, I have to go out in half an hour, so if you'll excuse me . . ."

"Time for a small glass of primrose wine?"

Gus made a big effort, and laughed. "Goodness no, thanks, Miriam. I shall need a clear head, so maybe later? Tomorrow, perhaps."

"If you're sure you're all right then. I'll see you later. Is Whippy coming to me this morning while you're out?"

Gus said that he would not be long, and so with no more suggestions to make, Miriam retreated to her own house.

WHEN HE ARRIVED at Tawny Wings, Gus saw Roy's trundle parked outside and knew that he and Ivy were there before him. He had still not made the big decision and stood on the front steps for a minute or so before knocking.

Deirdre's head appeared at an upstairs window. "It's not locked. Come on in, Gus. Come straight up."

He climbed the stairs and went into the office, where Ivy and Roy sat drinking coffee. Their greeting was pleasant, as always, but he thought there was a little less warmth, a certain reserve.

"Right," said Deirdre. "First on the agenda is the need to marshal our thoughts before we are asked to help the police with their enquiries."

"Me and Roy, we've already done that," said Ivy. "It's up to you and Gus to tell us what conclusion you've come to."

"Or which direction your thoughts are taking," said Roy kindly.

"You first, Deirdre," Gus said.

"Well, as you can imagine, what with me having spent some time with Ulph, and him coming back here, and so on, there is quite a lot I have to try and recall. The first time he came, it was just to ask me to speak up for him with the county orchestra. I have a contact there. Then, the second time, he turned up asking to swim in my pool."

Here she paused and looked conspiratorially at Gus. "I must say he warmed up a lot after we'd had one or two drinks, and then we were a bit silly fooling around in the water. He was nice, really, not presuming or anything like that. You know me," she added, with another sly look at Gus, "I'm always ready to enjoy life."

"Are you going to tell the police about that lovable side of your character?" Ivy said sarcastically.

"If it's Inspector Frobisher, he'll know that already," answered Deirdre, happily trumping Ivy's ace.

"Now your turn, Gus," said Roy. "Take your time, old chap. We know that you are in a rotten situation, knowing Ulph in the past and still being in touch with your ex-wife. How do you see it all?"

It was Roy's sympathetic old face that finally cleared Gus's muddled head. Here he was with people he could trust and to whom he owed a considerable loyalty. After all, they had got him out of tricky situations in the past.

"Thanks, Roy," he said. "I do, as it happens, have something new to tell you. It is not easy for me, as you'll see, but it is obviously important. What you decide to do about it after I've spoken is up to you, of course. It's about Katherine. She left a message on my phone the other evening, and it was brief and to the point. She gave me no opportunity to reply, and I have been consumed with worry about it ever since."

Then he told them that Katherine had been intending to visit Oakbridge and Barrington very soon and did not want to have any contact with him. If he saw her, he was not to acknowledge her.

"She had business to conclude, she said," he added. "After she had ended the call abruptly, I could not help thinking the worst. I convinced myself she was intending to see Ulph, threaten him with exposure of crimes unknown to us, and retrieve her jewellery. She's very tough, and what would have happened next I have no idea . . ."

His voice tailed away, and the others murmured sympathetically.

Then Ivy spoke up in her usual sharp tones. "So you didn't see her at all?" she asked. "You didn't even meet accidentally?"

"Oh dear," Gus said. "Now I see what you have been thinking. No. I did go into Oakbridge but to the hospital. As I was forced to own up to Miriam Blake, I suffer with piles. You know the sort of piles I mean? Ah, Roy, I see you do. Well, I had an early appointment with the specialist, and then I did some shopping, had a snack lunch, walked around the park for some fresh air and then came home. Met Deirdre in the lane, and she will no doubt know what time that was."

And now, he thought, my decision to tell all will have ended for good any chance of a permanent romance with the widow Bloxham. Who would want fun in bed with a man with piles?

Forty-four

"SO, ARE WE digging or not?" asked Deirdre, hoping that Gus had changed his mind about excavating holes on private ground. Several new avenues of enquiry had been decided upon by the team. Ivy and Roy had agreed to go back to Folgate Street and have coffee in the same restaurant where they had met Ulph. They would get into conversation with regulars, maybe even one they recognised from before and see what was being said around town about the possibility of a murder having happened in their midst. Then, if the street was now open, they would meander down Folgate and once more buttonhole a likely looking source of gossip.

Meanwhile, Deirdre had said firmly that she and Gus would search in the woods for any further clues. After all, if it had been Ulph burying jewellery, he was obviously in a hurry and might well have dropped another piece somewhere close to the mound. Ivy said helpfully that she could still remember roughly where the mound was and could give them directions. And then perhaps Whippy could do a retrieving job?

"All you have to do," she advised, with very little knowledge of dogs, "is give her the scent of something belonging to Ulph, and she'll lead you to the jewellery."

Gus had smiled. "Not as easy as it sounds, Ivy. First, where do we get something belonging to Ulph? And second, I don't know about other whippets, but Whippy has never retrieved anything in her life. She is much more likely to make for home."

"That could be interesting," Ivy had muttered, and Gus had changed the subject.

Now Deirdre said she would fetch a spade from the gardener's shed. Gus, still reluctant to excavate, proposed a better plan. "Let's walk down Hangman's Lane and collect a walking stick from my house. I doubt if Theo would object to me thrusting a stick into the ground in the appropriate place. We'd soon know then if there was anything solid buried there."

"Oh, for heaven's sake!" Deirdre said. "Don't be such a wimp! Theo won't suspect us of poaching! I didn't know you would be so law-abiding. But still," she added, seeing a bleak look on Gus's face, "we'll do as you say."

Gus nodded gratefully, and they set off.

Halfway through the village, they met Miriam on her way to the shop.

"Hi, Gus!" she said cheerfully. "Good meeting? Are we anywhere near finding the solution to the missing hand? I'll be pleased to assist, if you need help. There'd have to be some adjustment to fees, of course. But it might speed things up?"

Deirdre kept quiet, and Gus politely refused Miriam's offer.

"She's a frightful woman, isn't she," Deirdre said, when they were safely on their way.

"Oh not really. She's a very generous person, and quite lonely, I think. I know she is unstoppable and has a hide like a rhinoceros, but as a neighbour, she could be worse."

"Point taken," said Deirdre. "Goodwill to all men. Come on, let's venture into the wild, wild woods."

MEANWHILE, BACK AT Springfields, Roy said he would book the taxi for the next day, having apparently convinced Ivy that there was not much chance of seeing regulars in the café, unless they went there at roughly the same time as before.

"I am sure there are useful things to do here in Barrington this afternoon," he said, and Ivy finally agreed. "I shall have my usual rest," she said, "and think of a line of enquiry we can follow up today. In fact," she added, mounting the stairs to her room, "a good idea is already germinating. . . ."

Roy once more marvelled at the resources of his beloved and retired to the lounge, where he happily indulged in a nostalgic conversation with his friend Fred. During the course of their talk, with both of them yawning and rubbing their eyes, Roy suddenly snapped awake at something Fred had just said.

"Did you say your father was a woodman?" he asked.

"Oh yes. He did other jobs for the Roussels, of course. Full-time employed there. But he always did all the wooding necessary, clearing away the underbrush and keeping an eye on the saplings. He loved it, did Dad. Knew all the birds and animals. You should've heard him on the subject of badgers! He knew every sett in those woods. Used to stay up all night, just to watch the young ones come out and play around. Just as well he's dead and gone, what with all this talk of culling. A bloomin' disgrace, if you ask me."

"So did you know your way around in there, in amongst the trees?"

"Good God, boy, yes! Used to go with Dad, when he'd let me. Young Roussel would come, too. Mind you, he weren't supposed to. Used to sneak out without telling. He was a dab hand at creeping about unseen like."

"You mean the Roussel who's still up at the Hall?"

"O'course. Mr. Theodore, it was. He was only a lad then. Even now, he keeps a close eye on those woods. Trespassers beware!"

Roy could take a hint. He left the lounge quietly, and made for his own room, thinking it was just as well Gus had won his point about spade versus walking stick.

IVY LAY STRETCHED out on her bed, with her shoes neatly tucked away where she wouldn't trip on them when she got up. Her eyes were closed, but she was not asleep. For the first time, she strongly disagreed with her Roy, though she had not argued. I'm learning! she said to herself. If, instead of waiting until tomorrow, they had got their taxi to take them to Oakbridge straight after lunch, they could have had coffee or, if too late, a cup of tea in the café and started asking around. The waitresses, for instance, would surely have remembered Ulph, with his shock of dark hair and hunted look.

Still, she had given way, remembering her mother's unlovable habit of always being in the right, positively, unassailably in the right. So now, what could they be doing usefully today? Gus and Deirdre had gone down to the

woods, so that was out. What about Roussel? Hadn't somebody said Ulph's father had been a friend of the Roussels?
Perhaps Mr. Theo would remember some useful snippets
of information. Deirdre had already done some enquiring
in that direction, but Ivy suspected two percent of her time
with Theo Roussel was devoted to enquiring and ninety-
eight percent larking about upstairs.

Yes, that was it. She and Roy would go for a casual walk
through the Hall park and maybe bump into the squire. It
was not open to the public, but Ivy did not believe in
STRICTLY PRIVATE notices. What harm could two old persons possibly do to a park that had been there for hundreds
of years?

She and Roy met at the top of the stairs, and she told
him what they would be doing until suppertime. "We can
skip tea, or, who knows, if we meet Theo, he might ask us
in for a cuppa? After all, he happily opened up the gates for
us once before."

Roy smiled. "Highly unlikely this time, I'm afraid, my
dear. He is much more likely to send us packing. Very
politely, of course. Anyway, the chances of meeting him
are slim, but I do agree with you that we should be out taking the air, after being cooped up in Tawny Wings all
morning. Give me five minutes, and I shall be ready."

The two were a familiar sight in the village now. People
smiled and greeted them warmly. Several elderly people
said they wished they could afford to live in Springfields. It
must be such a splendid place, if that pair was an example
of Mrs. Spurling's brand of care.

As they approached the park gates, Roy was hoping to
see them closed. He was not a natural trespasser. But they
were wide open, and Ivy sailed through as if she lived
there. He followed a few yards behind but soon could see

the familiar figure of the squire standing on the flight of steps that led up to the main door of the house.

"Good afternoon, Miss Beasley, Mr. Goodman," Theo said politely. "Can I help you? We are not actually open to the general public."

Ivy frowned. "We are not the general public. We are here on Enquire Within business. We were hoping you could perhaps help us with a case we are investigating?"

Theo thought hard. He remembered Ivy Beasley only too well as the fierce old duck who had helped to solve the big problem he had had with his housekeeper. And dear little Deirdre had asked him something to do with the enquiry agency quite recently. He could not for the life of him remember what it was about. He was, he recalled, fully occupied with something else at the time! Was it about his friend Ulph's son?

"Well, now, I haven't much time, I'm afraid, but fire away. What was it you wanted to know?"

Grasp the nettle, thought Ivy, and said firmly, "I believe you were a friend of a Mr. Ulph? He's dead now, so we have learned, but his son is known to have been in the village and around, and we are anxious to contact any of his friends."

"You mean Sebastian? The one who jumped off a roof to his death in Oakbridge? Terrible business! Glad his father is dead, you know. Such a nice family, but Sebastian was a bit of a black sheep. Got mixed up with an appalling woman, I remember."

"That's the one," said Roy, who was now feeling reassured by Theo's willingness to listen. "He played the saxophone rather well."

"Played up here, at the hunt ball, didn't he? I was too busy for a chat, but you could tell he was streets ahead of the other so-called musicians. Frightful business. Now, what was it? Oh yes, do I know any of Seb's friends. I'm afraid not, unless you count Sid and His Swingers. Oh, and yes, there was this woman. Something to do with one of my tenants in the cottages. Halfhide, wasn't it? Divorced, of course, but someone said he'd had a visit from her. Stayed overnight with Miriam Blake—might have been Miriam who told me. Memory going, you know! Advancing old age—might be joining you in Springfields soon! Mind you, Miss Beasley, even as a schoolboy I could never remember things. Dates, kings and queens, that sort of thing. Now, I really must be going. You'll be fine with the gates. We won't shut them until after you've gone. Good day to you both!"

Forty-five

UNAWARE THAT THEIR colleagues were also out collecting evidence, Gus and Deirdre had reached the woods and plunged in. In no time, they were completely lost, circling round and round, arguing about which way to go. Then they began to see odd holly bushes and a rabbit warren that they recognised and found themselves in exactly the spot where Miriam and Rose had seen the severed hand.

Gus stopped, and said, "I remember Miriam said it was by this tree. See? It has been marked in blue paint as one to be felled. Diseased, she said, and a danger to the others."

"I reckon these woods are a danger to more than just trees," Deirdre grumbled, picking her way through brambles and nettles. She was happier in an urban jungle, with pavements and signposts.

"Hold my hand, Deirdre love," said a sympathetic Gus. "If we go straight ahead from here, like Ivy said, I guarantee we will come across the badgers' sett."

"Okay, I'll believe you, though thousands wouldn't. But oh, hang on a minute, Gus."

"What is it?" said Gus, as he watched Deirdre bend down to pick up something half buried by brambles. "Here, let me do it. You'll scratch yourself to pieces."

But Deirdre was pulling out something covered in earth that looked to Gus like a filthy glove. "Now," Deirdre said triumphantly, "how about this! A rubber glove, in exactly the same spot as those women found the hand—or should we say glove? What'd'you bet it is the same one? D'you know what I think, Gus?"

He shook his head. "Go on, tell me."

"I think Ulph or someone else buried something here and then dug it up again and took it to the new place. Being a musician, he would obviously not want to damage his hands and used rubber gloves. In a rush to get away, he probably left one behind, pushed under the leaves and stuff. Maybe he was rumbled and needed to find a better hiding place for the jewellery? Here, you take it. It's horrible!"

"It's just a dirty rubber glove. Anyway, let's get going and see what else you can find."

This time they went straight to the mound of earth, Gus leading the way. A couple of yards away from it, he stopped. "Oh no!" he said. "Just look at it, Deirdre."

"Blimey! Grave robbers," said Deirdre. "They got here before us."

In front of them, they could see that the mound had been taken apart, with heaps of earth in all directions. They walked forward and Gus poked around in the loose soil, but found nothing.

"What a mess!" said Deirdre. "If it was Ulph, you'd have thought he'd have tidied up a bit, just to cover his tracks."

"In too much of a hurry, I suspect," Gus replied. "Look about for footprints."

They walked around, eyes down, but their own footprints were inextricably mixed up with others in the loose earth.

"I suppose we've failed, then?" Deirdre said sadly.

"Oh, that's where I disagree, Mrs. B.," said Gus, smiling at her mournful face. He walked away a couple of paces from the mound. "What about this?" He speared a piece of screwed-up tissue. "Ta-ra!" he shouted. "Perfectly clear, I reckon. Someone has risked being discovered digging for buried treasure, and we can be sure the stuff has gone. Not likely to have been Ulph, at least, not since he got ill. But whoever took it, he or she is very possibly touting it around for sale amongst insalubrious buyers."

"SO WHAT DO you suggest we do next?" Deirdre and Gus were making their way back down Hangman's Row, when they caught sight of Roy in his trundle outside the village shop.

"We'll catch them up and have a talk at Springfields. Ivy will certainly be able to rustle up a cup of tea in the summerhouse. Then we can swap the results of our enquiring this afternoon. No doubt, Deirdre love, that we shall have the most important piece of news."

"And then?"

"The police," said Gus. "From past experience, they'll be close behind us, but we must do our citizen duty and tell them what we have found."

"Including the earrings? After all, they point directly at your charming ex-wife."

Gus thought for a moment. "You may be right," he

acknowledged. "But Kath is unlikely to have taken on a dirty digging job. She would have had help. And if so, who? Her erstwhile lover is dead."

"Dirt never hurt anybody, and she might have been desperate."

"Mm. But there's bound to be another swain. Rich, young and probably strong, with an emphasis on the 'rich.' Kath only trawls around for her kind of love in the upper echelons of society."

"So you fell into that category?"

"Not telling," he said, and laughed. "Come on, girl, let's give the others a nice surprise."

"YOU'D BETTER TAKE off your shoes, both of you," said Ivy. "La Spurling is very strict about mud on the carpets."

"But aren't we going to the summerhouse?" Deirdre said, looking at her soil-caked sandals.

"She's put carpet down in there," Ivy said. "Sometimes I think she does it to annoy."

Gus and Deirdre dutifully took off their shoes and stepped onto the grass green carpet.

"I've got muddy feet," said Deirdre. "Shall I take them off as well?"

"Don't be ridiculous," said Ivy. "No need to be childish."

Roy abandoned his trundle, and they arranged themselves in a semicircle in the shade. Sunlight filtered through the trees, and the summerhouse was a cool retreat.

"All we need now is tea," said Gus. "Would you like me to petition the gaoler?"

"No need," said Ivy, and at that moment Katya appeared with a tray of tea and scones.

"Mrs. Spurling says to tell you the rest of us had tea

some while ago, but she is once more bending the rules. What does that mean, 'bending the rules'?"

"Just that she is very kindly taking care of us, my dear. And thank you. Did you bake those scones?"

Katya nodded. "My boyfriend is coming soon, and I shall try him out on them."

"Try them out on him," corrected Ivy, with a fond smile. "Run along now, and get yourself prettied up."

How does she do it? Roy wondered. So sharp with everyone else, even me sometimes. And yet Katya can do no wrong. Ah well, there's no explaining the contrary ways of my Ivy.

Tea poured and scones buttered, Ivy took the lead. "So what did you find out in the woods?" she asked.

"You tell." Deirdre looked at Gus and nodded encouragingly.

"Well, it was rather extraordinary," he said. "First Deirdre risked life and limb to delve into the brambles and brought forth a filthy rubber glove." He looked at Ivy and Roy for gasps of surprise but met none.

"Well," said Ivy, "I for one had already decided that the hand was nothing more than a work glove, left behind by somebody. Ulph could have had to move jewellery buried there and, being a musician, would have worn gloves to protect his hands. He was most likely in a rush and so dropped one of them. Or could've been anybody, blackberrying maybe. I reckon we've all come to the conclusion that there was no dead body. So what else?"

Deirdre and Gus looked crestfallen, but Gus continued bravely. "And when we finally found the so-called badgers' sett, it had been desecrated."

"What do you mean?" Roy said. "You're not telling us it was a grave?"

"No, though you could say it was a burial place of sorts."

"And?" Ivy was losing patience with Gus's customary love of spinning out a story.

Deirdre took over. "It was a real mess. Earth everywhere, and the mound levelled to the ground. I reckon he'd dug out all the stuff, then put some earth back into the hole and chucked the rest around to cover footprints."

Ivy nodded approvingly. "Very succinct," she said. "So when you say 'he,' are you referring to Ulph, and do we need three guesses to decide what 'stuff' was hidden there?"

"Jewellery. Valuable jewellery," Roy said. "Almost certainly. But I think we must think carefully about *who* the excavator might have been and *when* the deed was done."

"Before Ulph's illness and death or after? That is the question." Ivy helped herself to another scone, and spread butter as if punishing it.

"Well, obviously not Ulph, not once he was dead!" said Gus. "Unless he really was the Green Man of the Woods and made a ghostly return. And dropped a very real used tissue?"

"Or," Ivy continued, "unless he had instructed someone else to do it for him."

"Like who?" Deirdre was desperately trying to keep up.

"Take your pick," Roy chimed in. "Could have been James from the shop or Tom, Dick or Harry from the pub. Or David Budd or his boss, Theo Roussel."

Ivy stared at him. "Are you being serious, Roy? If you ask me, this is not a matter for levity."

Fortunately, Katya appeared once more. "More hot water for the tea?" she said. "I am just on my way out but thought you must all be thirsty, being out in the sun all afternoon. But it must have been lovely, strolling around the village and watching the children playing in the recreation ground. There now," she added, filling the pot, "second cups for all."

Deirdre suggested finishing up the last scone and took it to her plate before any of the others could stake a claim. "Exhausted from all our investigating," she explained.

"Half for me, then?" said Gus. "No, no thanks, Deirdre, only joking."

Ivy cleared her throat. "Well now, we should correct Katya's assumption," she said.

"Eh?" said Roy.

"I mean she said we were out for a stroll, but in fact we, too, were investigating, weren't we, Roy?"

"Oh yes, of course, my love. It was Ivy's idea, and we went down to the Hall and up through the gates, straight in without a by-your-leave, and progressed up the long drive. As we approached, we could see the Hon Theo standing on the front steps, staring at us."

"And he would have sent us off with a flea in the ear," said Ivy, with a smile. "But I reminded him of our previous encounters, and he softened. Right, Roy?"

"Right, my dear. We had a chat, and then we came back down the drive and out into the village. But, before you interrupt, Deirdre, during our chat we brought up the subject of Ulph. He was most helpful. Confirmed that Ulph's father was an old friend, now dead, and that Ulph—Seb, he called him—was a black sheep, with a history of minor transgressions, who had got involved with an unsuitable woman." He paused, and Ivy took up the story.

"Foolish man, on the whole. Butterfly-minded. Skips from one thing to another. Still, the mention of the unsuitable woman was very useful confirmation."

"Very useful," Gus said. "Certainly something to bear in mind. Thank you, Ivy."

Forty-six

IN A SMALL modern pub smelling strongly of last night's beer, anonymously sited between two Oakbridge suburban housing estates, the landlady trudged wearily upstairs to clear out the two bedrooms that had been occupied. The first had been inhabited by a regular commercial salesman on his rounds in the east of England. It was neat and tidy, with the sheets and pillowcases folded into a pile ready for the wash.

She hoovered round and dusted where necessary and moved on to the second room, where things were very different. The bed was exactly as the occupant had left it, with screwed-up newspapers and dog-eared magazines strewn over the floor. She stepped into the tiny bathroom and gasped. The hand basin and shower tray still had the remains of scummy, bright red *something* lingering round the edges.

"Good God!" she said aloud. "Blood!" She still had in her mind the case of the man pushed to his death from a lodging house in town. But when she gingerly rubbed a finger around and sniffed it, it smelled strongly of cheap scent. Then she looked in the waste bin and pulled out an empty packet of Flame Red hair colouring. "Flaming cheek!" she said, and added, "And my best white towels!"

Downstairs she checked her visitors' book. Jean Smith had been the last entry, and she fumed. "Well, Miss Smith," she muttered, "that's the last time you visit my establishment."

IN THE ENTRANCE hall at Springfields, Ivy and Roy sat waiting for their taxi to take them to Oakbridge. "Ah, there he is," said Ivy. "Come along, my dear, we can meet him halfway down the path."

Mrs. Spurling emerged from her office. "Off out again, Mr. Goodman?" she said. "And where are we going this morning?"

"Oakbridge," answered Ivy, helping Roy into his trundle. "We shall be back in time for lunch."

"Which is at one o'clock," said Mrs. Spurling acidly.

"And delicious as ever, I'm sure," said Roy as he allowed Ivy to precede him down the path and out into road, where their taxi was waiting.

Elvis had the door open ready, and Roy drove up the ramp with confident panache.

"Oops!" said Ivy, as he bumped into the back of the seats. She started to laugh, and Roy noticed once more that small catastrophes amused his beloved. It was as if she wished to take the sting out of an embarrassing or not too painful moment.

"All set, then," Elvis said. "Off we go. Straight to the coffee shop?"

"Yes, as ever," said Ivy.

Elvis was in a good mood this morning, having had a long and fruitful run to Heathrow and back yesterday. "And if you don't mind my saying, when shall I have the pleasure of running you two to the church? I guarantee to get you there on time!" he added, and burst into a selection from *My Fair Lady*, which kept them entertained all the way to Oakbridge.

When they were welcomed to the café and comfortably settled at their usual table, Roy reached under the table and took Ivy's hand.

"So maybe we should think about booking Elvis for one morning next spring?" he said. "It's time I made an honest woman of you, don't you think?"

"I have never been anything but an honest woman," retorted Ivy. "And if you mean when shall we get married, I have been giving it some serious thought."

For one horrible moment, Roy thought she was about to break off the engagement. But no, she smiled and said that if anyone asked her, a Christmas wedding might be a very good idea. Everyone was already geared up for the season, and they could save on decorations and probably refreshments, too.

Roy could not contain his excitement and beckoned to their favourite waitress. "I just have to tell someone, my dear," he said. "This wonderful woman has just agreed to marry me at Christmastime!"

"Very nice, too," she answered. "I hope I'll get an invite! Now, have you got all you need for the moment? Those doughnuts are especially nice today."

"There was one more thing," Ivy said. "It's just a question, really. Can you remember a regular customer for coffee, a man with lots of dark hair and a hangdog look about him?"

"Oh, you mean Mister Mystery. That's what we girls call him. Or should I say, *called* him. Poor devil threw himself off a roof in town. Dreadful shame. He was quite nice, really, when he warmed up and started talking to us. Why do you ask?"

"We were surprised when he got quite friendly with us one morning. Just before he, um, died."

The waitress nodded. "Did he tell you about his wife? Divorced, apparently. He was sad about that. I reckon that's why he jumped. Yeah, he did look miserable as sin most of the time. But I reckon he had a good heart. You could tell, couldn't you?"

At this point, a portly customer lost his patience and called the waitress over to give his order.

"Well!" said Ivy. "His *wife*, eh? I wonder who that could be. Not Katherine, surely. Gus would have told us if Ulph had been married to her."

"Perhaps Ulph was telling a good story. People do, you know. But it is certainly worth reporting to the others. Not a wasted journey at all. I think we have a useful new piece of the puzzle, and, to me more important, my fiancée has named the day!"

"Not finished here yet," Ivy said, smiling warmly at him. "Don't forget we are going to Folgate Street when we've finished our coffee. We asked Elvis to pick us up in the marketplace, so it will be a nice stroll."

The doughnuts were so good that they had two each and then made their way through the shoppers to the entrance to Folgate Street. All trace of the tragic accident or incident had vanished, and the usual straggle of people passed along the narrow street.

"Must've been terrible traffic jams in the days of horses," said Ivy. "I wonder if they had one-way streets in those days."

"Good question," said Roy, who was concentrating on negotiating his way on the pavement. "I guess the noise would have been deafening."

Ivy stopped suddenly. "Roy, do you realise what we've missed in all of this?"

"So sorry, madam," Roy said to an unfortunate robed and veiled woman who had collided with him.

"Roy! We have not once thought of Ulph going over the edge to his death, *screaming*! It would be a certain reaction to being pushed, surely. But maybe not if he intended to jump? We should find out if anyone around here heard him go."

To Roy's dismay, Ivy stepped up to number seven and knocked firmly.

The door opened at once, and Mrs. Feather looked out. "Yes?" she said, and then recognised them and opened the door wider. "Well, it's you two!" she said. "Nice to see you again, and in happier circumstances, I hope," she added. "Are you coming in for a cuppa?"

"Just had coffee," said Ivy, "but I have a favour to ask, if you don't mind."

"Come in anyway, and rest your weary legs," said Mrs. Feather. She had taken a liking to Roy and a kind of admiration for Ivy, who had survived so well under close questioning that fateful day.

Roy parked his trundle somewhat reluctantly as he mistrusted the local lads, but he followed Ivy into the house with Mrs. Feather.

"Now, Miss Beasley, what can I do for you?" Mrs. Feather looked forward to a postmortem of the tragedy, but Ivy surprised her.

"If it's not inconvenient, I'd like to take a look at the rooftop where Ulph used to sunbathe," she said. "Just need to satisfy myself on a point that's been niggling in my mind. You know how it is, I'm sure. Oh, and before I forget, can you remember any more about what his visitor looked like? The one who came to see him on that dreadful day?"

"No, 'fraid not," said Mrs. Feather, shaking her head. "It really was too dark in my hallway. I only saw her when she went up, and she had gone by the time I came back, as you know. Tallish, dark, I think. I've been lying awake at night going over and over the whole thing, wondering if I could've prevented it in some way."

"I'm sure you did your best," Roy said. He was beginning to worry about Ivy going out on the roof. He supposed she would be safe enough, just so long as she did not go peering over the edge.

"Be very careful, my dear," he said mildly.

"I would let you have a look out there," Mrs. Feather said, "but I have a lodger in Mr. Ulph's room at the moment. I make it a rule not to trespass! But I tell you what," she added. "I could take you into the next room. It's not a room, really, but a large walk-in cupboard, where I keep all the bed linen and so on. Would that do? It's got a window, if you want to look out."

"Fine," said Ivy. "Let's go."

WHEN THEY WERE safely settled in Elvis's taxi and on their way home, passing the long string of nineteen thirties bungalows more suited to the seaside than an ancient market town, Roy decided it was time for an explanation.

"So, did you find anything interesting in the linen cupboard?" he said.

"Sorry about all that, Roy," Ivy said, not at all contrite, "but it struck me so suddenly that anyone living in the next

house could look out of their window and see Ulph's terrace rooftop. There's a passage between some of the
houses, so they'd certainly spot anything going on."

"And?" said Roy kindly. He didn't want to discourage
Ivy, but he was certain the police would have thought of
this at a very early stage.

"I know what you're thinking," Ivy said. "But it might
not have occurred to investigators that even if nobody had
seen anything, they could well have heard Ulph yell as he
went down. That is, if he really screamed with terror, an'
that."

Roy shivered. "Don't, Ivy dear," he said. I can't bear to
think of it. Poor young man." He shook himself. "Anyway,
what did you discover?"

"There is a window opposite, and somebody was looking out of it. It was a boy, about ten years old, I should
think, and he waved to me. I waved back, of course."

"So, are you planning to find the boy and ask him if he
saw or heard anything that day? I can't think of any reason
why his parents would allow such a thing, especially as the
police must already have been asking if he saw anything."

"Not necessarily *heard,* though. And I recognised the
child," Ivy said smugly. "He helps at the market sometimes, behind the fruit stall, and his mother has sold me
oranges. You couldn't mistake the boy. He is unfortunately
overweight, obese even. I don't know what these women
feed their children on these days."

"So next market day," said Roy with a sigh, "we are
going to Oakbridge again, hoping the fat boy is not at
school?"

"It's still summer holidays," Ivy said triumphantly.
"And he could well be on the stall. Very good at helping his
mother, I noticed. Good memory, too, with counting up

change and so on. And don't forget," she continued, "we must tell Gus again about that visitor Mrs. Folgate mentioned. I expect the police will be onto it already but may not have discovered the woman's identity yet. So, here we are, back at Springfields."

"Back home, you could say," Roy suggested. "And a job well done."

Forty-seven

IVY MADE GREAT play of checking her watch against the old grandfather clock in Springfields' entrance hall. "Absolutely on the dot," she said loudly, as they passed the window of Mrs. Spurling's office, where she sat absorbed in a telephone call.

"I must just pay a visit, then I'll meet you in the dining room," said Roy. He had parked his trundle and now walked to the gents' as quickly as old age would allow, thinking that if only the good Lord, when making Adam, had invented a tap fitted in the right place, many an embarrassing situation would be avoided.

Everyone was seated in the dining room when Ivy and Roy made for their table.

"Ah!" said an elderly lady, known to dislike Miss Beasley and her autocratic ways, "so now I suppose we can start lunch! The VIPs have arrived." A number of residents laughed, but Roy's friend Fred said loudly that it was a pity some people were jealous of the grit and determination of others he could name.

Ivy took no notice whatsoever, and Roy did his best with a charming smile at the jealous old duck at the next table. "I was going to make an announcement about our wedding date," he whispered to Ivy. "But perhaps now is not the time."

Ivy shook her head. "Have to consult the gaoler first," she said. "You can bet she'll find a reason why it won't be convenient."

"Oh, come now, Ivy! Fair's fair. Don't forget how cooperative she was with your birthday celebrations."

"Mostly Katya's doing, that was," Ivy replied.

"But how about Tiddles? That was a real triumph over inclination for La Spurling. She hates cats and took some persuading."

"That was your undoubted charm," said Ivy, her eyes twinkling. "Now then, when are we going to tell the others what we discovered in Oakbridge?"

Roy looked at his watch. "I suppose we could walk up to Tawny Wings? The forecast is for a thunderstorm over the coast, but it may not reach us here. Do you feel like more exercise, my love?"

"Of course," Ivy said. "An hour or so with our feet up, and then we shall be ready for anything. I'll ring Deirdre after lunch, and see if she'll be at home."

GUS ALSO RECEIVED a call from Ivy and agreed to a meeting at half past four. He said that he would take Whippy for a walk first and then call at Tawny Wings on his way back.

"She hasn't had a proper walk for weeks," he said.

"Mind you, Ivy," he added, "it has not been the weather for long trudges round the countryside. But it is a bit cooler today, don't you think? A storm forecast. So, see you there at four thirty."

He had just locked up and put Whippy on the lead when Miriam appeared in her garden. "Hi, Gus! Going for a walk? Mind if I join you? I haven't had any exercise today, what with writing letters and paying bills. I'll just get my wellies."

Gus's heart sank. His intention had been a longish, solitary walk with only Whippy to distract him. He needed to think about the subject he least wanted to consider. His ex-wife, Katherine, who had been out of his life for so long, and now seemed inextricably bound up with him, appeared to be closely connected with the death of a relatively inoffensive young man.

Who else either knew about or wanted to retrieve that jewellery, which had most likely been buried in the woods? Kath, having bullied Ulph into telling her the whereabouts of the jewellery, could have gone straight to collect it.

Miriam was not in the least discouraged by Gus's obvious lack of enthusiasm, and the two of them plus dog set off. "I am sick of the woods," Miriam said as they shut the garden gate. "Let's go across the park and round the fields. The ground is so dry, it will be fine. Mr. Theo has told me it's okay to go anywhere round the estate so long as we don't leave gates open or disturb the game. That only applies to Hangman's Row tenants, of course."

"If you like, then," Gus said. "Last time I walked round the fields, I met the squire, and he was very pleasant. I think he's a bit of a fool, but his heart's in the right place."

Miriam looked at him with a smirk. "*Very* pleasant in my past experience," she said. "Still, that's all over. And now I've got you!"

Oh no you haven't, said Gus to himself. "Yes, well," he said. "Enough said about that. Come on, Whippy, you can sniff all you want when we get to the park."

Gus was thankful that Miriam could keep up a monologue without requiring an answer, and after a while he stopped listening. His thoughts went back to Katherine, wondering where she was now and whether the real truth about Ulph's death would ever emerge.

They reached a stile into the next field, and Gus automatically offered his hand to help Miriam over. She grasped it firmly and then quite deliberately lost her balance, falling straight into Gus's hastily outstretched arms.

"Oops-a-daisy!" yelled Miriam. Gus set her straight, and then withdrew until he was at a safe distance from her.

"Oh, look! There's Mr. Theo with his dog, old Wullie. Do they get on, Gus? Maybe we should put Whippy on her lead?"

All this cosy chat was increasing Gus's irritation, and he answered sharply that since Theo's dog was a male and Whippy female, he was sure they would be fine. Unfortunately, Miriam took this as an acknowledgement of her presence and tucked her hand through Gus's arm.

"Afternoon, Halfhide! Miriam." Theo raised his hat politely. "Out for a walk? I hope I haven't interrupted anything," he added, with a wink at Gus.

"Absolutely not!" answered Gus, firmly detaching himself from Miriam.

"Are we in for a storm? I do hope not. Best get home, I think, all of us." Theo turned to go but then said, "Oh, and by the way, I am expecting a visitor. If you see someone lost in the park looking for me, kindly say I am on my way. Thank you so much. Good afternoon!"

So not Deirdre, then, thought Gus as he and Miriam

hurried on, looking up every few paces at the approaching heavy bank of cloud.

By the time the two of them were back in the park and heading for Hangman's Row, large drops of rain had begun to fall, and Miriam chirped that she did hope Theo's visitor would have found him by now and would be safely warm and dry inside the Hall.

"Oh, look, Gus," she said, pointing at the kitchen door as they passed. "There they are. Just in time," she said.

Forty-eight

"I AM AFRAID I can't give you much time, Miss . . . er . . . Now, what was your name?"

Theo stood in his study, facing his odd-looking guest, whom at first he had taken to be a young man. However, he had turned out to be a woman, with inexpertly dyed red hair and a thin, sunburned face. Or was it heavy makeup? He thought of Deirdre's attractive apricot curls, so natural-looking, and her fresh, smooth complexion. She would no doubt have known exactly where nature had been improved upon. He was vaguely aware that hermaphrodite people existed and wondered if this masculine-looking person was one of those. The clear blue eyes fixed on him were cold, stone cold.

"Elizabeth Woodville," she said. "My father is Sir Richard, MP for Dennington, in the north. I expect you have heard of him."

The name was certainly familiar to Theo, but he could not place either the woman in front of him or her illustrious father. "How can I help you, then, Miss Woodville? I am afraid I have to be somewhere else in half an hour or so."

"I need a place to live for a couple of years, and you were recommended to me as having an empty cottage on your estate. I am willing to pay six months' rent in advance and can assure you that I shall be a very well-behaved tenant!" A wintry smile flickered across her face and then disappeared as she opened her bag and took out a letter.

"This is a reference, and I can give you more if required."

Theo opened it. It was written on House of Commons paper, and the handwriting was bold and firm. It was not, as he first thought, from her father, but from a woman whose name he did not know. Signed with a flourish, he noted. Well, he could check her out on the internet.

"Um, well, I am not too sure," he said finally. "My cottages in Hangman's Row are all taken, but I do have a gamekeeper's lodge at the edge of the woods. Hasn't been occupied for a few years and would need a bit of attention. Could you get in touch in a month or so, and I could be more certain?"

The woman shook her head. "Sorry, no. I need somewhere more or less straightaway. Like today! But don't worry about the cottage. I am very good at do-it-yourself, and would happily make any necessary improvements at my own expense."

Good grief! thought Theo. This was all too good to be true. He could certainly do with the extra rent, and it would be a very handy way of getting the cottage smartened up.

"Well, Miss Woodville, if you are prepared for spiders and mice, then of course you may have the cottage. I will get my farm manager to show you where it is. He might give you a hand, if you ask him nicely!"

She did not smile. "I shall manage perfectly well on my own. And I think I know the cottage. At the end of the track through the woods, on the Oakbridge road?"

Theo nodded. "Come with me to the kitchen," he said, "and I'll give you the key."

He walked ahead of her and felt as if he was being swept along by an unstoppable force. When she left, he went into the drawing room and watched her walking smartly down the drive. How extraordinary! And she really did look faintly familiar. He tried to imagine her without the lurid red hair but gave up. Tonight was bridge night at the Conservative Club in Oakbridge, and he turned his thoughts to hoping he would be partnered with someone who knew how to win.

Must warn David Budd about the gamekeeper's cottage, he remembered, as he folded the reference and tucked it into his pocket. Maybe ask him to keep an eye on Miss Woodville.

IVY AND ROY arrived at Tawny Wings at exactly four thirty and were ushered up to the office, where a tray of freshly made tea and coffee cake awaited them. "Not my own baking, I'm afraid," said Deirdre. "I gave up wrestling with sponge cakes that sink in the middle years ago. No," she added, picking up the cake to show them. This is from the village shop, believe it or not. They have homemade cakes once a week now. And guess who's the baker?"

"Miriam Blake," said Ivy flatly.

"Got it in one! Oh, that'll be Gus at the door." Deirdre set down the cake and went downstairs to let him in.

"Can't say as I fancy cakes handled by that Blake woman," said Ivy.

"You liked her Victoria sponge. But don't worry, little love, I'll have your slice," said Roy with exaggerated concern.

"Oh well, I suppose it'll look funny if I don't eat it," Ivy backtracked. "I just hope she washed her hands."

"Afternoon all," said Gus, appearing with a smile. "Nice drop of rain. Did you two go to Oakbridge as planned?"

"Oh yes, we went," Roy answered, "and I'll leave Ivy to tell you what we achieved."

"Sounds good," said Deirdre.

"Well, it was certainly worth the visit," Ivy began. "I'll keep it brief, but there's a lot to tell. The waitress in the coffee place remembered Ulph and said she and the girls liked him. Felt sorry for him, as he always looked sad. He talked to them a bit, now and then. Said he was divorced and living on his own. Then she was called away, and so we set off for the market."

She paused and Roy took up the story. "We went down Folgate Street, and then Ivy had a moment's inspiration. We had been speculating on how noisy it must have been in the days of horse carriages. It was *noise* that triggered her good idea."

So then Ivy carried on and explained about Mrs. Feather and going up to the linen cupboard, which had a window with a view across the terrace roof. "I said I was curious to see again where he had lived," she said. "Thankfully, she agreed to take me up. Not to his old room, which was let again, but to the linen cupboard next door. Oh, and by the way, I asked Mrs. Feather if she could describe Ulph's mysterious visitor the day he died, but she said her husband never got round to fixing the light in the hall and stairs, and it was too dark to see anybody clearly. If you ask me, it was lucky for her nobody fell downstairs."

"I'm lost," said Deirdre. "Why on earth should you want to go up there?"

"To see what would have happened if he yelled as he went down," said Ivy bluntly. "If he jumped, he'd have more than likely gone quietly, but if he was pushed? He'd have yelled, all right. Screamed, I'd say. So, *noise*, you see, Deirdre. If he'd made a noise, would anyone have heard him? No doubt the police questioned all around for anyone seeing anything, but *heard*?"

After that, the others were quiet as she told them about the boy in the window opposite, and him being the son of a fruit seller in the market.

"So," said Roy, with a mock sigh, "my beloved's next idea is to revisit Oakbridge next week on market day and chat up the boy. Can't mistake him, Ivy says, as he's a regular Billy Bunter."

"Heavens," said Deirdre, "I think we all need stronger refreshment. Anyone fancy a buck's fizz alongside their cuppa? Got some in a bottle, ready mixed. Ivy? Gus?"

Ivy refused, but Gus and Roy nodded vigorously. Deirdre got up to go downstairs and paused at the door. "D'you reckon he really was married and divorced? That would put a whole new complexion on things, wouldn't it?"

DAVID BUDD WAS having his tea when Theo Roussel knocked at his door. Rose got up to open it and greeted the boss with a big smile.

"Hello, Mr. Theo," she said, "just in time for a cup of tea. Come on in."

David thanked God he had just finished a nice piece of

cod and chips so was able to give his full attention to Theo. He had a habit of calling at mealtimes, and David was subject to indigestion if interrupted while eating.

"Afternoon, Mr. Theo," he said. "Will you have a cup of tea with us?"

Rose had already refilled the pot and handed Theo a cup of tea so strong that it was a vivid orange colour. He sipped it cautiously and said that there was nothing urgent, but there would be a new tenant in the gamekeeper's cottage, and he would be glad if David could offer help if needed.

"She's a strange sort of woman but with a good reference and makes a fair impression. What's more, she's offering to do some restoration on the cottage at her own expense."

"Goodness!" said Rose. "We'd better be extra nice to her, then. Will she be living there on her own. It is rather a lonely spot."

"I don't think that bothered her at all. In fact, she seemed to like the idea. One of those 'I want to be alone' people, I expect."

"Oh, well, in that case, I'll pop up and offer help but not be too pushy," said David.

"And I'll go with you. We won't take the kids, though! She doesn't sound like she'd appreciate their little ways!" Rose added.

Theo drank his tea manfully, and got up to go. "Well, I won't keep you any longer," he said. "Oh, and you can't mistake her. She's a Miss Woodville, and she has the reddest hair I've ever seen. Cut very short. Looks like a man. Quite awful! Thanks for the tea, Rose. Bye, children."

Rose saw him to the door and then returned to David.

"So," she said, "at least she doesn't sound like another candidate to add to Theo's list of conquests."

"What's conquests, Mum?" said their eldest.

"Never you mind. Go and wash your hands before you watch telly. Off you go, now."

Forty-nine

GUS HAD BEEN feeling restless since coming home from Tawny Wings. It was not just the missing hand turning out to be a rubber glove. That had now been generally accepted. Coupled with the fact that no dead body had been found, and no missing person reported, he had put Miriam's case to one side. That would leave him with Kath and Ulph, and he decided to review what he knew.

First, Ulph was dead. That was sadly irrefutable. Then he, Gus, had had a connexion with Ulph through Kath. He had never seen him in Barrington until that whoopee swim with Deirdre. Both of them had been tipsy. Kath spoke of him as being an ex-lover, and now it seemed they might have been married. It was certain that Ulph had played in Sid and His Swingers' band and that he had left on a trumped-up excuse about going abroad but had not gone, since he turned up at Deirdre's soon after. Playing in the band had perhaps been too public?

Unless Kath was lying through her teeth, she had definitely had her jewels stolen by Ulph and was being blackmailed by him. That much she had told him in Scotland. But she could have been lying? He would list only what was certain. Whippy looked up at the biscuit tin, and Gus gave her three. He couldn't remember whether she had had her daily six, so gave her three more, just in case.

Now, back to known facts. Gus settled in his chair with a small whisky and considered. The pearl earrings found in the woods were Kath's. Gus had designed them for her and had had them made by a London jeweller for a small fortune. They were found near the rubber glove site and could well have been part of the hoard moved to the mound for safer keeping. More speculation but useful.

The mound. It was reasonable to decide that the rest of Kath's jewellery had been hidden in the woods and, considering Ulph's earthy spade, more than likely in the mound at some stage. This mound, according to countrywoman Ivy, was very much like a badgers' sett. But no further jewellery had been found around the site, and now it had been raided, and nothing remained except a used tissue.

As he proceeded with his list, Gus could see more clearly where the next step would have to be. He reluctantly admitted to himself that everything seemed to rest on whether Katherine was telling the truth about any of it. And that was unfortunately doubtful. He would have to find Katherine and question her more closely, though this did not give him much hope. She was the best liar he had ever met. He was painfully aware that some unfriendly person, even his own ex-wife, could still attempt to trace back Ulph's death to himself. He had already had a call from Inspector Frobisher asking him to call in at the police station as soon as possible.

He sighed, poured himself another drink, and turned on the television. Nothing caught his attention, and he turned it off again. He looked at his watch. Eight thirty. Perhaps he would have an evening stroll with Whippy. The woods would be cool and quiet, and he shook himself into action.

"Come on, small dog," he said. "Let's go and clear our heads. The rabbits will be out in the woods now, so lots of fun for you."

Miriam, sitting by her front window, saw him go and wondered whether to run after him to keep him company. Poor old Gus, he looked like a man with the cares of the world on his shoulders. She turned away and looked up the television programmes. Her favourite quiz was about to start, with the acid-voiced quiz mistress making fools of the contestants, and she decided to stay at home. Perhaps she would catch him later for a nightcap.

GUS WAS SOOTHED by the evening chirruping of roosting birds, and his pace slowed. Whippy was having a fine old time down rabbit burrows, wriggling round and then emerging covered with sandy soil. She seldom caught anything, and he hoped this would not be the one time she presented him with a small half-dead baby rabbit.

The trees were dense now, and light was going from the sky. Lost in his thoughts, Gus strolled on, not watching out for landmarks to find his way back. He came to a fork in the path and stopped. Which way? He had no idea, so took the footpath that seemed most used and carried on his way, calling Whippy to follow him. This time, there was no answering scuttle through the dried leaves. He called again, but Whippy did not appear. He walked on, fairly sure that she would follow his scent and find him without too much trouble.

He came out into a grassy clearing and stopped again. This was completely new territory for him. He looked across the clearing and saw a small cottage with a broken wooden fence and an open front door. A man stood by the gate and, to his surprise, turned swiftly and retreated into the house, slamming the door.

How odd, Gus thought, and walked forward towards the cottage. He had been hoping to ask for directions, so he went through the broken gate and knocked at the door. Perhaps when the man saw he was nobody's idea of a gamekeeper, he would answer. A few minutes elapsed, and Gus was about to leave, when the door opened a crack. A man—or was it a woman?—peered out at him, then opened the door wider. It *was* a woman, with bright red hair, cut very short. She was wearing jeans and a man's shirt and was not smiling.

"So it's you," she said. "You'd better come in."

He felt the hairs on the back of his neck prickle and stepped through the open doorway. "Good God, Kath!" he said. "What on earth do you think you're doing here? And what the hell have you done to yourself?"

Fifty

"WHAT DO YOU want?" Katherine said coldly.

Gus shook his head. "Nothing," he said. "And please don't think I was looking for you. Pure accident. I've lost Whippy. Must go and find her."

"Are you all right, Gus?" she said. "You sound a bit fuzzy. Not been at the bottle, I hope."

He shook his head. He felt a bit fuzzy, but his head was clearing. It had been a shock, and not a nice one, to see Katherine with her good looks deliberately concealed, if not destroyed. She was thinner, and her face had unsightly patches of dry skin.

"Oh, look, Gus," she said. "There she is! Here, Whippy! Here, little one!"

Whippy approached in hangdog mode, ears back and tail down. She was expecting chastisement from Gus, but he picked her up protectively and stroked her head. "There, now," he said. "We must go straight home and give you a nice drink of milk. Poor little thing's shivering, Kath."

"I've got milk," she answered, opening the door wider. "Come in, Gus, and don't be so stupid. I'm not about to take you prisoner."

"Katherine," he said sadly, "I wouldn't put anything past you."

"Never mind," she said, "you'll win one of these days. I need to talk to you, so *please* come in."

"But why here? The place is falling down."

"No it's not. And I'm renting it from the lord of the manor. I shall restore it to its former glory, which frankly is not very glorious. I had a vague idea, sown by a friend and more or less confirmed by a conversation with Seb, that my jewels are hidden in these woods. I mean to recover all of it, Gus, if I have to dig up every square yard. And, equally important, the cottage will be a bolt hole when I need one. Like now. I suppose I can rely on you to forget you've seen me?"

She disappeared inside, and Gus reluctantly followed, still holding Whippy in his arms.

"Now, Whippy, if your foolish master will put you down on the floor, here is a nice drop of milk. I found an old bowl. Not very clean, I'm afraid, but the milk's fresh. I bought a few supplies at the supermarket."

Gus put the dog down, where she shivered and failed to drink. "She's not sure about it," he said, and bent down to dip his fingers in the milk. He offered them, and Whippy licked his fingers, then began to drink.

"Just like the king's chief taster," Katherine laughed. "Well, no poison in there, Whippy-dog."

"So, as there's nowhere to sit, and I really must be

getting back, will you please tell me whatever else you have to say."

"We can sit on the stairs. Come on, you at the top and me on the bottom. Then you can be sure I won't push you down."

Gus stared at her, and noticed her sharp intake of breath. "Kath?"

She slumped down on the bottom stair and put her hands over her eyes. "Christ! What did I say? Oh Lord, Gus, I didn't mean him to go over the edge. . . ."

Gus's heart was beating wildly now, and he stepped over her hunched figure to the next step. He put his hands on her shoulders, and said, "Go on. There's more to tell, isn't there. And no lies this time, Kath. Just the plain truth."

She was quiet for what seemed to Gus like ages. Then she began to speak in a small, almost childlike voice.

"Seb was not a bad person," she said, and in her heart she knew that her future life now depended on convincing Gus that she was telling the truth.

HEAVY CLOUDS WERE massing over the woods, and Miriam strode along, glad that she had put on wellies and a rainproof jacket. It was cooler now, and there were densely thicketed parts where the sun did not penetrate, and so never warmed up.

She knew every inch from childhood and was sure she would be able to find Gus. He had looked so alone, walking off down the road, even though Whippy was his companion. A dog, however intelligent, could not replace a warm, caring human being. There could be no harm in following him, just in case he got lost. Spurred on by this thought, Miriam began to sing.

* * *

"WHAT ON EARTH is that noise?" said Katherine. She had recovered from her tears, and she and Gus sat in silence after she had told him a convincing story in such detail that he had nothing to say until he had digested it.

"Sounds like someone singing," he said now. "And I have a feeling I know who it is."

"Who? Not a musical policewoman, surely?"

"Don't be silly, Kath. Though I'm afraid you must expect the police in due course. No, I think it's Miriam Blake. You remember, the one who lives next door and gave you a bed for the night?"

"Ah, that one. Do we want to hide?"

Gus sighed. He longed for Deirdre, clever, straightforward Deirdre. "No, of course not. Miriam has a good heart, and I have no reason to be unkind to her."

"Oh my God! Gus Halfhide with a conscience! Whatever next?"

"That's enough, Katherine. Let me pass, and I'll speak to her."

Miriam had now arrived outside the cottage and was staring at the open door. Gus walked into the garden, and Whippy followed.

"There you are!" said Miriam, with a big smile. "I came to rescue you. I was sure you'd get lost on your own. Are you snooping? That cottage has been empty for years. Must be a wreck inside. Are you ready to come home, love? It'll soon be dark."

At this point, Kath appeared in the doorway and leaned against the frame. "It's not that bad inside," she said in a gruff voice. "I am the new tenant."

Miriam stared. It was the same youth she'd seen with

Theo up at the Hall. Who was he? And what on earth would Gus want with him?

"Must go now," Gus said, anxious to avoid a confrontation. "I'd be glad of a guide back to the village, Miriam."

He turned to Katherine and said he would be in touch. But not soon, and not for long. She looked at him oddly, but nodded and went inside, shutting the door behind her. Gus joined Miriam, with Whippy now on the lead, in case she should wander off again.

"Who *was* that?" Miriam asked. "We saw him outside the Hall that day. He looked so familiar, but I couldn't place him."

"Just somebody who's taken the cottage on a short let. Now, which way do we go?"

They were nearing the place where Deirdre had found the rubber glove, and Gus decided it was time to put an end to speculation on that score.

"By the way, there is some good news. Mrs. Bloxham and I were walking in the woods and saw something that looked exactly like a whitish, dirty hand, covered with earth and hidden by brambles. We got it out and realised it was an old rubber glove, and nothing more sinister than that. It was close to where you had seen it. Badgers and rats and all kinds of animals push around in the undergrowth looking for things to eat and could easily have buried it again."

"And the earring?" said Miriam. "I still have it, you know."

Gus frowned. "I thought you'd lost it?" he said.

"I found it again," said Miriam blandly. "How do you account for that being in the woods?"

"I have its pair. I can only think my ex-wife put them in her pocket and they dropped out in the woods that day she spent around here, after she left your cottage. I believe earrings can get painful, is that right?"

"So my case is solved? I must say I'm rather disappointed. I was thinking in terms of a dismembered body at the very least! Anyway, that's just my fevered imagination, as you would say. Thanks, Gus. I'll send a cheque to Ivy Beasley—or give one to you? Who's the boss of Enquire Within?"

Gus laughed. "That's a tricky question," he said. "We have never actually appointed one. I think Ivy considers she is, and the rest of us go along with that. Now, here we are. Thanks again, Miriam. I'd certainly have got lost without you."

His voice was so sweet, Miriam thought. And he is definitely much more friendly now. Her spirits rose, and she hummed her favourite song as she unlocked her cottage and went into the kitchen to prepare a sandwich.

Gus's mood, on the other hand, darkened considerably when he was alone in his cottage. He poured himself a whisky and sat down to consider everything that Kath had told him. According to her story, her calculations and contacts had revealed where Ulph was living and she had gone there in order to persuade him to hand over her jewellery. She reckoned she could win a battle of wits, and since it would be a case of both sides revealing secrets to appropriate authorities, she had arrived at Folgate Street well armed with evidence against him.

"We had a drink on the roof terrace," she had told Gus, as they sat on the stairs. "Not really a proper terrace. Just a flat roof on top of an extension. No guardrails, or anything like that," she had added pointedly. "That's when he foolishly hinted to me where the stuff was hidden. Never was good at keeping secrets, our Sebastian. I suppose he thought

I'd never risk digging around to find it." Her smile was
chilly.

After that, she confessed, the arguments had begun.
Ulph had had a wine bottle at his side and was drinking
steadily. He had stood over her with it in his hand and
threatened her with it. She had tried to get around him
and go back into the house, but he had dodged and shoved,
and in the end they were close to the edge. He had swung
the bottle at her, and the action had taken him over to his
death. He was very wobbly from some unnamed illness.
She had sobbed again at this memory but not for long.
And in due course Miriam had come along.

So glib, thought Gus now. Perfectly worked out. Kath
the innocent victim of a drunken blackmailer. Why, then,
the need for disguise? And not just a false moustache or a
concealing hat. No, Kath had, as usual, not done anything
by halves. She really looked like a man, and though the
voice was a bit strained, she sounded like one. Miriam had
been deceived and suspected nothing.

It was Miriam's question about who was boss at Enquire
Within that finally decided Gus what he should do next. He
was one of four. They were an agency, and the others had a
right to know. He would call an emergency meeting tomorrow, and put the whole thing before the others. Ivy, certainly, would have strong views on where to go next.

Fifty-one

"HE SAID AN emergency meeting," Ivy reminded Roy as they prepared to leave for Tawny Wings next morning. "Sounds as if he has discovered something interesting."

"I do hope so," said Roy. "The poor chap has looked very miserable lately. I think his ex-wife has become a heavy burden for him to carry."

"Specially after years of them not communicating. One thing I promise you, Roy dear. You'll have no such trouble from me. Once we're married, it'll be like we're stuck together with superglue. Not a chance of unsticking me! Beasleys are known for it. A vow is a vow, and made in the sight of God."

"Thank goodness for that, dearest! Have you had any thoughts of retiring from Enquire Within once we're wed?"

"Heavens, no! We'll still be here, stuck in Springfields. You're not suggesting we take up bingo and EastEnders, are you? No, no. Enquire Within will go from strength to strength. Ah, now, here we are. Gus has arrived already, I see. Looking out of the window, waiting for us, bless him."

There were solemn faces all round as Gus began to tell them what had happened. His chance encounter with Katherine dropped like a bombshell in their midst.

"You didn't know she was there? Honest?" said Deirdre.

Gus shook his head. "I had no idea, and actually I think she was pretty taken aback seeing me. But in a way, it gave her no chance to brush up her story. At least, so I think. I can never be quite sure of Kath, I'm afraid."

"No matter, lad," said Roy. "Carry on, and may I suggest no interruptions until Gus has finished what he has to tell?"

Deirdre shrugged. "All right with me," she said huffily.

Gus had had time overnight to sort out Katherine's emotional outburst and gave them what he hoped was a factual account of what had happened on the rooftop. "And so she fled in panic, leaving Folgate Street without anyone seeing her, she said. But Mrs. Feather had let her in, and she decided all evidence gained by police would point to her. Which is why she has gone to great trouble to disguise herself. 'I've killed off Katherine Halfhide,' she said to me, 'and metamorphosed into Elizabeth Woodville.'"

"As in wife of Edward IV," muttered Roy.

"Roy!" said Ivy. "Go on, Augustus."

"Well, she has made a good job of it. Hair dyed a terrible red and cut like a man's, and clothes that disguise her figure. Mind you, she seems to have lost a lot of weight. No flesh on her bones, and a dry skin. I think she must have been having a bad time lately."

"Sounds like she deserves it," said Deirdre. "And don't tell me off, Ivy, because Gus has finished, haven't you, Gus?"

"No, there is a little more. After she had told me all this, and we were sitting on the stairs saying nothing, Miriam Blake hove into view. I could see then how effective Kath's disguise was. She came out into the garden, and Miriam did not recognise her at all. And, don't forget, Kath had spent a night in Miriam's cottage."

"Correct me if I'm wrong," said Ivy, "but as I see it, and I'm surprised she hasn't done this, she could easily have upped sticks and disappeared without trace for a very long time. Still could. So should we report to the police and be quick about it?"

"Oh God," said Gus. He had not intended to tell the others of Kath's chief reason for staying around. "There is another thing," he croaked. And then he told them that his ex-wife was determined to find her jewels, come what may. I told her nothing about the raided badgers' sett," he added. "She obviously hadn't found it yet."

"Not so clever, after all," Deirdre said. "I think maybe we should have a coffee while we think."

"No need," said Ivy. "Our duty is clear. Beasleys know their duty. We have to report to the police immediately. Deirdre, would you like to make an appointment with the inspector right away?"

"No," said Deirdre, looking at Gus. "I think we should leave it to Gus. He has to see Inspector Frobisher anyway. What do you think, Roy?"

"I rather think as you do, Deirdre," Roy said, risking all.

"Then it is left for me to do what I know is right," said Ivy. "Excuse me, I shall go and make a call."

"My phone's out of order," said Deirdre desperately.

"I have my mobile," said Ivy, and left the room.

Fifty-two

IT WAS NOT long before Ivy returned to her colleagues, with a smug expression on her face.

"Did you get hold of Frobisher?" Gus asked. He was looking beaten, and Deirdre sat with clenched fists. Really, Ivy had gone too far.

"No. And I wasn't trying to. But I did speak to Mrs. Feather, and the results were excellent."

"Tell us more, dearest," Roy said gently. He could see the others were very near losing their patience.

"Well, if you remember, Roy and I were going back to Oakbridge to try talking to the boy on the market. Things seem more urgent now, so I got Mrs. Feather to give me the name and number of her neighbour. The boy's mother wasn't keen but has agreed we can go and see him this afternoon. She said she had felt very sorry for the poor man and supposed she should help find out what had really happened. Three o'clock this afternoon, Roy, so we'd better ring for our taxi."

Gus sighed. "Well done, Ivy," he said. "But what am I to do about seeing Frobisher? I can't just ignore a polite request from the police."

"I think Gus should come with us and then go on to the police station," Roy said. "Or even go instead of me, Ivy."

Ivy shook her head. "We can see if Mrs. Feather will let us take Gus, but she said she had told the neighbour—Rickman, the name is—that nice Mr. Goodman would surely put the boy at his ease. Perhaps I should step down and let Gus go instead of me?"

Deirdre took a deep breath. "Oh, for God's sake, Ivy! You know perfectly well you have to go, and wild horses wouldn't stop you. No, I'm sure if the three of you ask nicely, this woman will let you in. If not, Gus will have to wait outside. My guess is that the boy saw and heard nothing, so Gus won't have long to wait."

"Very well," Ivy said icily. "We shall see. Now, if everyone is agreeable, we should get back to Springfields and organise ourselves for this afternoon."

After they had gone, Gus remained with Deirdre after an invitation to have lunch. He was silent and frowning, almost unaware of her presence. In the end, she took his hand and kissed his cheek. "Don't fret, Gus. I'm sure nothing will come of Ivy's plan, and you can tell Frobisher just what Kath told you. What happens after that is out of your hands. No doubt they will go to pick her up immediately, but whether she is still there is anyone's guess. Come on, now, have a bite of lunch and then you can go off to Oakbridge with Ivy and Roy."

*   *   *

MRS. RICKMAN HAD been sitting behind her lace curtain keeping watch. When she saw three people approaching her door she went quickly to open up.

"Alan!" she shouted up the stairs as she went. "Come on down, love. Those people are here."

To her surprise, her son had cheerfully accepted that nice people were coming to talk to him about the man who fell to his death in the yard. "I've already told the police I didn't know nothing. Might be interesting to hear what they say," he had replied. Now he clattered down the stairs and stood by his mother at the door.

"Good afternoon," Gus said, "I do hope I may meet your son with my friends here?"

"I spoke to you this morning on the phone," said Ivy, moving forward. "This is Mr. Halfhide, and this is Mr. Goodman. I do hope three of us won't be too many for young Alan."

"More the merrier," said Alan, nothing like the sulky boy they had been expecting. "Let them inside, Mum. You can get the kettle on while we're talking."

Ivy glanced at Roy, and he shrugged. It was all too good to be true. Too easy by half.

When they were settled in the best room, Ivy took over.

"Now, Alan, you remember that day when poor Mr. Ulph fell off the roof? We still do not know what *exactly* happened and wondered if you could help us."

"Are you relatives?" said the boy. His voice was firm, commanding even.

"No, not close," said Gus. Diplomacy needed here, he thought. "But Miss Beasley had met him and liked him very much. She has asked us to help find out more, if possible."

"And so," said Ivy, "I wonder if you saw anything that day? Any visitors standing on the roof with Mr. Ulph? We are not sure what time it was, but probably latish in the morning."

Alan shook his head. "Nope. I didn't see nothing." He smiled angelically.

"Or heard?" asked Ivy, using all the force of her personality to will the boy to tell the truth.

Again, he shook his head. "Plenty of noise around here but nothing out of the usual. What d'you mean? Something like a scream?"

"Yes, that's it," said Ivy. "A shout or a scream?" She was sure now that the boy had heard something.

"No, nothing like that," Alan said, and reached for another biscuit.

"May I ask you a question, Alan," said Roy. He had been helped into the house and a comfortable armchair by Mrs. Rickman, and she had warmed to his gentlemanly ways.

"I think that was all you remembered, Alan dear," she said. "It was around that time that you were playing on your computer."

"What's the question, Mr. Goodman?" Alan was enjoying himself. It was nice to have people being so friendly and himself the centre of attention.

"Does your bedroom window look over towards Mr. Ulph's rooftop? I'm sure he would have waved to you, just like Miss Beasley here. He must have been pleased to see a friendly wave."

"Oh yeah. We often waved to each other. I reckon he was lonely, poor old sod."

"That was kind of you, Alan," Roy continued. "I expect you sometimes wondered if it was safe for him out there. No guardrails or anything like that."

"Yeah, I did. I said to Mum, didn't I, Mum, that he often got too near the edge."

"And you were quite right. Well spotted, Alan." Roy smiled encouragingly.

"Mind you, that woman didn't help, giving him a push."

In the horrified silence that followed this revelation, Alan's mother reached out for her son's hand, but he brushed it aside. "It's no good, Mum. I did see it, and even if it does get me into trouble for lying before, I should speak out."

Ivy shook her head slowly. "I think it would be best if you just told us in your own words what happened, and then it'll be up to your mum. She'll know what to do."

"Well, I was fed up with my computer game. Went to look out of the window, which was open. Sometimes we get police helicopters. Not that day, though. The only thing to look at was that bloke and a woman. They had drinks in their hands, and I waved, like I always do. But they didn't look at me. I thought maybe they were having a private discussion and I ought to shut my window. It stuck, and then just as it started to move, she shouted something. Looked like she'd lost her temper. Then the next thing was, she chucked her drink in his face and began to push him backwards. I thought she'd stop, but she kept going, and he screamed something awful as he went over the edge. I rushed down to tell Mum, didn't I, Mum?"

Mrs. Rickman nodded. "Oh my God, Alan," she said. "I'm sorry, boy."

She turned to the others and, scrubbing away tears, said that she had done wrong telling him to keep quiet about it, but wanted only to protect her son. "There wasn't nothing we could do. It was all over for the poor man. And then the police come round, and I decided the best thing would be for us to say nothing."

"Did you tell your husband, Mrs. Rickman?" asked Gus.

"Him! Haven't seen him for years. He ran out on us. I don't want him back, an' that's part of the reason I didn't want our names splashed across the local paper. My Alan is man of the house now. Every word of what he just said is true. You can rely on that."

Gus got to his feet. "Thank you very much, Mrs. Rickman," he said. "What you and your son have told us is invaluable, and I know you will want to call the police at once. I am sure they will be very understanding of your situation, and children's privacy and rights are very well protected these days."

They filed out slowly onto the pavement, and Roy climbed into his trundle. "Say good-bye to Alan for us," he said. The boy had disappeared but was there again suddenly, holding out something to Roy. "Here," he said, "this is for you. Thanks, Mr. Goodman."

WHEN THEY WERE safely in the taxi and on their way home, Ivy said, "What was that piece of paper he gave you?"

"Not a piece of paper, Ivy. It's a comic." He unfolded it and held it out to her.

"Oh my goodness," she said, with a crooked smile. "Just look here. 'Speedy Sam, the Mobile Detective.' And look, Roy, here he is, in a trundle just the same as yours!"

"Nice lad, young Alan," said Roy, and returned the comic to his pocket.

Fifty-three

GUS LOOKED AT his watch. It was six o'clock, and Inspector Frobisher had finally left the room, saying he would be back in a few minutes.

It had not been exactly a grilling since the others had left him at the police station, and at no time had the interview become threatening, but there was no questioning its thoroughness. From the day he first met Kath, to their conversation yesterday, he had explained everything, including her relationship with Ulph, and her present whereabouts in the gamekeeper's cottage.

Frobisher had immediately taken action in sending a car to bring her in. Then, in his turn, he had given Gus information the police had already collected. He told him that they had discovered from marriage records that Ulph and Katherine had actually been wed, and their marriage had lasted exactly six weeks. A police contact in Katherine's circle had reported that Ulph had left when he discovered her flaunting an affair with another man, unashamedly boasting about it to mutual friends.

Gus put his head in his hands, trying to shut out memories best left undisturbed. There would be much more to get through, but at least an end to it all was now possible. He didn't care what happened to Kath. With her lies and selfishness, she had effectively erased all feelings he had ever had for her. He had no doubt whatsoever that she would wriggle out of this one, if only by negotiating a short sentence on grounds of self-defence. When Frobisher returned, he said there had been a further development.

Gus stared at him. "What else?" he said.

"I am afraid that when my lads got to the gamekeeper's cottage, at first they thought nobody was there. But the door was unlocked, and they pushed it open, calling out to see if there was somebody around. One of them thought they heard a moan from upstairs, so he went up. Found your ex-wife, recognisable from your description, lying on a sleeping bag on the floor. She was unconscious, barely breathing, and looked in a bad way, so we got her to the hospital, where she is expected to recover. The usual thing, sir. Empty pill packets beside her. The lads were just in time."

"Oh my God," said Gus in a hoarse voice.

The inspector reached into a file, then pulled out a folded piece of paper. Gus saw his own name on it in familiar handwriting.

"This was also found beside her," said Frobisher, "and it seems to be addressed to you, Mr. Halfhide. You are known as Gus, aren't you?"

Gus nodded and took the paper. He unfolded it and read the short message.

Gus—it's no good, is it? This is my last escape. Be happy. Kath.

"Are you all right, sir?" The inspector was very experienced and gave Gus time to take it in.

Then he said that there was a friend waiting in reception. "Been there for hours. You are free to go now, Mr. Halfhide. We shall be in touch. Oh yes, and I'm afraid you won't be able to see your ex-wife. The law, you know, has to take its course."

DEIRDRE STOOD UP as he approached. She held out her arms, and he submitted gladly to a bear hug. "Come on, now, Gus. Time to go home."

"Where's Whippy?" he croaked.

"Miriam's got her. She'll be waiting for you."

"Who? Miriam or Whippy?"

"Both, you bet," said Deidre, "and, if you ask me, Cousin Ivy and Roy as well."

"WHERE ARE WE going, Deirdre?"

"To Tawny Wings, of course. I guess you've had nothing but a sandwich all day. Miriam's been having a cook-up, so we can look forward to a good supper."

"I'm not sure I'm hungry," Gus said, and then added that he was very grateful, but he'd really rather go home to the cottage and Whippy.

Deirdre ignored him. She drove up to Tawny Wings and held the car door open for him to alight. "Come on, Augustus," she said. "Trust me."

They were all waiting in the drawing room, Ivy, Roy and Miriam. And Whippy, who shot across to greet Gus, sensing, as dogs do, that her master was not a happy man. He fondled her ears, and for a moment Deirdre was afraid he would break down. But then Ivy saved the day.

"If you ask me," she said, "that dog needs to go out into the garden." She sniffed. "It's not exactly Chanel No. 5, is it."

Miriam laughed, and after a short pause the others joined in, even Gus, who wiped his eyes with the back of his hand and said he would take her out. And yes, he had a plastic bag in his pocket.

"Don't be long," Miriam cautioned. "Supper's ready, and it's one of my specials."

The supper was, as promised, delicious, and they all lingered over coffee and chocs, until Gus said he really must be going. He had not talked much, listening to the others conduct a kind of postmortem. Most of the conversation had been about Katherine. He was able to contribute a few facts, items the police had discovered and Inspector Frobisher had told him. It had not taken them long to find the pub where she had left her room full of telltale red dye stains. The landlady had hardly recognised her as the pleasant-looking woman who had arrived, she said. Katherine had apparently slipped in and out of the pub like a shadow.

"But what was she doing? Surely Oakbridge was the last place she should have risked staying around?" Ivy felt she had to ask this question, even though Gus looked beaten. But it was important to know. There was still no confirmation of the whereabouts of the jewels.

"It was avarice, I suppose," Gus said wearily. "She took on that gamekeeper's cottage in order to search the woods. Ulph had told her they were buried there, and she meant to troll every square metre, however long it took."

"And never thought of giving up?" Deirdre had her own idea why but hoped Gus would confirm it.

"Not really," he said. "She'd had a quick look round the morning she went missing from Miriam's. Of course, then she realised it was going to be a big job, searching such a large area. So she went back to London and planned how to do it. But first she intended to put the pressure on poor Ulph, in case he would save her the trouble and lead her to it. So that's what she did, and after that, we know what happened."

"Do we?" said Ivy.

"Well, she had not intended to kill him, I'm sure of that," Gus answered. "One of her quick flashes of temper, more than likely. She had to adjust her plans, of course, and came up with that hideous disguise. But she hadn't given up."

After a half a minute, when nobody interrupted, he continued. "And then, although I hope this was not true, I think she planned that we might get together again. God knows why! She had taken everything from me, including my faith in women! But there it is. She was making overtures of at least friendship, and I'm afraid I made it clear I was not interested. Do you think that's why she, well, you know, swallowed those pills? Perhaps that was the last straw?"

"Absolutely not!" said Deirdre angrily. "That woman never did anything without it being advantageous to herself! I should be very surprised if this suicide attempt wasn't carefully planned to enlist sympathy. See how upset you are, Gus! No, I shall be pleased to see her behind bars for a good long time."

"Deirdre Bloxham!" said a shocked Roy. "Compassion, my dear, is surely needed in this case. And now," he said, as he saw a tear run down Gus's cheek, "I think we should get Gus home to rest. Deirdre? Will you see that he gets a proper sleep?"

"No need for him to go home to that decrepit cottage," she said. "Come on, Gus, upstairs. Spare bed made up ready. And Whippy, you come, too. I've found an old dog basket, and it's all ready with a clean blanket."

"Very kind, Deirdre," he said. "But don't worry. I'm all right. Just a bit tired. And at the moment I'd rather be back in the old routine."

"And Gus's cottage is quite comfortable now," chipped in Miriam defensively.

"Then I think we should leave it to Katherine to find that the mound has been dug over and nothing found. That is, if she is free to continue her search, I should perhaps add," Roy said gently. "I think our job is done now. A dirty rubber glove found by Deirdre has satisfied Miriam and Rose Budd that nobody's hand was severed. The rest is now safely with the police, who, without doubt, have benefited from Enquire Within's investigation."

"So what's next, I wonder," said Ivy gently. "Roy got talking to a stranger he met outside the shop. He was waiting for the bus and happened to mention that he was having trouble sorting out his old mother's will. Everything left unexpectedly to his cousin. He gave Roy his card and said to get in touch if we were interested."

"Roy!" Deirdre patted his arm. "So there's no talk of retiring?"

"If you ask me," chipped in Ivy, "once you retire, you might as well book your eco-friendly casket. Now, who's for taking on the man at the bus stop?"

"Not a bad title for a book, that. The Man at the Bus Stop," said Roy. "So, are we all agreed?"

All except Gus, who was studying his folded hands.

"And you, Augustus?" Ivy asked quietly.

"Mm," said Gus.

"What does that mean?" Deirdre was looking anxiously at him.

"Well, of course, yes. You'd get nowhere without me," he said, looking up at her with a fond smile.

Fifty-four

NEXT MORNING, GUS woke up and for a moment could not remember where he was. Most of the previous day had been so long and horrendous that he thought for a moment he was still in the police station where they had given him a cell for the night.

Then he saw Whippy curled up on the end of his bed and knew that he was home. This was a relief, but there was still the future to get through. Deirdre and the others had been marvellous, and he remembered now what she had repeated to him several times. She had reassured him that his part in all of it was over. He had done the right thing, and nothing he could have done would have saved Ulph.

But that left Kath, and she had meant to die. Gus repeated to himself her scribbled message and knew that she had given up. How would she feel when she realised she was still in the land of the living, a place that held nothing but trouble for her? Or had Deirdre been right in supposing it had been a bid for sympathy?

He went downstairs to make himself a cup of tea, and then sat by the window, looking out at the peaceful scene. A parade of Theo's sheep passed by, followed by David Budd and his dog. As the baaing and whistling faded, Gus felt better. There was an ordinary world out there, getting on with everyday matters. He could join it and attempt to set Kath and Ulph to one side.

A knock at his door sent Whippy into a frenzy of barking. Gus sighed and went to open up to the morning.

"Mr. Halfhide, so sorry to disturb you. May I have a word?"

It was Theo Roussel, and he walked in, ignoring the fact that Gus was still in pyjamas and bare feet. He refused politely Gus's offer of tea and said that he would not stay long.

"It is just a small matter. Well, not all that small. The thing is, David was working in the woods some days ago and came upon an unfamiliar mound. He knows every inch of those woods and was suspicious, so he kicked the earth to one side. Found a couple of very dirty supermarket bags buried just under the surface. They were tied up tightly and, as far as he could see, full of Bubble Wrap. Fortunately, he brought them straight to me, and we opened them."

"And found a hoard of beautiful jewellery?"

"Well, yes! How did you know? Costume jewellery, we decided, but I thought I should come to everyone in the Row to see if they know who is the owner. And you are the first, and seem to know about it?"

"Yes, I do, and it is certainly not rubbish. It is the real stuff, Mr. Roussel. I can prove it is my ex-wife's, but I shall be very glad if you could hold on to it for the moment. It is a long story, but it would be a great favour to me."

"Oh, of course, old chap. You're not looking well, you know. Take it easy! Now, I must go. Would you like to come up and have potluck supper with me this evening? Then you can tell me the whole story. Sounds most interesting. I do hope there's a happy ending!"

THE NEXT EXCITING TALE IN THE LOIS MEADE
MYSTERIES FROM AUTHOR

Ann Purser

FOUL PLAY
AT FOUR

A mother's work is never done—especially when she runs her own cleaning company and moonlights as a secret sleuth. No matter what the hour, day or night, when a mess is made in the village of Long Farnden, Lois Meade is there to clean up—and find out whodunit.

PRAISE FOR THE AUTHOR

"Purser's expertise at portraying village life and Lois's role as a working-class Miss Marple combine to make this novel—and the entire series—a treat."

—*Richmond Times-Dispatch*

"Notable for the careful way Purser roots every shocking malfeasance in the rhythms and woes of ordinary working-class family life." —*Kirkus Reviews*

penguin.com

ANN PURSER

The Measby Murder Enquiry

The author of *The Hangman's Row Enquiry* presents a brand-new mystery, as cantankerous spinster Ivy Beasley finds that spending her golden years in the quaint village of Barrington won't be as quiet as she thought.

Ivy hasn't been in assisted living at Springfields for long, and she's already found new friends, formed a detective agency called Enquire Within and solved a murder. Now, as autumn falls, Ivy and her team—Roy, Deidre and Gus—have more mysteries to solve in between card games.

Enquire Within has been asked to look into a murder in the village of Measby—a crime that, to Ivy's surprise, hasn't even shown up in the papers. Similarly intriguing is the new Springfields resident, Mrs. Alwen Wilson Jones, who claims she was conned out of a large sum of money. But as clever old Ivy discovers, Mrs. Wilson Jones, like everyone else in Barrington, has secrets—like a possible connection to the murder in Measby . . .

"Purser always comes up like roses." —*Shine*